I0673864

Cowboy in the Moonlight

Sheryl Marcoux

Cowboy in the Moonlight
COPYRIGHT 2015 by Margaret S. Rychwa

Contact Information: titleadmin@pelicanbookgroup.com

Scripture quotations, unless otherwise indicated are taken from the King James translation, public domain.

Ville du Havre (It Is Well With My Soul) - written by Horatio Spafford , 1876 –public domain

Cover Art by *Nicola Martinez*

White Rose Publishing, a division of Pelican Ventures, LLC
www.pelicanbookgroup.com PO Box 1738 *Aztec, NM * 87410

White Rose Publishing Circle and Rosebud logo is a trademark of Pelican Ventures, LLC

Publishing History
First White Rose Edition, 2015
Paperback Edition ISBN 978-1-61116-500-5
Electronic Edition ISBN 978-1-61116-499-2
Published in the United States of America

1

"I heard some men in town talking about getting wives."

Zachariah Keane's jaw froze as he looked at his partner, Molly Crammer. He'd bet she'd waited for him to take a mouthful of her delicious beef hash before making that statement. He chewed, swallowed—and intended to put an end to the subject fast. "Ain't interested in a mail-order bride."

She scowled. "You ain't heard everything I have to say."

"Heard enough." He filled his mouth again.

Molly and Zachariah were the most unlikely team on the cattle trail, and had settled under a rain-battered tarp for supper. She was a widow, sixty-eight years young, lean as a maypole, but strong-boned, with an even stronger will. He was twenty-two years old and single.

She heaved the cast iron frying pan off the coals. "It ain't mail order," she said. "It's a scientific matchmaker doing the hitching. He takes a strand of hair and looks at it under a microscope so he can find the compatibilities between a gal and a feller."

"A strand of *hair*?"

"It's science."

"It's hogwash."

"It's satisfaction guaranteed."

Satisfaction? "Your hash is going to cool off," he

said.

Molly gave him a hard look. "You deserve yourself a good woman just as much as that old goat-faced Malachi Moore."

As far as Zachariah was concerned, if old Malachi wanted a wife, that was his business. But maybe he could use Malachi to get her mind off him. "Now Molly, name calling ain't Christian-like."

"Ain't Christian-like, huh? If I said Malachi looked like a stallion, that'd be Christian-like, wouldn't it? So if God made the horse, and God made the goat, what makes one creature better than the other?"

"Malachi's got a suiting place for a lady to live."

"You call that a suiting place?" Molly said. "I call it an outhouse. Besides, your ma left you a fine home."

Gone months at a time with money spent on women, whiskey, and making a rumpus, typical cowboys didn't have a home.

But Molly and Zachariah weren't typical cowboys. They had Ramsden, Texas to call home.

Molly would return to the house her late husband Danny had built for her.

Zachariah had recently started fixing up his mother's old house, which had been abandoned for eleven years to the wrath of storms and the ravages of just plain neglect, while he'd been away cowboying. "The place needs a lot of work." He bit off the food on his fork.

"Just needs a few comely touches, like some curtains and maybe a tablecloth."

"And maybe an upstairs that ain't all rotted out, and some windows that ain't busted-"

"You *need* yourself a wife."

He pushed an empty dish at her. "I *need* myself

more of that hash."

Slinging more chuck into his dish still didn't make her drop the subject. "Good Book says that a feller who finds himself a wife finds a good thing."

"I got myself something better," he said. "I got you. You do my cooking, you do my wrangling, and you do my nagging." He filled his mouth and mumbled, "You're real good at that last one."

"I ain't going to live forever," she said. "Besides, it ain't good for a young man to be spending his days with an old lady and a bunch of cows."

"First of all," he said, "I reckon you'll live another hundred years 'cause God's enjoying the peace. And second," he gave her a long look, "I ain't the one complaining."

"Yup," she said after a pause, "that's right. You ain't the one complaining. You ain't never the one complaining."

"That's right." He always made it a point to act as if he was satisfied with his lot in life, even when that lot wasn't so satisfying.

At nine years old, he'd lost his pa to a wagon accident, and two years later, lost his ma to tuberculosis. Just as he was getting up the gumption to ask his sweetheart to marry him, he'd lost her to a fire. A big piece of his heart got cut out with each loss. Especially the last one. He rubbed the rough skin on his face over a scar the fire had left on him.

Lonely. It seemed his lot in life was to be alone, and the scar was fate's way to keep him that way. He thanked God for Molly's—albeit meddling—company.

Molly heaved a sigh. She had a look on her face he didn't like. She was up to something.

~*~

The sea breeze rustled Lillian Rauling's dress as she stood on the deck of a ship, bound for matrimony.

Night had fallen, and the vessel swayed soothingly. Waves slapped in a restful rhythm. The full moon cast a glow over the ocean. It would have been so calm, so romantic, except for one thing.

She was here because she had solicited the services of a matchmaker. Worse, it was a matchmaker who referred to himself as *The Love Doctor*.

"If the lady don't like the chap," one of her cabin mates and fellow brides had said, *"she's got to pay him back every penny for the fare and the Love Doctor's services—plus damages."*

Lillian had learned that what those so-called damages entailed was vague and determined entirely by the gentleman. But those were the terms of the contract she'd so hastily signed.

"If she ain't got the money," the girl said, *"that constitutes stealing, and she'll wind up in the clink."*

Prison. Lillian felt a chill beyond that of the crisp night air. She clutched her shoulders, wishing she had a shawl in which to wrap herself.

A couple came out on the deck as romance drew them to the side. They looked at the moonlight magic, and then kissed.

Would the man she married hold her like that? Who was the man waiting for her beyond the shimmering ocean? Could he be a godsend? Someone who would put an end to the chaos her life had become?

If the so-called Love Doctor had taken any note of her upon her visit to him in London—other than the fact that she had unusually black hair—her chosen match would likely be an accountant or a man of some profession. Her gentility would dictate such an arrangement. And that's all it would be. An arrangement. Indeed, the last thing she wanted was a business partner.

She drew near to the warmth of a mounted oil lamp with a chimney of etched glass and a brass cherub base. She stared into a flame glowing through a globe as transparent as her own heart felt. The core of her being burned with loneliness.

But she knew what she wanted. She wanted someone who was brave and kind and uncomplicated. Someone with smiling eyes who would draw her out and strong arms that would catch her as she passionately threw herself into them. Most of all, she wanted someone who would see past the pretty globe and into the caged fire that was Lillian Rauling.

She could hear a pianist in the dining hall playing, most appropriately, Beethoven's *Moonlight Sonata*. It brought back memories of a time long past when she was learning to play such pieces, before she'd been forced to live with her aunt and an uncle who couldn't keep his hands to himself. Before she'd been sent away to school. The memory that stirred was back in a time when she was simply Lilly, her father's delight, talkative and expressive, and proud as could be of him.

Papa performed in opera houses all over Europe—in Stuttgart, Vienna, and Paris—and on several occasions entertained royalty. He was the sunshine in her life, and without him, every day seemed dreary. Unfortunately, month-long engagements were common for the well-known tenor.

She couldn't wait until he was home, when she'd

run into his arms, and he'd catch and twirl her. One day when she was eight years old, he returned with some sheet music. It was a song he'd written especially for her, and he asked her to play and sing it for him.

"*Papa, you sing it,*" *Lilly said.* "*You have the best voice in the world.*"

"*Not so, my darling.*" *His eyes filled with tenderness, and he perched her on the piano bench.*

Perhaps he sang so often that he was tired of doing so. So she pressed her hands to the ivory keys and played with the hesitant chords of a beginner, and sang with the small voice of a child.

> *When it's cold,*
> *And skies have turned to grey,*
> *When the sun that's been shining in my world*
> *Has suddenly gone away,*
> *I close my eyes and see with the eyes of my heart*
> *Because I know*
> *God's given me a promise*
> *And sealed it with a rainbow.*

Her father assigned her to play "*Sealed with a Rainbow*" *once a day every time he went away, until he returned.* "*That's to remind you that your Father in Heaven is always watching over you, even when your earthly father can't be.*"

> *When troubles rise and flood beyond the brim,*
> *I stand my ground, I close my eyes*
> *I put my trust in Him.*
> *I know He's up in Heaven*
> *And watching me below,*
> *I know because He promised*

And He sealed it with a rainbow.

Lillian's body was still on the ship's deck, but her spirit had gotten caught up in the fond memory. So much so that the words to the song slipped through her lips, and she sang toward the moonlit horizon.

"When storms are over,
I always lift my eyes
Sometimes I can see it there
His name up in the sky.
It reminds me of His promise
That my longings will come true
He sealed it with His rainbow,
So I know He will come through."

It was too late in the evening for rainbows, but the moonlight glistened over the water just as magically. Her eyes and heart became fixed upon the softly glowing blue-black horizon. She could swear she saw in the moonlight the silhouette of a tall, gallant cowboy, with her name in his pocket.

~*~

Molly finished washing the dishes in a bucket she'd set out to catch the rainfall off the tarp.

A gap in the clouds to the west allowed the sun to break through for a while before more rainclouds rolled in.

She spotted Zachariah on the crest of a hill overlooking the river valley. He was a fine figure of a man, majestic on horseback against the slate gray sky. He had a secret he shared only with the animals, with her, and with the Almighty.

That grand singing voice.

At the end of each day, he'd ride to the highest point and sing a hymn. His voice would spread over the valley like a blanket of peace. But watching him up there singing, alone and solitary, made her heart ache. That's why she'd done it.

She'd snatched a hair from his hat when Zachariah had come over for Sunday gathering before they'd left on the cattle drive. Selling her old piano gave her enough money to pay the Love Doctor's wages and the girl's fare. Even though Molly no longer had the one piece of furniture she had insisted her late husband drag across the country forty years ago, she smiled contentedly as she watched Zachariah on the hilltop.

It didn't matter if a hymn was meant to be sung soft throughout. He sang each verse the way his heart said it ought to be sung.

The beauty of his voice filled Molly with so much awe that she couldn't take her gaze off him.

The air was still. The cattle and horses grazed calmly. She bet that even the angels had settled among the bluebonnets on the hillside to listen.

Zachariah was as close to God as a man could get.

She hugged her shoulders anticipating the end of the hymn. He always gave a grand finale that gave her goose bumps.

Zachariah finished the hymn, but Molly continued to stand there spellbound. "If that don't beat all." Amazed, she rubbed her shoulders and shook her head at a rare phenomenon, which held her in holy awe. Zachariah's back was to it, so she knew he didn't see what she was looking at.

From where she stood, he was standing right

underneath the arch of a rainbow—so that it looked as though God had painted a big, glorious circle around the man.

2

"Nate! Get that calf!"

"If you want it, *you* get it! I'm not risking my neck for a piece of veal!"

The rain started up again, and the storm had swollen the river into rapids.

Just as Zachariah suspected, someone was in a hurry to cross it.

"You made the decision to push them across the river!" Marcus Powell shouted over the pelting rain and the bawling cattle to his twenty-two year old son, Nate.

Safely on the other side of the tempest, Nate just spurred his horse and rode away.

That left one thrashing creature fighting a losing battle.

Some cattlemen didn't bother with the calves born during a drive. But Marcus respected that these creatures were being driven to the slaughterhouses and deserved to have their last days on God's earth to be pleasant ones. Marcus tried to rope the calf, but missed.

Zachariah's lasso hit the mark. "I heard the ruckus," Zachariah shouted over the storm and the cattle. "Thought you could use some help."

"Is that a polite way of saying, 'I knew some fool would be headstrong enough to try to cross the river'?" Marcus shouted back.

Thunder had panicked the cattle, and the ones behind pushed the ones ahead to bottleneck and crowd into a rushing river that was getting too wild and too deep to cross.

Zachariah didn't want to get involved in a father/son dispute between Marcus and Nate, so he just got down to business. He let the current carry the calf a ways farther to take the fight out of the little beast and get him away from the panicked herd. Cattle perceived a man on horseback as part of the herd, but a man on foot would only spook them more.

He dismounted and followed the rope into the cold, churning river. The current pulled his legs out from under him and tried to wash him away, but he got back on his feet. When he grabbed hold of the calf, the river pulled them both under. Zachariah broke through the surface for a gasp of air. He summoned all his determination and strength to haul himself and the calf out of the roiling water. He stayed on the riverbank with the calf until it got back its kick, and then he draped it over his saddle.

Now, to face Nate.

Zachariah coaxed his sure-footed horse through the river.

Nate met him on the other side, but as Zachariah peaceably offered over the calf, Nate acted pretty much as Zachariah suspected he would.

"We don't need charity," Nate said. "Not from a man with the mark of Cain."

Zachariah didn't say a word. He just let the calf down, and let Nate's words pour over him like the battering rain. Nate blamed him for the fire that killed Sally, Nate's sister, five years ago.

"Start gathering them cattle before you lose them

all," Marcus yelled through the lashing rain.

Nate glared a moment longer at Zachariah before spurring his horse to head off the cattle.

Zachariah crossed back through the river, bid Marcus farewell, and rode off to tend to the forty-six head that made up his own small herd.

~*~

"Some fool tried to cross the river, didn't he?" Molly looked up from her cooking fire and saw that Zachariah was soaked. She grabbed a blanket and wrapped it around him. "Bet it was Marcus," she continued at him.

They'd spotted the dust from another herd a week ago, and the campfire two nights before. "That son of his is always in a hurry. Going to ruin his pa. If he inherits nothing but ticks, it'll serve him right, the way that feller treats you."

Everybody knew Nate's side of the story, that he blamed his sister's death on Zachariah's irresponsibility.

There was more to the story, because Zachariah never told his side. All the nagging in the world couldn't drag it out of him, either.

"Now get ready to eat."

Zachariah's horse nudged its nose against him, and he obliged it with an apple from the chuck wagon.

Then Dusty, who'd been watching the herd, ran over and greeted him, and he gave her a piece of jerky. The dog's bushy tail swung over Molly's frying pan.

"What do you think this is? A barn? Now tether that horse and get that matted old dust mop out of my kitchen." It didn't matter that Molly was under a tarp.

Cooking was serious business, and wherever she cooked, there was her kitchen.

Zachariah took the horse away, shooed the dog, and then joined Molly under the tarp. He was so tall, he had to duck. Being the gentleman he was, he took off his hat. His dark brown hair had grown scraggly and hung in his face.

It was a face that broke Molly's heart.

"This rain's given me a hankering for that hash and them sourdough biscuits you got stinking up the air," he said.

She planted her hands on her hips. "Stinking up the air, huh?"

He nodded to the side. "That's why them cattle are standing over there."

She followed his gaze to the herd. The cattle were *standing over there* because a cook kept a distance in case of a stampede, as he well knew. "That so?" she said. "I'm the best chuck cook in Texas, and you know it." Her secret was a pinch of cinnamon and a peck of caring. She'd never been blessed with children, and she loved the man like a son.

They'd partnered up two years ago.

When Nate quit college, Zachariah quit working for Marcus.

Molly had just lost her husband to a thief who broke into the house and shot him for eleven dollars and a sweet potato pie.

The town formed a posse and hung the killer, but it couldn't bring her Danny back. She didn't know what she'd have done without Zachariah. That's why it hurt her so much to see his face like it was.

He'd once been a good-looking son-of-a-gun, and it was no wonder Sally Powell liked him. But the fire that killed her had left him scarred. The hollow of his cheek on the left side of his face was red and rippled. The beard that had grown while they were out on the cattle drive never did fill it in.

It was a crying shame no one had taken a hankering to him since Sally, and as far as Molly was concerned, it was the woman's loss. Because if a lady was willing to look beyond what was on the outside to see what was on the inside, she'd find she had herself a gem of a man.

~*~

Lillian returned to her ship's cabin, but hesitated with her hand on the doorknob. Inside, she could hear her cabin mates and fellow brides talking—about her.

"She brought nothing with her but the clothes on her back." That was Aggie's voice. She was a full-figured woman with a pretty face and a wardrobe of dresses with daringly low necklines. With the scrutinizing glares she'd cast, Aggie had made her dislike toward Lillian obvious from the beginning. "And that's another thing. That's a governess's dress she's wearing."

"And you don't think a governess wants to marry as much as the next woman?" That was Rosie's voice. She was an aging woman with frayed red hair, a face caked with rice powder, and she seemed uninterested in prying open the Pandora's Box that was Lillian's business.

"I think a woman raised in high society would rather be a slave to her own class than mingle with the likes of us." That was Aggie again. "I'm telling you, there's something ain't right going on with that little prissy."

"Well, I think she's a pretty little thing," Rosie said. "She can't be more than seventeen years old."

Thank you. Lillian appreciated her advocate, but wanted to correct her by saying, *the little prissy is nineteen.* Instead, she took a deep breath and opened the door.

Rosie was dressing Aggie's hair, a daffodil-colored mass of ringlets, by the mirror.

Both women fell quiet, and the gazes of their images fell askew.

Lillian found her own faraway image to be a stranger's. A stranger who had the impassive expression of an old spinster and the radiance of a young woman. A stranger whose severely drawn, blue-black hair framed an oval face of ivory skin. A stranger donned in a black dress on a petite frame that moved fairylike. Not only was the image in discord with its circumstances—but it was especially out of harmony with the soul that inhabited it.

"So, Rosie," Aggie abruptly said. "What brings you across the Atlantic?" The ice-gray gaze of Aggie's image peered into Lillian's core. It wasn't Rosie Aggie wanted to ask.

A groan reminded Lillian that the fourth cabin mate, Prudence, still lay bedridden with seasickness.

Lillian welcomed the opportunity to escape Aggie's glare by dabbing at Prudence's forehead with lavender water.

"I'll tell you what brought me here." Rosie took the hairpins out of her mouth. "I was fed up, that's what." Her tone suggested Rosie was especially fed up with Aggie's suspicions about Lillian. "I was through with working for hours, standing half-naked and shivering like a twig in a blizzard 'cause the boss was too cheap to put a log on the stove, and 'cause my bosom was popping out so the ladies could gawk at a dress they'd never look good in, and their gents could gawk at me." With a final jab, Rosie finished Aggie's hairstyle.

"What about you, Prudence?" Aggie asked, though her gaze never budged from Lillian's mirrored image. "What brings you here?"

Rosie hushed her. "If you must know, Prudence is a widow. She didn't know her husband had a gambling problem until after he died. The creditors took everything." Rosie was the only one who hadn't gotten seasick, and she'd tended to the other three.

Lillian had overheard Prudence disclose her history with no caution of confidentiality.

Aggie altered her question and sweetened her voice. It seemed the widow roused some understanding. "So, Prudence, what are you looking to marry?"

Prudence had the figure of a preadolescent boy, and she barely made a bulge beneath the covers. Behind the damp cloth Lillian pressed to her forehead, and in a voice filled with pure misery, Prudence answered, "A doctor."

The humorous answer eased the mood for a moment, until Aggie turned away from the mirror and flatly demanded of Lillian, "What's your story?"

Lillian looked into Aggie's eyes. It was like looking into the twin barrels of a coach gun.

Lillian may have done something irrefutably wrong that drove her here, but one thing she was *not* was a liar. And one thing she could *not* conjure up was a credible answer.

"I'm starved." Rosie's statement interrupted the tense moment. "Pudding. All I want is a good dish of plum pudding. I bet the rich are in the dining hall this very minute feasting on roast duck and plum pudding." Rosie's rescue was a fine attempt, but for one thing. She should have curbed her critical culinary tongue. "The slop they served *us* last night tasted like swill. I swear, the cook took all the scrapings from the night before, mixed it in a pot with fish entrails, and-"

And Prudence shot up in bed. "Fetch the bucket!"

Rosie stretched for the bucket, but Lillian beat her to it and reached Prudence just in the nick of time.

When Prudence finished, Rosie offered Lillian a soft and thoughtful, "Thank you."

But Aggie had a one-track mind. She stepped away from the mirror and put her hands on her femininely rounded hips. "So what are you looking for in a bloke from America that you couldn't find in a bloke from England?"

"A-?" Not only did Lillian have to come up with an answer, but she also had to translate the question. It took a moment to figure out what a *bloke* was, and when she did, she quoted the Love Doctor. "I'm looking for a-'a compatible connubial companion,' of course." With a strained smile, she tried to convince Aggie not only of that, but also of her urgency to get rid of the bucket.

But Lillian's answer only stimulated an inquiry from Rosie. "You're going half way around the world to marry a stranger. Ain't you been thinking about what kind of man he'll turn out to be? That's all I been thinking about for months, dearie." It came out more as a sentiment of sympathy.

Aggie wasn't as understanding. "Sounds peculiar

to me."

Peculiar? Lillian had tired of Aggie's prying. *Who's calling who peculiar?* The situation they'd *all* gotten themselves into was outright ludicrous.

The Love Doctor had claimed to be the founder of a field destined to revolutionize the course of connubial combinations. *"This is 1880,"* he'd said to Lillian, *"and it's time the haphazard primitive pairing of persons is replaced with logical modern methods."* He referred to his logical modern methods as Scientific Matchmaking and assured her, *"Don't worry; satisfaction guaranteed."* Then he plucked a strand of hair from her head, placed it under a microscope, and started mumbling things about *"an elongated follicle"* and *"a relatively thick medulla..."* Judging by the tone of his voice, he frowned upon *"a particularly large follicular orifice."*

"I don't believe you," Aggie said.

"I'll tell you what kind of man *mine* better be," Rosie the rescuer said. "Somebody rich. Rich as an earl. He can be as old as Methuselah, for all I care, so long as he's wealthy. And there'd better be a match, and a good one at that, waiting for me at the end of all this, or I'll hunt down that Love Doctor, and make curtains out of his hide."

And *that* was another issue.

Although they were underway to meet their husbands, they didn't have the names of their matches. The Love Doctor's final instructions to the women were to call their own names out loud when they reached their destination, and their husbands would claim them.

Lillian thought Aggie should be more concerned about knowing who her husband was, rather than what a governess was doing among them.

Aggie spat on her palm and smoothed her hair. "Ain't this a little below the likes of you?"

As far as Lillian was concerned, this was *below the likes* of them all. She held up the bucket to draw Aggie's attention to it, and with that in tow, Aggie let her pass, but not without eyeing her.

Once again, Lillian left the cabin and decided she'd do well to avoid it as much as possible for the rest of the trip. But she hesitated by the door to listen in on Aggie's final comments.

"Why are you picking on the poor thing?" Rosie asked.

"Because no respectable high society prissy would sign up with a matchmaker. There's something ain't right about her, I'm telling you. And I'm willing to bet my bloomers I know what it is."

Lillian put a hand on her chest, over a heart that had gone rock still.

"It ain't a husband she's looking for, so much as-"

As what? Lillian couldn't even swallow. Had Aggie figured her out?

"-as a father for her baby."

"What?" Even Prudence spoke up after hearing that accusation.

"Not a well-bred thing like that," Rosie said.

"What else could it be?" Aggie snorted. "Can you fancy her matched with one of those American cowboys? Ha! That would fix her good."

A father for my baby? The statement appalled Lillian, but not enough to barge in and set things straight. Because even that scandal was better than the truth.

And as for being matched with *one of those*

American cowboys, it would not *fix her good*, because Lillian had no intention of even meeting the man.

3

"'Am finished perfect matches,'" Clayton the telegrapher started to decipher.

Finally, Molly thought. She had gone to town every day since she and Zachariah had returned from the cattle drive to see if the name of his bride had come in.

At long last, the telegraph clattered away.

She watched as intently as the three bachelors, as if the machine would start spewing out the ladies themselves.

"Brawley," Clayton said, "yours is first. You got a Miss-"

"Wait a minute," Brawley said. "Ain't this kind of, you know, personal?"

Everyone looked at Brawley, including Molly, who stood undetected with her elbows on the windowsill and an ear leaning into the office.

"I mean," Brawley said, "I'd like to know her name before everyone else does."

Molly rolled her eyes. She was in a hurry for the men to get their business over with. She wanted to be alone with Clayton to get Zachariah's match in secret. If someone told Zachariah before she could ease the news to him, it would be all over with. "It's just a name, for Pete's sake," she muttered.

"Just a name?" a chorus of voices said.

Molly had been discovered. She pulled her elbows

off the window sill, and tried to make it look like she'd just stumbled across the commotion. "Well," she barked, "it ain't like the lady's standing here in front of you on your wedding night."

Meanwhile the telegraph machine clattered on with the whole list. Clayton accommodated everybody by writing down the matches on pieces of paper. "You're all set," he said.

The bachelors flocked around him like geese trying to snatch bread out of the man's hand, while Molly kept her eye on the piece of paper Clayton had folded in half and set aside.

Finally, the men left the telegraph office all goo-goo eyed, and headed to the barbershop. All except for one. Old, goat-faced Malachi Moore. And he was the one who needed cleaning up the most.

Molly snapped, "What's the name of the poor thing who got stuck with you?"

Malachi hesitated. "I can't rightly read."

She grabbed the paper from him. "Her name's Rosie. Rosie Reed."

"Rosie," he repeated, dreamy-like. "Ain't that the prettiest name you ever did hear?" He stood there, repeating the name over and over as if he were already in love.

But Molly needed to move him along. "Ain't you going to get yourself some new duds and get prettied up like the rest of the bunch?" She'd never seen him in anything other than those worn-out buckskins and an old knapsack the color of dirt. "You could at least shave them whiskers."

"I reckon this is as pretty as I get." Malachi offered Molly a hairy grin that looked half human and half mutt-hound. "If the gal's going to love me, she's going to have to love the whole kit and caboodle."

Molly couldn't imagine kissing a caboodle like that. She shuddered for poor Rosie. "Then go buy her a box of candy, or something."

"A box of candy?" His eyes lit up. "That's a good idea."

Molly watched as he headed off to the general store, his gaze nailed to that piece of paper. *How can he afford a wife, anyhow?*

She was now alone with Clayton. "Place needs fixing up," she mentioned. Up until now, the peeling paint on the walls hadn't bothered her. "This town's getting in some real ladies."

"You're right," Clayton said. "The place could use some repairs." Then he gave her the special, folded piece of paper. "Here you go, Molly. I didn't tell a soul."

She snatched the paper from him just as eagerly as the bachelors had. "I knew I could count on you." She started to open it, but suddenly stopped. "I reckon Zachariah should be the first one to see his wife's name."

"Sounds like the right thing to do," Clayton said. "Have you told him yet?"

Molly huffed. "The opportunity ain't exactly popped up."

Clayton cocked a brow. He knew Molly and Zachariah had been out on the trail together for months, and that she was stalling.

"Matters like telling a feller he's getting hitched take a little finesse," she said.

"I can't argue with that," Clayton said. "But you'd better use a little less finesse. The women are due here Sunday evening."

~*~

Although Lillian's irrational heart nudged her toward the vision of the gallant cowboy on the moonlit horizon, her rational mind drove her in another direction. *I've signed an agreement with a man who calls himself the Love Doctor and matches people based on the characteristics of a strand of hair. What kind of simpleton would actually pay for such a ridiculous service?*

Certainly not a man she could honor in the sanctity of marriage.

When the ship finally docked in Boston, and while the other women disembarked and headed toward the train station, Lillian lagged behind. She couldn't let any of the women know of her intentions, not with Aggie disliking her as much as she did and *'being thrown into the clink'* hanging over Lillian's head if she got caught.

After the others disappeared from sight, Lillian headed toward the hustle and bustle of a congested city. She ducked into an alley. *Free at last.* She contemplated what to do next.

"What are you doing here?" A voice came up from behind

Lillian turned.

"You can't be wandering around. Not in a place like this." A concerned Rosie had found her. "It's too easy to get yourself lost and no telling what could happen to a sweet thing like you. What were you thinking?" Rosie scolded as she led Lillian by the hand to the train station.

Lillian found a second opportunity to escape when their train stopped for passengers in Oklahoma. The same concerned Rosie discovered her missing. "I don't blame you for wanting to stretch your legs, but you can't go wandering off." Once again, Rosie foiled Lillian's plot.

~*~

"You watch." Aggie leaned across the table at a hotel in Kansas City. She spoke to Prudence as she nodded toward Lillian. "I'll give her seven months from now."

Tomorrow they'd reach their final destination. Tonight was Lillian's last chance to get away. She sipped her soup, unfazed by the slander, because she had no intention of being around these women seven more *hours*, let alone seven more months. This time, she'd come across the best escape plan of them all.

She'd spotted an empty barrel behind their hotel. All she had to do was slip away after Rosie, her roommate for the night, had fallen asleep, and hide in the barrel. This plan was foolproof. Rosie would never find her there.

"Whose baby do you think it is?" Prudence whispered to Aggie. At least Prudence tried to be discreet.

"Her husband's, of course. It'll just come early." Aggie said with a wink and a laugh.

Rosie's chair scraped the floor. "First of all, if Lillian here was having a baby, I'd say she'd at least show by now, seeing we set off months ago. And second, I've had it up to my eyeballs listening to you talk about her."

Lillian tried to spare Rosie the redundant heroics, but she gallantly continued.

"You don't like the way Lillian here talks. You

don't like it when she don't talk. You don't even like the dainty way she eats. Well, let me tell you a thing or two, missy, at least Lillian here considers other folks. Not once did you haul out a bucket or clean poor Prudence's face when she got sick. And speaking of which, Prudence, you of all people, should be ashamed of yourself for even listening to that—that twaddle." Rosie snatched Lillian by the elbow and dragged her up the stairs. "If Aggie insists on being jealous, we're going to give her something to be *really* jealous about."

Who is this woman?

Rosie opened her trunk and pulled out the most extravagant clothes Lillian had ever seen, even on the women in the society in which she'd lived all her life. Lillian was speechless. With awe, she stared at Rosie.

"My boss made these dresses for Anastasia Mikhailovna."

"The Grand Duchess of Russia?" Lillian gasped. "What are you doing with her clothes?"

"Let's just say I borrowed them and I ain't returning them anytime soon."

Rosie sat Lillian on the edge of the bed. "There's one dress in particular I want you to see." She laid a royal blue, velvet day dress with a red satin waistband and intricate white lace trim across Lillian's lap. It was the most beautiful of all the dresses, and too magnificent to touch.

"That one's yours," Rosie said.

"I couldn't possibly," Lillian whispered.

"You ain't going to go meeting your bloke in that dress. He'll think you're a widow in mourning. Now take that thing off."

Lillian caught a glimpse in the mirror of a young woman dressed in black, with her hair severely pulled back into that usual tight knot at the nape of her neck.

Rosie was right.

She looked as if she'd never stopped mourning the life she'd lost. Against her better judgment—she was planning to slip away tonight, wasn't she?—Lillian pulled off her black clothes.

Rosie helped her put on the velvet dress, and Lillian's image transformed into something that looked as if it walked out of a palace.

If she were going to meet the man of her dreams, this would be exactly how she'd like to meet him.

"It needs hemming and a couple of darts, but I can do that." Rosie produced needle, thread, and pincushion, and started pinning the hem.

Lillian came out of her stupor. No matter how beautiful she looked, the man she was doomed to meet would still be the same foolish, one-strand-of-hair-tell-all believing husband.

She stepped away from the mirror and stammered to Rosie, "I–it's not necessary." She tried to pull off the dress, but was trapped by the many buttons in the back that she couldn't reach.

"It *is* necessary," Rosie said, "because I want to see the look on Aggie's face once she gets an eyeful of you in this dress." Rosie stuck another pin in the hem. Rosie stayed up all night working on Lillian's dress.

And Lillian finally fell asleep, unable to proceed with her plan.

~*~

Criminy!

Sunday morning had arrived, and Molly still hadn't found the finesse to tell Zachariah he was marrying a woman who was arriving that very day. And she had an even worse problem—the rapping on her door. Zachariah had come over for Sunday gathering. If he discovered her piano missing, he was bound to figure out why. Knowing him as she did, that was the *last* way she wanted him to find out.

She'd been racking her brain since sunrise, and the only plan she could come up with was to buy more time. She'd put her nightdress back on, tied a rag around her head from chin to crown, and cracked open the door to meet him. "Can't meet today, Zachariah. I got the mumps."

He took a good look at her face. "I don't see any swelling."

"It's there. I can feel it."

He headed toward his horse. "I best fetch Doc."

"I don't need Doc." She leaped out of the doorway and grabbed his leg before he could swing it over the horse. That's when she'd noticed he'd shaved as he'd always done for Sunday gathering, and he looked handsome dressed in his Sunday duds. But she wanted him to look especially nice for this evening, so she abruptly suggested, "Why don't we go to your place? I'll give you a haircut."

He threw her a *where-did-that-come-from* look followed by a *not-a-chance* stare. "There's no way you'll get near my hair with a pair of scissors since you discovered a scientific matchmaker."

"A scientific matchmaker? Now where would I get the money to do that?"

"I don't know. But I know you, Molly Crammer."

"Then you know I'm as poor as a church mouse," she said.

It took a minute for him to digest that. Then he

headed for her door. "If you're well enough to go to my place to give me a haircut, I reckon you're well enough to have Sunday gathering at yours."

She barred the doorway with her body. "You can't go in there."

"Why not?"

She paused to think up a reason. "Cause I ain't dressed, yet."

He knew her too well. "What do you got in there you don't want me to see?"

She watched as his gaze moved from her face to over her head, through the open door behind her, and then land right smack where something wasn't.

"Where's your piano?"

"I moved it to the bedroom." She flexed an arm muscle. She was a whopping ninety-nine pounds.

"The bed-?" Zachariah picked her up and moved her aside. He stepped inside. "What'd you do with your piano, Molly?" He found a folded piece of paper on the dining table, and before she could grab it out of his hands, he opened it. He grew awfully quiet, and she knew he'd figured it out.

"You sold your piano for a mail-order bride."

There was no use fibbing, so she argued instead. "It's scientific matching."

"I told you plum out. It's hogwash. What you done ain't right, Molly. Some men ain't meant to get married, and I reckon I'm one of them. Seems I can accept that better than you can."

"What I done is right. The Lord made Eve for Adam, didn't He?" She tapped the paper he was holding. "Well, this here's your Eve, and she's coming in this evening on the stagecoach." She paused. "I want you to be happy, Zachariah."

"I know that," he said. "But this time you went too far. A man wants to be loved, and there's got to be something about him a lady finds handsome."

"You *are* handsome. You're a fine figure of a man, and—and you've got the prettiest heart I ever done seen in a person."

"Things ain't as easy as you think." He buried the paper in his pocket, as if he were taking the matter out of her hands and into his own in order to somehow fix it. He headed toward the door.

She chased after him. "But you'll still be there when the stagecoach comes in, won't you?"

"First of all, I reckon I'll be too busy trying to get back your piano, so we can have Sunday gathering again. And second?" He mounted his horse. "At the moment, there ain't no second."

4

The morning of the fatal day had arrived. But instead of finding herself hiding from that fate in a barrel, Lillian found herself facing it in front of a mirror.

Giving painstaking attention to every detail, and humming cheerfully as she did so, Rosie styled Lillian's hair. By the time Rosie was done, Lillian looked more beautiful than the Grand Duchess herself. The dark blue velvet of the dress showed off the light blue in her eyes, and complemented the creaminess of her skin. It also put a shine in her black hair, now pinned in soft curls on her crown. A blue hat trimmed with white lace and red silk rosettes finished the look with grand elegance.

Rosie put on a green dress, and the two looked like royalty as they headed toward the stairs for breakfast.

The other brides were already in the dining room, and Aggie was enjoying the attention she was getting from Prudence and the staff. Anticipating their meetings with their husbands later that day, the ladies had changed into their best attire.

Prudence was wearing a conservative walking suit, and didn't stand out.

But Aggie did. Aggie was wearing a melon-colored evening dress that left no doubt it was a woman inside, because of the flesh straining out of its low-cut neckline. She was the belle of the ball, and she was thriving on the "Oh's" and "Ah's."

"I worked sixteen hours a day for nearly a year to buy this dress," Aggie said. "When my husband sees me, I want his eyes to pop out of his head." She twirled around to show off the dress, but stopped short halfway in her pivot.

That was when the regally-clad Rosie appeared on the stairs.

All gazes abandoned Aggie, and locked onto Rosie.

And when Lillian appeared on the stairs behind her, jaws dropped.

"She looks like a storybook princess," Prudence said.

Aggie did a double take. From her expression it was obvious she was thinking that the little governess who had no business being with them had indeed transformed into someone who looked as though she'd walked off the pages of a fairytale. Having lost her admirers, Aggie tromped off to a table, plopped herself into a chair, and remained utterly speechless for the rest of the trip.

Lillian also remained speechless. She'd missed her last chance to escape.

~*~

Where's Zachariah?

Sunday evening found Molly standing with the rest of the bunch waiting for the brides to arrive. She was ashamed to be meeting decent women in front of the saloon, but that's where the stagecoach stopped, because that's where the only hotel in town was—on top of that den of degeneracy. Molly wasn't all too happy she lived in a town full of heathens. She hoped these ladies would add some saints to their population.

It seemed every man in town, whether or not he had a special interest, was there—*except* Zachariah. Those men who had a special interest were all dreamy-faced and dolly-duded up, and, by the sound of them, anticipating their perfect women.

"I feel like I already know Aggie," Doc Hinkle said. "She's a modest and refined lady, and someone to keep me organized."

Molly frowned. *Organized?*

"I bet my Prudence is a hearty woman with nice, child-bearing hips," Brawley said. He had the same goofy look on his face as Doc Hinkle. "I can see her now, working the farm with me, and bearing me a dozen little helpers."

Molly felt compelled to speak up. "If all you want from a woman is a bunch of hired hands, why don't you just hire yourself some of the school boys?" *Organized? Hired hands?* She thought, *These men are about as romantic as the hiccups.* With one unexpected exception.

"I bet my Rosie's as delicate as a teacup." Malachi had his loving gaze on that piece of paper, but his usual getup—those old buckskins and tattered knapsack—were still on his back. His gray hair hung down to his shoulders, and his scraggly beard reached his chest. He hadn't changed his appearance a mite since the last time she'd seen him, except for the box of candy she'd shooed him off to get. In fact, it was a mighty big box.

Where'd he get the money for that? Molly had never seen him work a day in his life. Just then, someone she wasn't too thrilled about walked up and joined them.

Doc Hinkle greeted him. "How are you doing, Nate?"

Nate returned Doc's greeting and then asked with a grin, "Are you here for a woman or for the show?"

Doc Hinkle laughed. "A woman," he admitted. "I miss having one around." He was a middle aged widower who'd lost his wife years ago. "I take it you're here for the show," he returned to Nate.

"That's right," Molly muttered. "You already got a woman." Hattie, the saloon girl, was sweet on him. *So you don't need to be all scrubbed down squeaky clean, decked out in a three-piece suit, and looking at that fancy gold chain-watch like it matters now, do you?* She was irked. There was nothing special about the other men—especially old Malachi.

But Nate, with his good looks and contempt for Zachariah, was definitely an unwanted presence.

What else can go wrong? Molly looked around. There was still no Zachariah.

She heaved a sigh, and resigned herself to the idea he wasn't coming because he was too ticked off at her for selling the piano, and he was bound and determined to get it back. It hadn't gone far. She'd sold it to the man who ran the general store. Then Molly realized she *did* have another problem. *If Zachariah ain't here, then who'll claim his gal?*

She planted two fists on her bony hips. *Lord, this ain't going as smoothly as I'd planned.* Just then, one of the men came running down the road.

"They're here!" he shouted. "The ladies are here!"

~*~

"Whoa, there."

The stagecoach came to a jolting halt. The women crammed inside were giddy and giggly.

Except Lillian. Burdened with a heavy heart and a velvet dress suited more for winter than this dry heat, Lillian looked outside. Somehow, some way, she, as unwilling as Jonah, had ended up in Nineveh.

Her journey had terminated in a place where top hats and teatime didn't exist. What did exist was a small, dusty town with a walk to keep one's feet out of the muck and the sour-smelling horse droppings. The buildings hosted the basic services, including a livery with a farrier, a telegraph office, and a Sheriff's office that announced with large black letters, "JAIL."

She assumed the gathering in front of the saloon was the entire populace, come to see those who would increase their numbers by another ten percent. Which meant there would be no disappearing into this crowd. She could count on one hand the number of women, and on the other the number of children. This town was predominantly male.

Lovesick, eager, and desperate-enough-to-fall-for-the-Love-Doctor's-loopy-science male.

Some of those men wore overalls, some wore suits. Some had mustaches, some were shaven. Some were young, some were old. But they all had that wide-eyed, languishing look. She looked from one lovelorn prospect to another, wondering to which one she was doomed.

And then one tall, slim figure wearing a black frock coat appeared behind the crowd, and captured her fascination. He stood a head taller than most, straight and strapping. Yet in his hands, he held a small bouquet of wildflowers as gently as though it were a lady's hand. A wide-brimmed hat tilted over his face made him look wonderfully mysterious. He had a dashing presence. A masculine tranquility. Here was a man who was calm about trivial things, and passionate about the things that mattered. A man who spoke softly, smiled easily, and would catch her when she playfully threw herself into his arms. His kisses would be long and tender, and they would make her close her eyes and forget the past. Most of all, he would love her beyond her beauty—and see into her very soul.

He's the one.

How did she know? If ever there was a figure who resembled the silhouette of the cowboy on the moonlit horizon she'd imagined that evening on the ship, this man was him. At last, this was the man who would coax out the Lilly who had hidden there inside long ago.

The door to her stagecoach suddenly swung open.

"Now remember," Rosie said, "all we have to do is say our names, and our husbands will do the rest. Lillian, you're by the door. You go first."

~*~

Molly took one more look around for Zachariah, and spotted him.

He stood behind the crowd, dressed in his frock coat, and looking more handsome than a rooster. They met eye to eye, until he pulled his gaze away with mild Zachariah-like disdain.

I knew it. Were she twenty years younger, Molly would have kicked her heels. She knew he'd been aching for a wife. And now she bet he was hoping the name on that piece of paper just might be the right one.

5

Lillian started to rise to meet her cowboy, when Aggie abruptly stood. "Those dresses of yours and Rosie's are going to outshine the rest of us. The least you two can do is allow us to make our grand appearances before you make yours." Aggie spat on her palm and gave her hair one last smooth over. "How do I look?"

The others assured her she looked lovely.

Aggie took a deep breath and, aided by two men, stepped down from the stagecoach.

Lillian watched, curious to see who would claim her.

A short but rugged young man, who appeared to be a farmer in his best clothes, stepped forward when he saw Aggie. He set a hopeful gaze on her.

"Aggie Morris," she said with a sigh. Her gaze fastened upon the farmer as well. It was love at first sight.

The farmer suddenly frowned.

A thin, intelligent-looking man a good twenty years Aggie's senior—and who bore the same perplexed look as the farmer—stepped to the front. He took off his glasses, polished the lenses, and put them back on. His perplexed look didn't disappear.

"Um, yes. How do you do, Miss Aggie. I'm your husband, Dr. Hinkle."

Aggie cast a distraught look at the young farmer

as the older gentleman took her aside.

Prudence came to her feet. "Wish me luck." She was a frail woman with a dry, but practical disposition. Without pomp and circumstance, she stepped out of the carriage and announced to the crowd, "Prudence Duldry."

Aggie's Dr. Hinkle took a second take at Prudence, as she did him.

"Did you say your name was Prudence?"

Prudence pulled her gaze away from her doctor and set it on the young farmer who, with a look as surprised as hers, stepped up to claim her.

It was now down to a befuddled Rosie.

"Well, there's got to be something more to it, and I know I'm getting myself a rich bloke," Rosie said, "because everything in my person has been wanting one. Even my hair. Good luck to you." She hugged Lillian, and then stepped out of the stagecoach. "Rosie Reed," she bellowed. She didn't need to repeat her name twice.

Lillian's jaw dropped when an old vagabond stepped forward and gave Rosie a box of candy. Of all the matches, the contrast between this beggar of a man and the elegantly-clad Rosie was the most extreme.

"What are you doing here, you old bum?" Rosie pushed the box away and shoved the man aside. She craned her neck, still looking for her match.

He took off his hat. "The name's Rosie Reed, right?"

Rosie crossed her arms. "It was when I left London. Who are you, and where's my husband?"

"The name's Malachi Moore, my sweet flower." He held his hat to his chest and bowed. "I am your loving husband."

"No, you ain't," Rosie said. "You ain't nothing like him."

Malachi handed her a piece of paper.

Rosie grabbed it from him, and froze as she read it. Then she came back with combinations of words that Lillian had never before heard.

Rosie, however, was the fortunate one of the women in that she had enough money to buy her way out of the marriage contract.

From the carriage window, Lillian glanced over the couples. Three unhappy women had met their husbands. Given the matchmaking method, it was no shock to her that not one match had happened as the ladies had hoped. In fact, each woman seemed to have gone as far as to have met her mismatch.

Lillian consoled herself that her situation would be different. She would be Rebekah meeting her Isaac, and like Rebekah lighting from her camel, Lillian would step off the stagecoach. Her Isaac would take her into his arms and then to his tent, where she would at last be loved. This was the man to bring her long flight to its end. She looked out the window for one last glance at her tall, gallant cowboy before going out to meet him.

But something was wrong.

~*~

Molly craned her neck, trying to see inside the stagecoach.

The onlookers were starting to walk away, leaving three pairs of uncomfortable people sizing one another up, and Nate something to snicker about as he headed toward the saloon and a good time with Hattie.

Zachariah stood behind the crowd back in the shadows between the buildings.

Come on, Zachariah, Molly mentally urged him. *Hang in there. There's got to be one more gal, and I know she's the right one for you.*

~*~

Where did he go? There was something else Lillian didn't understand. *With one couple yet to meet, why was everyone leaving?* A terrible thought struck her. *Could it be they dislike the man with whom I've been matched? They don't care what becomes of him?* Was her husband-to-be a tyrant detested by his own community?

Fear flooded her senses. She searched desperately for the tall man in the wide-brimmed hat, but he was nowhere to be seen. Finally, her rational mind convinced her that her foolish heart had deluded her. The heart-throbbing vision of that tall, mysterious cowboy waiting for her on the horizon, and then standing behind the crowd, had been nothing more than a figment of her hope. And the man she was about to meet was nothing but a gullible fool, duped by a so-called scientific-matchmaking crock.

She stared dismally past the wooden structures of a sun-beaten town. Dismay gave way to panic as she envisioned a familiar, but horrifying image of a stocky man with bulbous eyes.

"Ma'am."

The stagecoach driver startled her.

"Trip's over. You're here, and I need to be on my way."

"Yes." Lillian parroted, "The trip is over." She forced herself to stand and face her doom.

The two escorts reached up. As she held up the hem of her dress, they took special care to aid her down from the stagecoach. Her feet met the wooden walk. She cast a final pleading glance for the cowboy to come and rescue her, but seeing him nowhere convinced her once and for all that the only place he'd ever been was in her heart.

And here she was. Stuck in Ramsden, Texas. Trapped in a tiny town in the middle of nowhere, with no escape. Her husband—whoever he may be—was her prison warden. Unlike Rosie, Lillian didn't have a penny to pay him for her release. She'd never felt more at the mercy of another.

Someone grabbed her arm, startling her. It was Rosie. "Call out your name," she prompted.

Even if she wanted to, after the fright Rosie had given her, Lillian couldn't. Indeed, she could barely breathe.

So Rosie belted out her name for her. "Lillian Rauling!"

The disbursing crowd came to a halt. Faces turned and their gazes settled on Lillian. They seemed confused. Weren't they expecting her?

Some faces stood out from the rest. Was her husband-to-be that rough-looking man with the crooked suspenders and stubbly jaw? Or that bony-faced old man with the cane and the shaking hands? Was God punishing her with such a husband because she should have stayed in England and faced the consequences of what she'd done?

The words of the headmaster at the boarding school she'd attended reverberated through her head. *"God chastises bad little girls to purify their souls while they're still on earth so they can enter heaven when they die."* The headmaster carried a rod with which he'd smack his students behind the knees. It was the only time she'd ever seen him smile.

Hellish moments trudged by. Moments during which the earth seemed it would crack open, and the devil himself would come forth from the fiery pit to drag her back down with him and make her his wife. She could have sworn an hour of agony had passed.

But no one stepped up.

The waiting began to enrage her. She was certain her husband-to-be wanted to torture her with the wait. Why else would he hesitate? He'd paid a good price for her. She was young and vibrant, and Rosie had groomed her so that Lillian was more beautiful than she'd ever been. And then something occurred to her.

Perhaps the man was so old he was hard of hearing.

Her gaze shot over to the emaciated old man with the blue-veined hand clutching a shaking cane. She could clearly envision that same quivering hand seizing her wrist and pulling her toward his home and into his bed.

Before Lillian had time to stop her, Rosie bellowed a second time. "Lillian Rauling!"

She stared at the old man. He was even worse than Rosie's bearded Malachi.

No, Lord, I beg of you. Lillian shut her eyes and pleaded until she figured she'd allowed enough time for the old gent to shuffle up to her. She opened one eye, anticipating the worst. But with relief, she saw he'd come no closer.

With enough volume to wake the dead and make Lillian's eardrums go numb, Rosie belted out Lillian's name a third time.

With the passing of each void moment, the throbbing of Lillian's heart in her throat eased. Until at last, she heard Prudence whisper, "Poor Lillian."

Aggie facetiously agreed.

But Lillian was overjoyed. Being unclaimed was an unexpected gift.

~*~

Molly had been standing with her chin to her chest, and her mouth opened wide enough for the flies buzzing around to fly in. She didn't like what she was seeing. She thoughtfully scratched the back of her neck as she addressed the Lord. *You sure this one's for Zachariah? I sort of had something a mite plainer in mind.* Actually, it was more like a heap plainer.

Lillian Rauling was a rare beauty. There was no other way to describe her other than princess-like, and that was bound to scare Zachariah off.

Molly had been a little uncertain about some of the matches. In fact, she was a bit iffy about all of them. Farmer Brawley and that pale, skinny lady who looked as if she'd never set foot outdoors a day in her life? Doc and that hand-spitting woman who dressed like a tart? And what about Malachi and that fancy-dancy Rosie?

Molly looked at Zachariah. Sure enough, he'd shrunk back even further into the shadows. He had his gaze fixed on Lillian, and a look on his face that indicated he wasn't too pleased. Which indicated to Molly exactly what she was afraid of.

Lillian Rauling was definitely the name he'd gotten.

Meanwhile, with Rosie hollering Lillian's name, the pretty little thing looked scared as a rabbit meeting a pack of coyotes.

With no one claiming her, Molly could just imagine how she felt. Abandoned and all alone. *Zachariah, why ain't you claiming your wife?* Molly turned back to cast him a nudging scowl.

But all that was left of Zachariah was the bundle of flowers he'd left behind on the ground.

6

The matches had given Nate Powell a good laugh. He was about to push open the door to the saloon and have himself a good time with Hattie, a real woman, when the town drunk came stumbling out.

Bart stopped short, his gaze fastened on something behind Nate.

"Now there's a fine–*hic*–fine spec-i-men of a wo-man. That one of them–*hic*–them sci-en-ter-ri-fic brides?" Bart was swaying in his boots. "Why–*hic*–ain't no one in town fit for that one, 'cept maybe–*hic*…" His wobbling head turned to Nate.

Nate laughed. "I've seen all three, Bart. Nothing out there interests me as much as what's in here." Namely Hattie.

Bart lifted a finger and starting counting. "One…two…well, I don't know. That fourth one's quite a looker."

That fourth one? Was Bart seeing double? And double of what? That riled Nate's curiosity to turn around.

Bart wasn't right about much, but this time he was dead on. There was a fourth woman. And it was no wonder the sight of her had nailed Bart's boots to the walk. She had the most refined feminine presence Nate had seen in his travels from Texas to Massachusetts. So what was she doing here? As far as he knew, there were only supposed to be three of them. *So who…?*

Something crossed his mind, and he turned toward the alleyway where he'd seen his sister's killer just a moment ago. *He wouldn't have. Not Zachariah.* He had thought Zachariah had come bearing flowers like the rest of the welcoming committee. But with Zachariah cowering in the shadows, the woman left unclaimed, and now just a bundle of flowers where he was standing…it all added up. *Well, I'll be.*

An idea came to him, and he thoughtfully rubbed his jaw. The idea evolved into a plan, and he liked where it was headed—and that wasn't marriage. *I'll lead her to believe she's marrying me, and when she's had a good taste of what she could have had, I'll throw her at Zachariah and enjoy the look on his scarred face when she gets an eyeful of what she's stuck with.* He snickered. Yes, he really liked where it was headed, to the point he spoke up. "With the way things have been going, I expected her to belong to Zachariah." Given the circumstances, he couldn't resist making the remark.

It was also a remark that put the town back into motion. Although none of the mismatched couples laughed, most of the onlookers did.

Nate looked over at Molly. There were bullets practically shooting out of her wrinkled orbs. She knew Nate had it figured out. Zachariah had ordered a wife, chickened out, and left Lillian unclaimed and certainly good enough to step up for.

Which is exactly what Nate did.

He took his derby hat off to the elegant English beauty. Shunning any hint of the Western drawl of his hometown, he put on the proper English he'd learned in college. "Miss Rauling, I apologize," he said with educated clarity. "I was taken aback by your beauty." He flashed her a warm smile and cast Molly an icy look.

Judging by her glare, that mother hen of Zachariah's knew exactly what would happen next.

Nate was counting on it. *You go tell Zachariah that this is revenge for what he did to my sister.* "My name is Nate," he said to Lillian. "Nate Powell." He added, "I sent for you."

One of the onlookers said, to the merriment of the rest, "Now *that's* the only match that looks right."

~*~

Lillian agreed. For all intent and purposes, this was the only match that indeed *looked* right. Mr. Nate Powell was young and handsome, with wavy blond hair and blue eyes. Everything about him declared him a gentleman—his three-piece suit, the manner in which he spoke, and the way he was now offering her his arm.

Their match was flawless. Or so it would seem.

Mr. Powell was, she estimated, too well dressed to be considered uncomplicated, six inches too short to be considered tall, and the brim of his hat was too narrow to be that of a cowboy's. But he apparently was not too intelligent to be duped by the tactics of a loony scientific matchmaker.

Still, she could have fared far worse. In fact, judging by the other women's matches, it appeared she hadn't fared all that badly.

This was where her journey ended and the rest of her life began. With a Mr. Nate Powell. He wasn't exactly the image of her cowboy on the horizon, but neither was he a quaking old man, and for that, she was grateful.

She reached for the arm of her young, polished husband so gracefully proffered, when suddenly-

~*~

"Hold your horses!" Molly butted up between them.

"What are you doing?" Nate said. "This is my wife."

Molly wanted to slap that lying look of surprise right off his face. He knew well enough what she was doing. She was preventing him from stealing Zachariah's bride. She just couldn't word it that way, so she tried another tactic. "You can't taste the pie until it's properly bought."

"But they *are* bought," Brawley said. "Paid in full." The other men agreed.

Molly snatched away all their wives. "I don't care if these here women are bought and paid for. They're human beings, not cattle, and you're going to woo them proper. They ain't your wives until a preacher says so."

"But there ain't no preacher for miles around," Malachi said.

"Clayton!" Molly bellowed to the telegrapher. "Wire us one up. Go ahead and put an ad in every newspaper you can think of. Wire up that there's going to be a bunch of weddings. And a bunch of heathens that need converting."

"I'll have to charge for it," Clayton said. "It could run into some money."

"Money's no problem," Molly replied. "The fellers here will pay for it."

The fellers who were stuck with the bill started

grumbling.

"No preacher will come here if there ain't no church," Brawley whined.

Molly knew that, too. It was part of her scheme to stall things. "There will be." She threatened, "You men can't see your betrothed women until I see a church floor. Ain't that right, ladies?"

Rosie, the one most displeased with her mate, was the first to side with Molly and agree to the delay. All the ladies followed suit, even Lillian offered a sweet little nod.

"Where will we get the money to do that?" Doc Hinkle asked.

"This will take too long," Brawley said.

Molly wanted to box his ears to drive that whimpering out of him. "How long depends on how interested you fellers are in seeing your gals again," Molly said. "Dig deep in them pockets, boys." The men dug deep, and Nate waited for Lillian to look at him before topping it off with fifty dollars. "That ought to get things started."

"Good," Molly said, although she'd hoped the progress would have been a lot slower. She also didn't like the way Lillian smiled at Nate's gesture. "You get that church floor built, and we'll have ourselves a getting-to-know-you dance on it."

"Where will the ladies stay until then?" Brawley said.

Molly decreed, "Them ladies will stay at my place."

The men chorused, "What!"

Rosie spoke up. "You heard what the woman said."

A chorus of unhappy women agreed, and they all

went home with Molly.

Molly, however, wished she'd kept her mouth shut. She knew a houseful of women would get on her nerves. But she had no idea how nerve-wracking a bunch of *unhappy* women could be.

7

How'd I get both feet stuck in this? Molly brought a stack of dirty dishes from the dining room to the kitchen. She had her house packed with women, and they were all just sitting around the dining room table. Not one was helping her. They were too busy bickering about whose man was worse than whose, and saying this one got the better husband than that one.

And Rosie wasn't very rosy. In fact, she was the worse one of the bunch, complaining about everything from her chosen husband—which was justified—to Molly's stew—which wasn't.

Lillian was the only one who didn't complain.

Molly supposed that was because Lillian didn't have anything to complain about. Nate, with his handsome face and education, looked like the finest catch in town.

How would Molly make Lillian fall in love with Zachariah after that?

With a huff, Molly put the dishes down and then served a nice pie for dessert. She figured that ought to at least sweeten Rosie up. Molly went back to the kitchen and picked up the bucket to fetch some water, when something froze her dead in her tracks.

"Cherry pie? Ain't you got apple?" *Ain't-So-Rosy-*Rosie was complaining again.

Molly set her fist on her hip. They were eating her delicious cherry pie, and how dare Rosie ask for apple.

"That woman's a fussy heifer," Molly mumbled.

"I'm surprised to hear you say that," Lillian said.

Molly turned to find Lillian following with another stack of dirty dishes. There was a mild look of shock on her face. It seemed the English expressed their astonishment by arching their eyebrows.

Nothing was going right, and Molly was in a sour mood, even toward Lillian. "And why's that?"

Lillian hesitated. She was the only quiet one of the bunch. "It's not very—well, not very conducive to one's expectations of Christian discourse."

What? Molly screwed her brow, until she sifted out the meaning from Lillian's fancy words. "You're telling me that what I said about Rosie being a heifer ain't Christian-like, ain't you?" Molly plunked down the bucket. "What if I said the woman was a dove? That would be Christian-like, wouldn't it? So, if the Lord made the dove, and the Lord made the heifer, what makes one creature better than the other?" *Didn't I have this conversation before?* Or something similar. And when she remembered with who and about what, she knew for certain that Lillian and Zachariah were a match paired up in heaven. Had to be. But with things so muddled up, how would she get that couple paired in heaven hitched up down here on earth?

Lillian picked up the bucket to help clean. "I think it was a wonderful idea, having the men build a church and sending for a preacher. What you did was right, and I wanted to thank you for your intervention."

You don't know the half of it. "Seeing Nate and none of the other fellers thought enough of you gals, I reckoned someone had to tell them to do what's proper." Molly had enjoyed the opportunity to knock Nate down a notch. Telling Lillian straight out that

Nate was sowing his oats with Hattie, or 'fessing up that it was her own big idea to send for Lillian for Zachariah—especially since the rest of the pairings were so odd—seemed a lousy way to approach things. But since Molly knew for sure that Zachariah and Lillian were paired up in heaven, she figured love would find its way.

With just a pinch of help from her, of course.

The building of the church would stall the marriage and give Molly some time to figure out how she would get Zachariah and Lillian to fall in love. But first, she had to figure out how to get them to meet. *Sometimes, Lord, I think You give us the brunt of the burden. I know. This was all my idea.*

"I can't eat this pie. It's too sweet."

And in the meantime, Molly had to put up with a bunch of fussy, squabbling, funny-talking English women.

~*~

Molly surrendered her bed to frail Prudence and spent the next few sleepless nights on the floor. She'd slept out under the stars plenty of times, where the ground had some give, but never before on the hard wood of her own house. The days found Molly cooking more meals for ungrateful women, and doing so many dishes she thought her hands might wrinkle up and fall off.

Lillian was the only one out of the bunch who helped out.

Finally one afternoon, Molly was through with all their jabbering and complaining and Rosie wanting this instead of that. Knowing the men would finish early with their regular day's work to hammer away at the foundations of the church, Molly sent the women and a jug of switchel to give the men incentive—and herself some peace. That left her in the middle of a mess, trying to figure out where to start.

She kept a clean house, and hated the sight of everything she owned, and everything these women owned, sprawled out all over the place. Every dish, cup, and pan she possessed had been used for lunch, and was sitting in the sink waiting to be washed.

Lillian had offered to stay and help.

But Rosie had coxed her into going by saying, *"Ain't you going to see your bloke? You got the finest of them all."*

"I don't want to leave Molly with the mess," Lillian stated.

Molly, having the big mouth she had, told Lillian to go enjoy herself.

With Nate.

After the girls left, Molly set about straightening the house. "Ain't you going to see your bloke?" Molly's drawl got in the way of mimicking Rosie's accent. She had a mind to straight out tell Lillian who'd sent for her, but that would cause the rift between Molly and Zachariah to get even bigger if he found out. As she bent over and picked up an old quilt, her back protested with a reminder that she would spend another night on the floor. She looked heavenward. "You sent them women to punish me for lying, didn't You?"

Someone knocked at the door.

She'd heard the horse come up, but had ignored it. It could be the preacher, for all she cared. She was in no mood to walk over and answer properly. "Come on in," she hollered.

Zachariah stepped in. He took one glance at the place, and then gave Molly an odd look. "What'd you do? Stampede some cattle through here?"

Molly didn't let Zachariah know what had happened to her normally neat and orderly house. She doubted if a stampede could have made more of a mess than these so-called ladies.

The odd look on his face changed to a grin, and he took a guess. He got some of it right. "So that's what all the hammering is about in town. You're holding the women hostage so the men will build you a church."

They were building a church so Molly could stall Nate and Lillian's marriage, and somehow get Lillian hitched up with Zachariah. But Molly didn't want to tell Zachariah that. Instead she came up with, "I didn't want the men to be with the ladies until they were properly wed in the Lord's sight." Molly put a finger in the air and a tremor in her voice. She was good at sounding pious. "I told the fellers they couldn't see their women until I saw a church floor."

Zachariah hesitated. He was good at letting things sink in. "So, where'd all your ladies go?"

"I sent them off to see their fellers."

"So much for making them wait." He laughed, and she felt like swatting him.

"Well," she barked, "what're you here for?"

"I brought your piano back. Clayton's out in the wagon with it. I reckon we'll put it right back where it was—if you can clear out some of the rubble." He was getting a good snicker out of her present troubles.

She let out a groan when she bent over to clean up the floor. She caught him smirking, and she cast him a *don't-you-dare-say-another-word* look.

Clayton helped Zachariah haul in the piano.

Once it was in place, Molly demanded, "Where'd you get the money to buy back that old thing?"

Zachariah didn't answer.

She looked at her comrade in cahoots.

Clayton kept his mouth shut, grabbed his hat, and promptly left. Apparently, he was in cahoots with Zachariah also.

But it didn't take long for Molly to put two and five together. "You used the money you got from the cattle, didn't you?"

Zachariah crossed his arms. "I like that old piano."

Molly planted fisted hands on both hips to prove she was just as stubborn. "And I'd like you to have a wife." She leaned toward him to emphasize her druthers, but abruptly straightened when her back smarted. But his gesture raised a good point, and she grabbed hold of it. "Lillian's your gal. By buying back the piano, you paid for her yourself."

"I didn't pay for anybody. Miss Rauling is free to do whatever she wants."

"Even it means marrying Nate?" Molly wanted to get a stir out of Zachariah, and that worked. But only for a moment.

"Look here, Molly. I *got* myself a dog, I *got* myself a horse, and I *got* myself some fine cattle. A woman can't be *got* because she has a heart and a soul, and there's things she yearns for. All Dusty wants is a pat on the head now and then. A woman's heart runs deeper than that. It takes two to fall in love, and I can't be happy in love with her unless I know she's happy in love with me. And a woman like that won't be happy with a man like me." The piano back in place and his piece said, Zachariah took up his hat and followed

Clayton.

Molly bit her lip as she watched them leave. Things had gotten muddled up enough even if she had Zachariah's cooperation. But without it?

Now what am I going to do?

~*~

Lillian and the rest of the women piled out of Molly's wagon when they reached the church building site. The switchel, which caused a stir, was hauled out to refresh their hard-working husbands-to-be.

Lillian and Rosie stepped aside while the other women fought to present the first glass, and bumped and splashed one another with the concoction of vinegar, ginger, and sugary water.

Lillian's Nate Powell wasn't yet there, and besides, she had too much poise to brawl.

Rosie just plain wasn't eager to see Malachi again.

As Aggie and Prudence presented their offerings to the men, Lillian noticed something. Prudence cast her gaze at the doctor, Aggie batted her eyes at the farmer, and their arms crossed over so that the glasses of switchel were poked at the wrong man.

It was Malachi who stepped in to put an end to the chaos. "Now that scientist feller said 'satisfaction guaranteed,' so you men best get back with your rightful gal."

And that, to a chorus of sighs and groans, corrected the problem.

"Now," Malachi inquired, "where's my lovely queen?"

"Wishing she was on the boat back to England, you old bum," Rosie called back. She hadn't budged from Lillian's side. "I suppose I ought to give the bloke a drink before he dehydrates into a piece of jerky," she said to Lillian. "He ain't far from that now."

Lillian watched as Rosie stomped over to offer Malachi some refreshment. But when he reached for the glass, she yanked it back. "What's that old rag you got on your back?" she demanded.

"It's my knapsack, Sugar Blossom."

"What's it got in it? Everything you own?" She finally proffered the glass to the desperately lovesick man. "You'd better be working hard for this, you old coot. I got a mind to give you back your money and get me a job as a saloon girl."

The saloon stood in the distance. *What a curse it would be to be married to a man who spent all his time there.* Lillian poured a glass of switchel and waited for Nate Powell to arrive.

The other women conversed with their husbands-to-be, but Lillian had no one to talk to. Finally, she decided she'd waited long enough. *Well, I know where I stand with you, Nate Powell.*

~*~

It was ridiculously hot, and the sun had soaked up every ounce of water from the ground on which Lillian was limping along. Thus far, she'd trudged one out of the four miles back to Molly's house. She was holding the heel that had broken off her shoe a half mile back, and she was getting angrier with each hobbled step. But she wouldn't turn back just to be disregarded.

If Mr. Powell can afford to donate fifty dollars towards the church, he can afford to get out of work at the same time as the others to build it. At least it would have spared

Lillian the humiliation of being left alone and Aggie's smug *that-put-you-in-your place* snigger.

I could—I could just spit! But of course, Lillian Rauling was too well-mannered to do so. It seemed Nate Powell had an aptitude for putting her in her place, and Aggie had an aptitude for enjoying it. Aggie who was naive enough to believe that a scientist could determine human qualities from a strand of hair. As did Lillian's own husband-to-be.

Nate Powell is handsome, he's educated, and he appears to be well off. Is he not the culmination of what every woman would want and more? Furthermore, he didn't know that Lillian would be coming this afternoon. Perhaps he had pressing work that kept him away.

She hadn't gotten over the romantic vision of a tall, quiet cowboy with her name in his pocket—and a love for her so deep he'd be willing to build the church all by himself. *You're being idealistic and ungrateful. You should be thanking the Lord instead of grumbling.* One should give thanks in all things, even when one was walking like a lame goose, up on one shoe, and down on the other—and each step down rubbing a hot spot on one's heel into a raw blister. And each disappointing thought about that noble cowboy chafing her soul.

She shoved aside the thoughts but kept on trudging. She yearned to stop and take off her shoes to get relief from that infinite abrasion, but refrained for dignity's sake and probably because, for the moment, she was enjoying the self-pity. Besides, taking off one's shoes in public was strictly taboo. Even if there was no one around for three miles.

Or was there?

A wagon was coming toward her.

8

"Whoa."

Limping up ahead was none other than Miss Lillian Rauling.

To Zachariah's relief, the reason for her affliction was just a broken shoe. Why was she out here by herself? A woman shouldn't be walking alone, especially on a path that rattlesnakes took a hankering to. She hobbled up to the wagon.

She sure is pretty. Too pretty to get tangled up with a scarred man. If only she knew who'd sent for her and why.

Being a straightforward man, telling Miss Rauling the whole situation should have come easy. In fact, on his way to meet her stagecoach the day she'd arrived, he'd determined to tell her everything. He had planned to make it clear she wasn't obligated to marry him, but if she was willing, he'd like to court her.

And then he saw her.

Seeing a name on a piece of paper was one matter. But after seeing how beautiful she was and how ridiculous the other matches were, Nate would have made a laughingstock out of him.

No two people could be more opposite, and that made him want to avoid her altogether. Especially when he found himself tongue-tied at the sight of her.

And still did. He tilted his hat to her, but made sure to hide behind the brim. The less she saw of him the better, and vice versa. "Ma'am." His tongue loosened. "I reckon you're heading to Molly's?" *Of course she's heading to Molly's. Ain't nothing else down this road except cactus and rattlesnakes.* And why was he so concerned about making a horse's behind out of himself, anyway? As far as she knew, she was Nate's.

"I am, and I'm in no mood to discuss it," she bit off.

Snappy little thing. If she was that irritable, Nate could have her. However, Zachariah wasn't thrilled about turning around and heading back to Molly's— especially with Miss Rauling in tow.

Just because Molly was a woman and she could ignore a patch of rippled skin right smack on a man's face didn't mean a pretty young lady could. No telling what that meddler would come up with if she spotted them together. But he couldn't leave the lady out here either, not by herself. "Get in. We'll give you a lift."

Clayton climbed into the back to allow her to sit on the bench beside Zachariah.

Zachariah offered a hand to help her, and when they clasped, hers felt small and silky. He didn't like the way it made him feel, as if she needed protecting.

Just as she placed the foot with the broken shoe onto the frame of the wagon, Zachariah heard the last thing he wanted to hear.

A rattler. The snake was in front of Thunderbolt, and it spooked the horse, who knew that sound from previous encounters. Thunderbolt reared, neighing as he skittered away from the reptile.

"Whoa, there!"

In the time it took to blink, Thunderbolt reared, the wagon jerked, and Clayton tumbled in the back.

Lillian's foot slipped, and it was a good thing

Zachariah had a solid grip on her, because he caught her just before she fell beneath the wheel. A long strand of hair tumbled across her scared blue eyes.

"I got you, ma'am." He hauled her up with one hand, using the other to keep Thunderbolt from bolting. The horse whinnied, reared, and fought the reins. Once Lillian was safely beside him, Zachariah instantly set his mind to stop the horse from panicking. There was a good reason the stallion was named Thunderbolt. *If he takes to running, we'll be in a heap of trouble.*

Clayton was still getting his bearings, and a lady as delicate as Lillian didn't look as if she'd be of much help.

Zachariah had to take care of matters by himself. "Hang on," he commanded. He stood up in the wagon, grabbed both reins in one hand, and used his weight and every ounce of strength he had to fight Thunderbolt's instinct to dash.

The horse fought hard, but finally stopped dancing, He stood, sides heaving, blowing air out of his huge nostrils.

The snake had moved under a small bush for protection, its beady eyes on the threat of the horse, and despite the heat, it was coiled, ready to strike.

Zachariah judged that taking out his pistol would make matters worse. Instead, he dug out his pocket knife. He flipped it in his hand, testing the weapon's balance. After a brief prayer, he aimed, threw, and speared the snake dead on, nearly severing the head. It wasn't the first time he'd done it.

He wrapped the reins around the break handle, jumped out of the wagon, and kicked dirt over the carcass. He grabbed Thunderbolt by the headstall.

The horse's eyes were rimmed white, crazed with fear, and he was stomping to and fro.

"Easy, boy." Zachariah held the stallion's head and patted his sweat-dampened neck, until Thunderbolt stopped hoofing the ground. "Easy."

Finally the horse nudged its muzzle into Zachariah's chest in a way Zachariah imagined was a horse's way of hugging a man. "That's it."

With Thunderbolt now calmed, Zachariah was about to climb back onto the bench. He brushed a hand across his forehead, wiping away sweat…and…he'd lost his hat. He looked up into the wagon.

Miss Rauling's gaze had locked onto his face. She was dead quiet.

He snatched his hat off the ground and retreated to the solace behind its brim. He recovered his knife and took the initiative to put the lady at ease. "Clayton, you take the reins." He climbed into the back of the wagon.

Clayton accommodated. "That was some fine horsemanship, Zachariah. And thanks for getting that snake with one throw. I'm mighty grateful."

Zachariah, in back where he kept his tools, thought of something else. "If you give me that shoe of yours, ma'am, I reckon I can fix it."

She loosened her fist, and then looked down into the palm of her hand. Amazingly, she hadn't dropped the heel in the ruckus. She hesitated, as if she didn't want to give up the broken heel. Or maybe she just didn't want to give it to him.

"Zachariah's mighty handy," Clayton attested. "He can have that shoe fixed for you by the time we reach Molly's."

"Or you can limp around until you're in town

again. The cobbler will charge you a nickel. I'll do it for free here and now. Your choice." Zachariah wouldn't twist her arm to do her a favor.

She surrendered the heel, and then, more reluctantly, the shoe. And she eventually thawed enough to hold a conversation with Clayton.

Zachariah, well aware of his mark of Cain, sat at the far end of the wagon and hammered the heel back on.

~*~

"How come you're back so early?" *Farmer's Almanac* in hand, Molly returned from the outhouse.

The wagon had taken off in a hurry and left someone behind.

Molly discovered that someone in the dining room.

Lillian was a mess, with hair tumbling in her face and dirt on her skirt.

"Why weren't you here a half hour ago when Zachariah came by? Oh, that's right, I sent the girls to town to get them out of my hair.

"Mr. Powell wasn't at the church, so I had no reason to stay, and since we'd left your house in such disarray, I decided to walk back and help you, when…" She looked around as she spoke, and her jaw dropped.

Molly was proud of herself. She'd already dried the last of the dishes and slammed the drawer shut on the last of the blankets. Even the women's belongings were neatly stacked to the side.

Apparently, Lillian was impressed to find that Molly was so efficient.

"A piano?" Or maybe not.

"Yup," Molly said. She put the reading material away. She'd barely finished cleaning the house when nature had called. The clock suddenly caught her eye, and she groaned.

"Where did it come from?" Lillian asked.

"Where'd what come from?" Molly asked absently. She had only an hour or so before all the women returned, and everything would be back in shambles.

"The piano," Lillian said. "It wasn't there before." She had genuine enthusiasm in her voice.

"You like the piano?" Molly asked.

"I love the piano. Where did it come from?"

Molly was just about to say that Zachariah brought it over, but changed her mind. "*Mr. Keane* brought it over." Using Mister and his surname made Zachariah sound as if he was just as fancy as any English gentleman. "He's the most generous feller I know. Why, he donated this piano to the church. Put it in my care in the meantime."

"Donated? How kind of Mr. Keane."

Molly knew that would impress her.

Lillian gestured toward the piano. "May I?"

"You play piano?" Molly feigned surprise. Of course, Lillian played piano. She wouldn't have been so happy to see one if she didn't. But Molly played naive because she had some pairing to do, and a plot forming in her head. "Why, be my guest."

With the happiest smile Molly had yet seen on the young lady's face, Lillian sat down on the bench. Then Molly figured out why she was so happy.

Lillian and the piano were old friends. The girl sure could play. And she had a sweet voice.

The hymn Lillian played was one that Zachariah sometimes sang while he and Molly were out on a cattle drive. The first time she'd heard him sing it, and every time thereafter, it brought tears to her eyes. Of all the hymns she'd ever heard, this one touched her heart the most, because it touched her in that wounded place her Danny's death had left behind. It wasn't fair she'd lost him the way she did.

"It is well, it is well, with my soul." Lillian ended the song prematurely by gently pressing the keys of the closing chord. She then folded her hands ladylike on her lap.

"That's my favorite hymn." Molly blinked away the moistness in her eyes. It seemed it didn't matter who sang it. "I'm willing to bet that old piano ain't never been played so good." She could testify since, to her knowledge, she was the only one who'd ever played it. "And your voice is pretty as a lark's."

Lillian's smile refused the latter part of the compliment. "My piano skills are adequate. But my papa—you should have heard him sing, Molly." The smile on her face broadened, and Molly could tell she had a special relationship with her father. "He had a voice so magnificent he brought the King of England to a standing ovation."

Molly smiled in turn, until something snagged her. "Your pa sang?"

Lillian nodded. "With a voice one would imagine the archangel Gabriel would have." Quietness swept over her. It was obvious Lillian's father was no longer alive.

"My condolences. It's hard losing someone you love." Molly wiped another tear from her eye as it struggled to get out.

"I was the world to him, and he was everything to me." Lillian's voice was soft and her gaze distant. "I always wanted to marry a man just like…" She suddenly apologized. "I'm sure Mr. Powell will make a fine husband, and I'm sure he had pressing business to which to attend, otherwise he would have been working on the church along with the rest of the men."

"Sure," Molly said. "Pressing business, all right." *Pressing business with Hattie, that is.* "I reckon by the time it takes them fellers to build that church, you ladies will have a chance to make sure you're happy with your matches. You know—before you go off and get hitched."

Lillian sat on the bench, her back straight and graceful. "I'm afraid that as far as the contract is concerned, we're all obligated. Except Rosie."

I'm afraid? Was that a tinge of disappointment Molly was hearing?

Lillian had also used another interesting word. *Obligated.* If that was so, then Lillian was obligated to the wrong man. If only she had known that Zachariah—albeit via Molly's meddling—was the right kind of man and that he'd given up the entire profits from this year's cattle drive for her, and that Nate was nothing but a smooth-talking, wife-stealing…Molly let her thoughts go quiet. She was getting that itch again. *So, her pa sang, huh?*

No, she wouldn't mention that Zachariah sang, too. Not just yet, anyway. She had some bread crumbs to drop, and she didn't want to throw them all into one pile. She had to leave a trail for Lillian to follow, but she couldn't resist dropping another morsel. "I was the only person in town who played piano, but my fingers are getting stiff with rheumatism. It's about time I retire them, so I'm handing the job as church piano-player over to you."

Lillian brought a delicate hand to her chest. "Me? I couldn't."

"You could." Molly insisted. "I won't take no for an answer."

That pleased Lillian and she broke into another smile. It was nice to see her light up. She seemed too serious most of the time. "Molly, I am thrilled to accept the job. I can't thank you enough."

"Thank *me*? It weren't me that donated the piano," Molly said. "I reckon Mr. Keane will be at the Getting-to-Know-You dance. You might save him a thank-you waltz." *You know, something slow, with hand holding?* She knew that talking Zachariah into going would be a chore.

"What a wonderful idea," Lillian said. "I would very much like to thank Mr. Keane personally for his generous donation, and to express my enthusiasm toward my new position."

"Why don't you play some more piano?" Molly suggested.

Lillian obliged.

Molly grinned. *Yup, I sure know how to drop those crumbs.* She wanted to drop a few more crumbs—about Nate. Because she could just image what he was up to at that very moment.

9

Hattie wore a dress that bared her shoulders and she stood behind a chair in a shadowed corner of the saloon, empty but for one man. The man sat in a chair, and he was swaying drunk. It seemed Nate had come in for an early supper, and the supper he'd chosen was a liquid one. He'd belted down one whiskey after another, until his tongue loosened, and he'd mentioned a woman's name.

Lillian Rauling.

Some of Hattie's regulars had ordered a so-called "scientifically-matched" wife, but she knew Nate wasn't one of them. With his good looks, plenty of money, and her at his beck and call, he had no reason to send for a wife. He did, however, have every intention of seeing *what*, as he'd put it, came in on the stagecoach.

Hattie guessed that something about this Lillian must have triggered memories of his dead sister, Sally.

"I'm going to fix that Zachariah," Nate mumbled. "I'm going to make him regret the judge let him go."

Of all men, Hattie thought. *Why did it have to fall on Zachariah?* They had a history together. They *all* had a history together.

Nate, Sally, Zachariah, and Hattie used to walk to school together. They weren't necessarily friends, though. They were just forced to take the same path. Zachariah, however, was friendly to everybody. Even her.

Back in those days, Hattie had always wished she could be like Sally.

Sally was self-assured and pretty as a picture in the clothes and ribbons she wore. She laughed a lot, and was as carefree as they come.

But it seemed those cares she'd tossed off were ones which Nate picked up and heaped onto his own shoulders, along with his own concerns.

Sally had made her affections for Zachariah clear by giggling and talking to him, and Nate wasn't keen on that.

When Sally would fall behind her brother to walk by Zachariah's side, Hattie would silently catch up with Nate and hope he'd strum up some conversation with her. Nate was nice-looking with yellow hair that curled around his face. His eyes were bluer than the sky, and he looked like the picture of Narcissus she'd seen in a mythology book.

She, however, felt like the nymph who'd fallen in love with him only to be spurned by his love for his own image. Not that she ever told Nate how she felt about him. The closest they'd even come to a conversation back then were his grumbled comments about how Sally was belittling herself by carrying on with someone of lesser stock.

Lesser stock.

Zachariah was poor, and he worked for the high and mighty Powells as a hired hand when school let out.

As for Hattie, she wasn't just poor, she was dirt poor. Her mother made her living washing clothes, and Hattie's hands were worn raw from rubbing on the washboard helping her. Hattie never knew who her father was. Her mother said he'd died in the Civil War, but Hattie suspected different, because her skin was considerably lighter than that of her African mother's.

So Hattie kept her feelings toward Nate hidden. That is, to everyone except Zachariah. Zachariah had a special kind of understanding, and Hattie found herself telling him things she could tell no one else. Even now, though she hadn't seen Zachariah in years, they kept their secrets—including the granddaddy of them all. That one belonged to Zachariah.

"Get me another drink." Nate interrupted her thoughts.

Contrary to her job as a saloon girl to keep the patrons dinking and the money coming in, she responded, "Don't you think you've had enough?"

"If I did, I wouldn't be asking for another, would I?" His eyes were bloodshot, and his gaze far off. "Make it a double."

It wouldn't take much to send him into a fighting mood, so Hattie bypassed the bartender and made Nate a double. A double of sarsaparilla.

Nate bolted it down. He was so drunk, he didn't know the difference.

"How about I take you upstairs?" she whispered in his ear. She never slept with him, or any other patron. She just wanted to put Nate to bed to keep him off the street and out of trouble. His mouth pressed hard against hers, and she wished he loved her with the same tenderness she loved him. "Come on." She took him by the hand and steadied him as he staggered up to her room.

He fell onto her bed, and Hattie slipped off his boots. "I'm going to get that killer, Sally." His glassy eyes looked straight ahead, as if he was talking to his sister face to face. "He won't get away with it."

Hattie sat on the edge of the bed while he talked to his sister as if Hattie wasn't even there.

"I'm sorry, Sally. I'm sorry." The quiver in Nate's voice diminished into weeping. "I'll pay him back for what he did to you. I promise."

Hattie offered a smile of pity and familiarity. This would be another one of those times when he'd be crying to Sally, telling her how much he missed her.

And Hattie would sit by his side stroking his sweat-dampened hair, and keeping him in bed every time he tried to stagger out, swearing he was going to kill Zachariah.

10

Molly found Zachariah at the general store where he'd just purchased two sacks of flour, two sacks of potatoes, and two sacks of beans. It was enough food to last him until kingdom come. Molly found it curious, but she had more important matters to tend to. Like figuring out how she would persuade him to go to the dance.

The church floor was in.

Nate hadn't helped out one bit, but the rest of the men were eager to get their wives. The Getting-to-Know-You dance was set up for that Saturday evening, and Molly made it known to the rest of the town everyone else was also invited.

Zachariah had made no commitment to go.

Molly followed him to his wagon. "You got to go to the dance."

He ignored her as he started heaving the sacks into the back of the wagon. He pitched in a sack of beans, and followed it with the other sack of beans, as though she wasn't even there. He picked up a sack of potatoes.

"Lillian wants to thank you for the piano," Molly said.

"For the piano?" That got his attention. "All I did was return…" He froze with the sack in tow. A suspicious look crossed his brow. "What'd you tell her?"

"Nothing." *Not really.*

"Molly?" That steely look in his eyes was as if the Lord Himself was staring her down.

"I told her you donated it."

"Donated…?" He nearly threw the sack clear over the other side of the wagon. "You know you ain't supposed to be lying."

"It weren't lying." *Not exactly*. "I reckoned you gave the piano back to me for Sunday meeting, and since we're going to have a church…"

"And that's another thing." He took up another sack. "You're holding those women hostage so their men will build you a church."

"It ain't hostage-holding."

"Then what is it?"

"I call it evangelizing."

He scowled at her and tossed in the last of the sacks. "You got a lot of scheming going on in that meddling mind of yours. What am I to do with you, Molly Crammer?"

"I don't care what you do with me, just as long as you do it at the Getting-to-Know-You dance. Her pa sang, Zachariah." As far as Molly was concerned, that was a sign.

"And that means what?" Apparently, he didn't see things as clearly.

"That means you two got something in common."

"Sure. We can both carry a tune. Anyone can do that."

"Not like you can. Promise me you'll go to the dance."

He climbed onto the wagon. "I ain't promising anything." Then he added, "I'll be by sometime to drop off some food for the ladies when I ain't so ticked off at your meddling." And with that, he snapped the reins.

~*~

The girls went to and fro in Molly's house, preparing for the dance.

Lillian had arrived in town wearing a dress fit for a princess, but since then, she'd been wearing a black dress fit for a funeral. And that's what she put on to wear to the dance.

"Ain't you going to wear another pretty dress like the one you came in?"

"I only have the two dresses," she said.

"What about that fancy dress?"

"It'll overshadow the other women."

You could wear a potato sack and you'd still overshadow those cackling hens. Especially that Rosie. Molly went into her own trunk and fished out a calico blouse and skirt she hadn't worn in years. Compared to what the other women were wearing, it was old fashioned and a little high on the neck, but it was modest and something Zachariah would find lady-like. Anything was better than that drab black thing.

"Put this on," Molly commanded.

Lillian complied. It made her look like a sweet little prairie girl. She filled it out nicely.

Molly had always been on the lean side, and had never been that curvy. "It's a little too long, but I can hem it up in no time."

~*~

"Lord, I know Molly's doing everything out of caring, but I sure wish she'd stop meddling in my affairs," Zachariah mumbled as he hauled one sack each of what he'd bought earlier into his house. The rest he left in the wagon to bring to Molly's.

What he called "home" since he'd quit working for Marcus was more of a disaster than a house. It was the place his mother had left him, and he, in turn, had left to the vermin, the elements, and the mischief makers. He'd cut back a decade's worth of overgrowth, cleared out most of the cockroaches, and burned the mice-infested bedding and cushions. It was six rooms, three up, and three down. The three down consisted of a kitchen that was no more than a cooking stove and a frying pan; a sitting room with nothing to sit on; and a bedroom with a pillow and a couple of blankets. He kept his spare clothes folded in a pile in a corner, and his Sunday suit hanging on a nail in the wall.

The entire top floor needed gutting because rain had gotten through the broken windows and rotted out the wood. He'd planned on using the money he'd earned from the cattle to buy lumber, and work on that for the next few months, but Molly and her meddling had sure wedged a rod in the gears of his plans.

"Yup," he said aloud as he looked around at all the work that needed to be done. "I want to go to this dance about as much as I'd like to have one of my teeth yanked."

Actually, having a tooth pulled would have been more pleasant than the way Miss Rauling had taken to him when he'd offered her that ride. The way she'd frozen up when his hat fell off seemed a sure sign she wanted nothing to do with him. He, in turn, wanted nothing to do with her. As far as Zachariah was concerned, Nate could have her.

But for some reason, as evening approached, he decided he could use a bath. Then he reckoned he should take a comb to his hair. And that stubble on his chin felt mighty scratchy when he rubbed it. The next thing he knew, he was dressed in Sunday duds that seemed to be getting a lot of wear lately and saddling Thunderbolt. He wasn't going to the dance to get a thank you from Miss Rauling, but rather to keep Molly from getting him into more trouble.

He held Thunderbolt to a slow, meditative pace along a well-trodden path, in no hurry. *So why does Molly want me to go to this dance? Oh, yes. So Miss Rauling can thank me for the piano that belonged to Molly, which she'd sold to pay the matchmaker, and which I then bought back and returned to Molly, who owned it in the first place, and Molly then donated to the church, so it didn't belong to her any more, and she then told Miss Rauling all the credit belonged to me.* "Lord," he concluded, "that Molly sure makes my life complicated."

At the last glow of dusk, Zachariah reached the church, but he'd still arrived before Molly's wagon. It made sense the women would arrive late, since they were the highlight of the dance, and because they were, well, women.

There were plenty of horses tethered to the hitching post, and plenty of activity up on the church platform. Malachi had brought his fiddle, Clayton had his harmonica, and the Sheriff had the jaw harp he often played on the bench in front of his office. The band was already in the swing of things, cranking out a toe-tapping jig.

Kerosene lamps lit up the staging, and a temporary grand entryway had been rigged over the stairway by nailing together a frame of two-by-fours, and then wrapping it with flowers. A rail had been built around the platform, so nobody would fall off. It made the 'church' look like a boxing ring.

This was the biggest to-do the town had had in years. Everyone was there, including the few local women and children, as well as all the men, whether they had a dance partner or not.

Molly's refreshments would soon fill the empty spaces on the table, and her wagon full of women would round out the event.

Zachariah dismounted from Thunderbolt.

"I had a feeling you'd come."

Zachariah's feet cautiously met the ground as Nate stepped out of the shadows. He didn't look at Nate's face, but from the corner of his eye, he took in Nate's fancy three-piece suit, silk tie and all.

"Are you here to claim the lady?"

He soaked in Nate's words. Miss Rauling wasn't just a woman, she was, indeed, a lady. And what exactly did Nate mean by the word *claim*?

Molly would have never let *that* slip out.

Zachariah avoided looking at the impeccably handsome Nate by tethering Thunderbolt's reins to the post with extra effort. "None of them ladies belong to me." It was the truth, regardless of Molly's intention.

"I'm glad you realize that." Nate added with a snicker, "Every so-called match offered the rest of us a good chuckle. If you had been matched with Lillian, why, that would have been the best laugh of them all."

A sickening feeling rose in the pit of Zachariah's stomach.

"In fact," Nate said, "the notion of you and Lillian together reminds me of a story." He paused, probably hoping Zachariah would be curious enough to ask which one.

Zachariah didn't care to know, and he supposed

that's why Nate continued.

"It's a story about a disfigured creature who becomes infatuated with a beautiful gypsy woman. Quasimodo and Esmeralda were their names. As I recall, the title of the book was *The Hunchback of Notre Dame*."

After a final yank on the tethering knot, Zachariah loosened Thunderbolt's girth to give the horse a rest.

"The beast rescues her, she tries to escape," Nate pressed, knowing very well Zachariah had read the book in school along with the rest of the class.

Zachariah moved to the other side of the horse, but Nate followed.

"And then she starts to pity the monster."

Zachariah paused. His face heated up, and he could feel the added sear of Nate's glare upon his scarred cheek.

"I figure that would be the only reason Lillian would succumb to marrying a creature like you. *If* she found out…"

"Found out what?"

"That you were so desperate for a wife, you had to buy one."

Thunderbolt snorted, and Zachariah caught himself being too rough. He eased up.

"That wouldn't be a marriage for a beautiful woman like her. It'd be a sentence." The humor dropped from Nate's voice. "You're a beast, Zachariah. You've got the mark of Cain on your face for good reason. That idiot of a judge might have let you get away with murdering my sister, but I guarantee that God of yours didn't. You don't deserve a wife, and God wants to make sure you don't have one."

Zachariah tightened the girth back up, and got

back onto Thunderbolt. "I reckon I ought to be going."

Nate's intelligent gaze hardened to a glare as he mocked Zachariah. "I *reckon* you ought to be."

~*~

When Molly pulled up with the wagon full of women, she wasn't too pleased when Nate walked up to them and offered a hand to Lillian.

He helped her down. "I apologize for not being at the church the other day," Nate said to her. "I understand you so kindly came by to offer me some refreshment. I found myself drafted into some impromptu entertaining."

Impromptu entertaining, all right. Molly kept her mouth clamped. *More like Hattie entertaining you.*

"You look lovely, Lillian."

Lillian? Molly noted that Nate had the gall to call Lillian by her first name, as though they were already married.

"And you, Mr. Powell, look dashing." By the slight smile on her face, Lillian was nibbling on that fake fly he'd put on the hook.

Nate then addressed Molly. "If you're looking for Zachariah, he decided to go home." He offered his arm to Lillian, which she took, hook, line, and stinker. "Which is a good thing," Nate added, "because I wouldn't want to upset this poor woman."

"Upset?" Lillian repeated.

"Molly didn't tell you about Zachariah?" He cast Molly a not-surprised look. "There's no need for details, but his face is grotesquely marred. His disfigurement would be shocking for a lady of your delicate constitution."

For some reason, Lillian looked down at her shoe.

The wagon emptied out, and Nate escorted Lillian onto the church staging.

The other men came for their women, and the band was warmed up and strumming a tune.

Malachi, however, cast love-sick eyes over his fiddle at Rosie. He'd gotten stuck providing the entertainment because, although he looked like an old shabby dog, he sure could play.

Molly hated to admit it, but he was the best out of the bunch. If only he'd stop with that knee-slapping ruckus and play a nice, solemn hymn.

Molly lagged behind to take care of the horses. *Nate makes that scar on Zachariah's face sound like his entire head is one big wart.* And the worst part was that Zachariah believed him.

It didn't take long for the couples to start dancing.

And then, Molly saw another problem.

Don't Prudence belong to Brawley, and Aggie belong to...? "Hold on there!" Molly butted up to the musicians and made them stop playing. "Why ain't you folks dancing with your matches? That scientist feller said his fixings were 'satisfaction guaranteed.' So quit cheating around."

The men and women hemmed and hawed, but found their proper mates.

Molly gave an approving nod of her head. "That's more like it." She ordered Malachi to start fiddling again.

He didn't budge. "Can I dance with my sweet Rosie now?"

Sweet ...? The name was getting under Molly's skin. She threw her hands up. This night was all washed out. "You can take her home tonight for all I care."

Malachi's eyes lit up, and he abruptly left his fiddle behind. He skipped down to where Rosie stood by the refreshment table, and bowed low. "May I have this dance, sweet love of my life?"

"Not a chance, you wretched old bum," Rosie said around a mouthful of gingerbread. Then she complained. "Ain't enough ginger."

Ain't enough....? Molly heard that, and she froze dead in her tracks. She indignantly planted a hand on her hip. *Why there's exactly the right amount of ginger*, and she knew because that recipe was tried and true. Nothing pleased that fussy, ain't-so-rosy Rosie. *So if they ain't good enough for you, why do you keep eating them?*

"How about dancing the next dance?" Malachi asked Rosie. He looked hopeful.

Rosie stopped chewing. "I don't want to dance the next one with you, or the one after that, or any dance for the rest of my life. That means no, not ever."

That shut Malachi up but only for a moment. "I don't blame you, my fragrant flower." He picked up a piece of gingerbread. "I'm partial to Molly's cooking myself." He finally left her.

The band started playing the waltz Molly had specially requested for Lillian to dance with Zachariah. Molly was grumbling mad when Nate asked Lillian to dance and she accepted.

~*~

Zachariah watched from the shadows at the shindig that livened up the night. There was one couple in particular that arrested his attention.

11

While the other couples in the center of the lighted staging looked as if they were just shuffling their feet, there was no doubt Miss Rauling and Nate were waltzing. She was the most graceful thing Zachariah had ever seen on two feet.

Nate looked dignified holding her, one hand set on the small of her waist, his other hand folded over hers. The top of her head reached Nate's eyes, so they were even the right height for one another.

Zachariah visually digested their physical and cultural harmonies as the couple moved in unison. They were one in accord; one of a kind. The only way they were opposites was in the color of their hair, but even in that, they were similar in a manner. Nate's hair was blond as blond can get, and hers was black as black can get.

Zachariah watched Miss Rauling, wanting to etch into his mind the way the lamplight shone upon her hair, and the way her simple skirt and shirt-waist showed off how pretty she really was.

The dress she'd worn the day she'd arrived had looked gaudy and uncomfortable. It was so tight at the waist it was a wonder she could breathe, and then all that fabric gathered behind in the bustle shaped her so she looked like the backside of a horse.

But the cotton dress she wore now skimmed her figure and made her look like what a woman ought to look like. And then some. There was only one thing that kept her from being perfect tonight, and he found that fault in her pretty smile.

It belonged to Nate.

Zachariah watched the couple until he'd soaked up enough, until he was convinced there was no reason for him to have stuck around. What else had he expected to find but two compatible people?

~*~

"I can't keep my eyes off you, Lillian," Nate said. "Despite the dress."

Lillian slipped her hand from his to touch the cotton neckline of the old-fashioned garment Molly had altered. It was light and loose and frankly, the most comfortable dress she'd ever worn. "Molly was kind enough to loan it to me," she said.

"It was kind of you to wear it for her. Where did you learn to dance so well?"

Lillian thought it interesting that Nate had turned the favor around and he had changed the subject so abruptly. Any argument from her would have to be wedged between an insult and a compliment. "I've had my opportunities, Mr. Powell." A brief response was best, especially since he'd touched upon a sensitive subject. Lillian was unwilling to divulge her plunge-from-heights history so soon in the relationship.

If Nate was as wealthy as he portrayed himself to be, then what would he say when he discovered she was just a governess—and worse, a fugitive?

"Where did you learn to dance?" she returned.

Since he was good at flipping things on their heads, she decided to try the same tactic.

But Nate Powell was a master at this game. He flashed a smile that would have made any lady swoon. The man was poised, dashing, and appeared to have every reason to be confident. "I've had my opportunities, as well."

Lillian, however, was not one to swoon. She could tell his statement was evasive. She pulled away from their waltz. "May I get something to drink?"

He escorted her to the refreshments and poured her some punch. "So tell me," he said. "What brought you to a scientific matchmaker?"

Lillian hesitated. She was quickly catching on to his game. "I suppose the same thing that brought you." She paused to allow him to interject, which he did not. So she offered, "Looking for a suitable mate, of course."

"Of course," Nate said. "Based on a single strand of hair."

"Amazing, isn't it?" She looked at him; he looked at her.

Both knew the other wasn't that gullible.

12

I never knew four ladies could be so much work. The next morning found Molly running back and forth from the kitchen to the dining room. Once again, she was catering to a bunch of bickering, funny-talking women who didn't give a fig about the feast Molly had set before them. They were too busy carping. Two of them were yakking louder than the rest.

"He ain't got one good word to say to me," Aggie said over a plateful of fluffy scrambled eggs and hash browns fried to a golden crisp. "The old fuddy-duddy does nothing but complain about what clothes I wear."

"As he should." Prudence plucked a slice of savory cinnamon bread from the serving dish. "The man is a doctor. He needs a wife, not a tart."

"Who are you calling a tart?" Aggie leaned her buxom bosom over a serving dish of crispy bacon, which had splattered Molly with sizzling hot grease while she fried it. "At least I don't look like an old schoolmarm."

"Old?" Prudence dropped the slice of bread into her plate. The bread could have been a piece of rawhide the way she acted. "Who are you calling old?"

Molly was going cross-eyed with all the bickering.

And then, one voice rose up above them all.

"Ain't enough cinnamon in this bread."

That did it. Molly had gotten up at four o'clock that morning to knead the dough, let it rise, pound it down, let it rise again, and bake it. She'd had enough, and she had a sure-fire way to cut things short. "Get ready for Sunday gathering in fifteen minutes."

Even though Zachariah wouldn't be showing up because Lillian was staying at the house, the Lord's Day was still the Lord's Day.

There was dead silence.

All gazes shot to Molly.

"Why," Aggie stammered, "it's almost eight o'clock. Time flies faster than a goose with its tail feathers on fire. I told Doctor Hinkle I'd meet him for— for a Sunday morning walk."

"As you recall," Prudence chimed in, "that walk was with Brawley and me."

"As I recall," Rosie said, "that walk was for all of us."

Before Molly could say "Hallelujah," the women had hitched the horses to the wagon, and were headed down the road.

All except Lillian. She sat at the piano, smiled, and started playing *Rock of Ages*. Her young hands looked like twin fawns skipping along a meadow.

"Ain't you going to see your Nate?" Molly asked cynically.

"It appears I'm the only one whose husband-to-be didn't invite her for a Sunday stroll. Besides, after we're married, I suppose I'll be seeing Mr. Powell everyday 'til death do us part.' No. Today is the Lord's Day, and I will celebrate it by playing the piano Mr. Keane so kindly donated." She paused a moment, and then added, "I regret I didn't see him at the dance."

"Regret?" That was the last thing Molly expected to hear.

Especially after what Nate had said to Lillian

about Zachariah's face being so "marred" and "shocking."

"I still haven't had the opportunity to thank him," Lillian said. Then she read the awed look Molly suspected had crossed her face. "I'm not as fainthearted as Mr. Powell thinks. For all the joy Mr. Keane has brought me by donating this piano, he deserves no less than a peck on the cheek."

Molly's jaw dropped. *Well, that's a start.*

~*~

"Did I tell you how lovely you look today, Lillian?"

"Yes. For the third time, Mr. Powell."

The next time Lillian saw her husband-to-be, she wore a dress borrowed from Prudence. More precisely, it was Prudence who had offered the dress. She had a trunk full, and she had handed Lillian the dress in private to express her gratitude for tending to her when she was sick.

Lillian rode beside Mr. Powell in the back seat of a surrey handled by a driver. They drove some distance, until a ranch came into view from afar.

Nate stopped the driver. "This is my father's ranch," Nate said. "And the estate I'm destined to inherit."

For a moment, the view held Lillian in awe. The house was a massive two-story log structure which stretched as long and wide as a mansion. The property had a bunk house, a barn four times as big as the house, and fences that stretched for miles. Within the fenced-in area, a seemingly infinite number of cows grazed on land that was vast and sunny. It was no wonder the tour required a surrey. It appeared the Powells owned more land than the Queen.

"I'd introduce you to my parents, but they're meeting with some other ranchers," Mr. Powell said. "They're trying to figure out what to do about open grazers."

"Open grazers?" Lillian had never heard the term.

"Cattle owners who don't have land of their own. They allow their cattle to graze wild on other people's property, and they've gone so far as to start cutting down our fences."

"How much land does your family own?"

"One hundred thousand acres. We've got over five thousand head of cattle."

She was astonished that one family could own that much land and that many cattle.

They drove in close enough where she could see and hear a dozen hired hands gathered around a fenced-in circle. They were waiving their hats and cheering a man riding a bucking horse, until it threw him onto the hoof-beaten ground. The man looked sore when he picked himself up, but everyone seemed to be having a good sport of it, except for the horse.

Lillian was also enthralled. Her heart danced with excitement. "So, you're a cowboy, Mr. Powell."

He laughed. "Heavens no. That's a job for slackers. My father made me get my feet wet in the business. He'd started at the bottom and figured I should do the same. But now I do something that's more to my liking."

"And that is?"

"Accounting."

The dancing in Lillian's heart came to a standstill. "You're an accountant?" *Yes,* she thought, *how—*

sensible.

She'd been too reserved to truly study her fiancé, but now a long-overdue look revealed he was not much taller than her five-foot frame, and not much heavier. In fact, the hand with which he'd helped her into the surrey seemed hardly the hand of a man at all. It was small, callous-free, and almost as delicate as hers. He was hardly the rugged man of her dreams. But he was a gentleman. He'd ensured they had an escort today, and not one of his comments had been inappropriate. Furthermore, he'd gracefully given in to Molly's insistence on a church wedding.

"So you work as an accountant for your father." Lillian tried to be content with her lot. She would marry a handsome man, and she would be wealthy. Wasn't that every woman's wish?

"Yes, I do the accounting. Although my father keeps harping on me to finish my education."

"You didn't finish?"

He glanced at her as though what she'd said was absurd. "Why do I need to know Greek, Latin, and Elocution," he said the latter word with exaggerated clarity, "in order to count cows? All one needs to do is count the legs and divide by four." His joke was stated too cynically for her to find it humorous.

"I'm sure there are other subjects taught that will help you keep up with the demands of a growing business, as well as the times in which that business is developing," she answered.

"My father didn't finish sixth grade, and he founded the most successful business in the county."

"If that's so, then your father is no fool. If he deems an education to be a wise choice for the beneficiary of his business-"

"I'm his only living child. My father has no *choice* but to leave me everything."

"But when the time comes for you to take over, you'd be all the more prepared, and-"

"And you're beginning to sound like my father."

As much as she believed his father to be right, young Mr. Powell had gotten red in the face. She thought it best to cut the subject short and find another topic with which he'd be more comfortable.

"So tell me, Mr. Powell. How do I look today?"

13

As the week passed, Molly's back got stiffer, but her rules for the women became more pliant. Lillian didn't spend as much time with Nate as the other women spent with their fiancés.

Nate had given her an excuse that he had work to catch up on. Nate had catching up to do, all right. Catching up to do with Hattie.

But Lillian didn't seem to mind when the other women took off and left her behind. In fact, Molly was beginning to wonder if Lillian liked it. After she'd help clean the house, Lillian would spend the rest of her time playing the piano. She'd close her eyes and smile, and Molly could just imagine Lillian was listening to her pa sing in her memories.

Molly stood in the doorway. Yes, she could live with Lillian as long as she wanted to stay. But that frail, bed-stealing Prudence, and that ain't-so-rosy Rosie who kept complaining about the food, and that other cackling hen, Aggie, all of whom kept Molly buried in clothes, blankets, and dishes, were another matter. She wanted to get them married off real soon.

Later that week, Molly encountered another problem. She'd gone with Lillian into town to check with Clayton to see if he'd gotten word from a preacher, when she noticed something.

Aggie and the Doc, and Prudence and Brawley passed one another on the walk, and the wrong woman was making eyes at the wrong man, and vice versa.

Rosie was yelling at Malachi, and calling him a bum in that funny accent of hers.

All in all, Molly counted everyone everywhere, except where they were supposed to be.

Building that church.

~*~

The next day, when the women were gone, it was just Molly's luck that Nate had taken Lillian out for a ride in his fancy surrey, because Zachariah stopped by.

Zachariah brought over sacks of food and a couple of squabbling chickens that Dusty started herding with Molly's other chickens. Zachariah heaved a sack over his shoulder, carried it into her house, and look manly doing it.

"I reckon you got some extra mouths to feed," he said, obviously not so ticked off this time.

"Some of them mouths are extra big," Molly mumbled, thinking of Rosie's in particular. She thanked him for the extra food, and then started grumbling. "It ain't right that Nate's stealing your gal. He don't deserve better than Hattie."

"First of all," Zachariah leaned low and placed the sack on the pantry floor, "Miss Rauling ain't my gal. And second." He stood upright. "It ain't right the way you talk about Hattie. She's had it harder than most folks." Zachariah was right.

Molly had once felt sorry for her way back when. Hattie had no pa, and she'd barely turned eighteen when her homesick ma left Hattie with a shack, a washboard, and a bucket. "I offered to take her in,"

Molly said.

"Times were just as tough for you as they were for Hattie," Zachariah reminded her. "Danny was faring poorly, and she didn't want to add to your burden."

"So she goes to work in a saloon, instead? I'd have found a way."

"I know that, Molly, but she doesn't. And if you don't stop talking about her like she's the devil's right hand, she's never going to come around."

"And if you don't start courting Lillian, she ain't never going to come around, either."

Zachariah shook his head as he walked out the door.

Molly chased after him. "Where're you going?" Eventually Lillian would return. How were these two going to meet if Molly couldn't get them both in the same place at the same time?

Zachariah stepped onto his wagon. "Molly, you're worse than Cupid. What will I do about your meddling?" He snapped the reins.

Molly scratched her head when she saw what was in the back of his wagon. Along with Dusty and his old toolbox, there were enough sacks of nails to build a whole new house.

~*~

Zachariah rode up to the abandoned, partially-built church. Now that the men could court their women, there was nothing motivating them to finish it. At least not until Molly could rustle up another one of her schemes. But in the meantime, he knew it had been Molly's dream to have a church.

"Molly," he muttered under his breath, "you sure

do pile a heap of work on me." He set to finishing the church by himself, unaware of the surrey in the far distance.

14

"Did I tell you how lovely you look today?"

"When you picked me up, Mr. Powell. As I'm sure you will recall, I responded that you looked dapper." Nate Powell found her more attractive wearing Prudence's clothes rather than Molly's. Lillian knew her response was a bit sharp, but she'd rather be playing piano than discussing how lovely she looked.

Or perhaps it was he—decked out in a three-piece suit, silk tie, and derby hat—who was fishing for compliments.

Once again, Lillian was riding beside Mr. Powell in the back seat of his surrey. This time he had taken her for a tour of the town outskirts. The flat scenery had long since become monotonous and the company more so.

That is, until he started taking subtle liberties. He draped his arm across the back of her seat. Avoiding his touch, she sat rigidly upright.

Her words had been few while they rode, but her head had been full of concerns. There was something particularly heavy she wished to discuss. The topic was important to her, but she didn't know how to approach it. Finally, she pushed herself to ask outright. "Tell me, Mr. Powell. Have you an interest in music?"

"I've been to the opera," he said with a disregarding shrug. "I found it ridiculous."

"Really? Why is that so?"

"Men that sing remind me of deep-voiced women." He laughed.

She didn't. "My father was an opera singer."

"I beg your pardon," he said with ease.

"And I beg yours." She eyed him. The fact his answer offended her didn't seem to faze him in the least. At the risk of being insulted herself, she added, "I play piano."

"I guess that's fine for a pastime."

You guess? "Of course, you'll allow me to play for the church."

This time he took a moment to respond. "I thought you knew. The work on the building has been cancelled due to lack of interest."

She hadn't known. "Perhaps you could use your influence and stir the men to finish it."

That stirred from him a small lecture. "That would be impractical. I'm willing to pay a preacher to come to town to perform your ceremony, if you insist on one. But to build a church for a one-time engagement? It's a lot of work and money for something no one but Molly Crammer wants."

Molly? What about your own wife-to-be? "But you donated fifty dollars towards the project."

"No, Lillian. I donated fifty dollars for you."

The thought raced through her head, and then darted out her mouth. "So I'm accruing damages."

He paused. "Damages?" Was he toying with her?

"As you recall, our contract permits me to renege so long as I reimburse you all your expenses, including those you further amass."

The manner in which he'd said, "Oh—yes," made it apparent he'd simply glanced over the contract looking for the signature line, just as she had.

"Head toward town." Mr. Powell's instructions to the driver avoided any further discussion on the topic. He then addressed Lillian. "I'm sure you could use something to eat. We have a quaint eatery in our quaint little town." He emphasized the word *quaint* both times in an effort to sound charming, when indeed she knew he was again being evasive. He started on another subject, but she couldn't get her mind off a previous one.

No church.

The more she saw of her fiancé, the more of a stranger he became, until it seemed her enthusiasm about playing the piano for Sunday services was all that had made the thought of marrying him tolerable. They had nothing in common—*except Elocution*, she thought to herself, with mockingly perfect diction.

The driver turned the surrey, and a dispirited Lillian looked to the side. She pretended to soak in more of that same old scenery, but there was nothing more to soak in. It was the same thing over and over. The grass was parched, prickly cacti dotted the ground, and the soil was baked to a cracked crust beneath that blasted noonday sun.

"What do you think of your new home, Lillian?"

Hearing her name brought her out of the stupor. The child inside wanted to stomp and sob, *It doesn't feel like home,* so the governess accommodated him. "It's— quaint."

He laughed lightly, but she failed to reciprocate even by forcing a polite smile. Since the depth of their conversation couldn't advance beyond *quaint* and *lovely*, Lillian avoided further repetition altogether by turning her head from him and steeping herself in more of that arid, barren, nowhere-to-escape scenery.

Mr. Powell kept rambling. She caught the word "parents," and thought it odd they were too busy to meet their future daughter-in-law. The notion also needled her as to why the highly eligible and apparently well-traveled Mr. Powell stooped so low as to order himself a bride. Specifically, a scientifically-matched bride. However, she knew straightforwardly asking either question would result in a verbal detour back to the *quaint* or *lovely.* Although Nate Powell had a broad smile, he was a closed man. This would not be a marriage of love.

As she stared out at her so-called new home, a familiar ache of loneliness settled into her chest. Every drop of hope had been squeezed out by the hand of her husband-to-be. She wished the cowboy who had appeared on the moon-lit horizon—the one she'd sworn she'd seen through the carriage window the day she'd arrived—would appear once more and rescue her from this fate. But all she saw were the spiny cacti of what was and what was to be.

She had to face the facts. The cowboy who had enthralled her was nothing but a fantasy she had to forget. She sat stiff and stifled by her reality, avoiding the touch of its unwelcome arm draped behind her.

The surrey bumped her along the sun-baked path. The town buildings came into view, and she found the tiny square of a partially-built church set off on a small hill in the far distance. She wanted to disbelieve what Mr. Powell had said regarding the lack of interest in it.

There was something about the image of a white steeple against the sky that offered the reassurance that even if she could never find herself again, at least God knew where she was.

The thought there was no longer the flurry of men

proving their honor to their future wives by their sweat and labor made her heart feel desolate. That there would be no place for the ladies to gather to show off their babies made her heart feel even more desolate. Finally, there was the most desolate thought of all—that of the kindly but marred Mr. Keane. His generous donation would come to naught.

Except to have brought her some joy.

"Lillian."

Hearing her name stirred her back to present company.

"Do you agree?"

Agree with what? Did it matter? Whatever it was, she knew he was merely tossing her a crumb by asking for an opinion he'd simply disregard. So she tossed him a crumb right back. "As you wish, Mr. Powell."

He paused. His lips smiled, but his eyes didn't. "Seeing we're engaged, shouldn't you be calling me Nate?"

She tried the name on mentally as she looked at a man who failed to care about the things that mattered to her. *Nate.* No. Calling him by his Christian name was far too intimate for an individual who was, in fact, so distant. Her quiet said it all.

He withdrew his arm from the back of her seat, and she leaned back at last.

This time it was he who turned away.

She studied his profile. Nate Powell was very handsome indeed. His face had a sculpted look, so that even his curls appeared to be deliberately set on his forehead. The light gray of his suit accentuated the light blue of his eyes and the yellow of his hair. She couldn't have asked for a mate with a more perfect appearance. But underneath that polished exterior, he was a passionless accountant with no interest whatsoever in music—and this dull ride was a bland appetizer of her life as his wife.

Nate Powell was no dreadful, wobbly old man, but neither was he a man who cared to know her heart. Nor was he one to share his own. All he'd been talking about was how successful his father was, and the only thing he'd revealed about himself was how straight his teeth were. Furthermore, the arm he'd rested on the side of the surrey, as well as the one he'd slung behind her earlier, weren't the arms of a rugged man in the least. Mr. Powell's ability to stand fast without getting knocked over when she passionately catapulted herself into his arms was definitely questionable. But there was one thing she knew for certain. He'd deem such behavior as childish and ridiculous.

As childish as a woman who loved to play piano, and as ridiculous as a man who sang…

This time Lilly had made Papa sing Sealed with a Rainbow *while she played the piano. Though he was in a rush, she wouldn't let him leave in peace until he'd done so. It had been raining that day, and the whole world seemed sad. The carriage was waiting in front of the house, with Papa's trunk tied to it, and Papa was singing at a faster clip than she wanted to play the piece.*

Papa finished and bestowed a good-bye kiss on her forehead, along with a reassurance that, God willing, he'd be back in no time at all. He left Lilly listlessly pecking out the tune with one finger. From the corner of her eye, she watched him open the door and glance back at her before closing it behind him. A moment later, he shot back in.

"Lilly, come here."

Had her pouting persuaded him to stay? It had never worked before. Judging by the fact his trunk was still mounted to the roof of the carriage, it wasn't working now, either. So what was he up to?

"Hurry! You're going to miss it."

His excitement piqued her curiosity enough that she followed him outside to where he had stopped short of the carriage.

The rain had ended but left a peculiar hue to the grounds. There was a bluish cast upon the grass, the cobblestone walk, and the Canterbury bells that lined it. Still, she had no idea why he was so excited.

"Well, Papa, what is it?"

"Look up," he said.

She did, a little. "All I see are big, gray, ugly clouds." It seemed they'd lingered there forever and were never going away.

"I see something far more beautiful than that."

He pivoted her and pointed to a spot way up in the sky where an arch of yellow, blue, and violet loomed.

She forgot he was leaving, and her mouth turned up. "I can see it, Papa! I can see it!"

He crouched and hugged her from behind. "Sometimes you just have to know where to look," he said over her shoulder.

With innocent awe, they watched the rainbow as the carriage waited and the bustling world came to a peaceful pause.

Memory tears were the most difficult to hold back, and against her will Lillian's eyes glazed over.

They had drawn closer to the church, and the angle of the view had changed. The church was now in the nearer distance behind her husband-to-be. Her hazy gaze shifted from his profile to it.

There was no steeple. There wasn't even a wall. Indeed, the building had been left as nothing more than a platform. She took in all the disillusionment, including, in her peripheral view, the indifference of her companion.

The realization her happiness had ended the day her father had died settled in. She doubted rainbows even existed in a place as dry as this. It was so far out in the middle of nowhere it seemed even God didn't care to go looking for it. *There will be no one to show me where the rainbows are any more, will there, Lord?*

Just then, the sound of barking roused her. *What would a dog be doing out here?* She spotted a horse and a wagon. After that came the sound of a single hammer striking something hard. The next thing she saw took her breath away.

There *was* someone working on the church. Someone whose tall, strapping form sparked her heart back to life. *Is my mind playing tricks on me again?* She attempted to blink away the vision, but when she reopened her eyes, the man was still there.

This time her elusive fantasy was wearing no shirt or hat. His bronzed chest was broad and brawny, and hard to look away from. His hair tumbled wild and unruly, concealing his face and keeping him a mystery.

He stood, both feet planted resolutely on the church platform. His stance expressed his conviction that despite the heat and that wretched sun, this building would be built. He raised powerful arms and slammed the hammer once again. His determination thundered across the hillside. He was steadfast.

As steadfast as her gaze.

Furthermore, the way Mr. Powell's gaze shot over to the man confirmed beyond a doubt this epitome of Lillian's ideal man was more than just a fleeting phantom.

He was indeed real.
If only she could see his face.

15

Molly had worked her way into a pickle. It was morning, her back was sore from sleeping on the hard floor yet another night, and the women had spent breakfast bickering about their fiancés, instead of telling Molly how delicious her flapjacks were. The worst thing was, in order for Molly to get any peace and quiet, she knew she would shoo them off to see their men—who were supposed to be building the church so they could hurry up and get married.

But of course, the men weren't working on it because they were content just to see their women. Or, rather, the other men's women. So maybe they were avoiding getting married altogether.

This isn't just a pickle, Molly thought. *It's more like a relish.* And then, there was still the matter of how to get Zachariah and Lillian together, when they hadn't even met.

Lillian was drying the last of the dishes, while the rest of the women were already piling into the wagon. Lillian was supposed to join them this time, and meet Nate in town.

Molly got an idea. *Desperate times call for desperate measures.* She put a hand on her back and let out a groan as if she were having a baby.

Predictably, Lillian rushed to Molly's aid and helped her to a chair. "Are you all right?"

Molly sat herself down with feigned effort. "Just

these old bones of mine acting up." She paused to look heavenward. *That's the truth, Lord.* Though her reaction was a mite exaggerated.

The dishes still needed to be put away and the house picked up, and after a long, sullen look around—and a theatrically heavy sigh—Molly knew exactly what Lillian would say next.

"I can't leave you alone. Not in this condition."

"I can't expect you to stay and do an ailing old woman's housework. Not when you got a young feller to see." *That no good, gal-stealing...*another hair-raising groan.

"Nonsense. You need rest, and I insist on staying." Lillian told Rosie to leave without her, and to tell Nate she'd had a sudden change of plans. She closed the door behind them.

Molly smirked inwardly. That was the easy part. *Now, what about Zachariah?*

While Lillian was picking the dishes up, and the rest of the women were riding away, Molly thought of a scheme to get him here.

After the wagon was almost out of sight, Molly asked Lillian, "Will you go catch up with the women and tell Prudence to tell Brawley to tell Clayton to tell Mr. Keane, that I need him as soon as he can get here?" The folks in the chain she'd mentioned were the most reliable. They'd get word to him soon. Molly paused. "Tell them I got something that needs fixing. Hurry now. Run."

So while Lillian raced out to catch up to the women to deliver the message, Molly snuck off to the woodshed.

A few minutes later, Lillian's mission was accomplished and she was heading back to the house.

Molly slipped back into her sick chair. She rocked and groaned.

Lillian finished cleaning. After the work was done, Lillian settled in and played piano for a while.

Molly made the request, because "it soothed her aches and pains." Molly reminded Lillian of how generous it was of Mr. Keane to donate the piano, and what a fine feller he was, and—"Did I tell you he brought over a sack of potatoes and some chickens to help feed you gals?" All the while, Molly kept an eye on one of the windows, until she suddenly asked Lillian something out of the ordinary. "Can you split me some firewood?"

Lillian's fingers froze on a chord. She looked up. "Split some wood?"

"There's some logs down by the woodshed. There's an ax there, too." *Don't you know how to split wood? Of course you don't.* That's exactly why Molly had asked. "To build a fire. That chill in the air has gone and made my back worse."

Lillian looked at her as if to say, *What chill in the air?* It was near noon, mid-autumn, and the sun was high in the sky, baking everything below it.

"I guess I could just use this here shawl." Molly pulled a worn rag over her shoulders, shivered, and put on her misery face. She stole a glance at the window again. She could see some dust way off. To hurry the girl along, Molly groaned loud enough to wake the dead.

"I'd be happy to—split some wood." Lillian reluctantly left for the woodshed.

After Lillian closed the door, Molly scooted out of her chair and dashed to the window. She wanted to make sure Lillian found the wood, and double sure she found the ax.

The girl dragged a log onto the chopping block.

So far so good. Molly then dashed to another window. *Perfect.* She then dashed back to the first window, where she had a clear view of dainty little Lillian picking up the ax—and looking at it as if it were some strange newfangled contraption. *Come on*, Molly urged.

Lillian clutched the handle of the ax in her lady-like manner. Then she raised it over her head. Just as Lillian was about to swing the ax, Zachariah rushed up and caught it from behind.

Yup, Molly thought with a grin, *timing is everything.*

~*~

"Hold on there, ma'am." Zachariah slipped the ax from Miss Rauling's hands. "That may not be the best way to split wood," he said. *But it's a good way to lose a foot. What was a delicate thing like her doing out here splitting wood, anyway?*

She turned to him with an awkward innocence. She'd worn her hair in a chignon, but one blue-black tress had slipped out, and it tumbled in a soft wave along an ivory cheek that looked soft to the touch. Her eyes were sharp and blue, and they looked too intelligent to believe that one of those strands could reveal enough about a person to find a proper mate. With or without that "satisfaction guaranteed" foolishness. She brushed the stray hair behind her ear.

Normally Zachariah wasn't a man to let a

woman's beauty set him off balance, but something about her made him weak in the knees. Maybe it was the lady-like way she carried herself. He said the first sensible thing that came to mind. "You never chopped wood before, have you, ma'am?"

"No—I...who?"

Since she'd already gotten a good look at his face when his hat had fallen off at their last meeting, Zachariah figured he had nothing to lose by introducing himself properly this time.

"Zachariah, ma'am. Zachariah Keane." Trying to be bold about it, he took off his hat to her. He was well aware of the rippled skin on his cheek where his beard wouldn't accommodate him by growing in enough to cover it. He was also well aware of the way she backed up a step.

"*You're* Mr. Keane? Yes, of course." She abruptly curtsied. "I'm Lillian Rauling."

There was a hesitation in her voice that gave Zachariah cause to speculate as to what *"Yes, of course"* meant. *"Yes," Nate told me about that scarred-up face of yours, so "of course" now that I have a good look at you, who else could you be but that ugly creature he was talking about?* He put his hat back on. Once again, he was behind the solace of its brim. "If I may ask, ma'am. Why are you splitting wood in ninety-degree heat?"

Miss Rauling stood with her hands crossed gracefully. She was as pretty as a fairy princess, and it was hard to keep from getting caught up in her enchantment.

"Molly's back is sore," she said. "She was catching a chill, so she asked me to get some firewood."

"Catching a...?" That broke the spell. He suddenly had an itch to look over at the house. Sure enough, he caught a glimpse of Molly's face in the window just before she ducked. Thoughtfully he leaned the ax against his shoulder. "I'll tell you what. If you'd go on ahead in the house and look after Molly, I'd be pleased to split plenty of wood." He looked over at the scheming little cupid peeking out the window again. "Yes, ma'am. You can tell Molly I'll take good care of the matter."

~*~

Lillian was coming toward the door.

Molly hightailed back to the chair. She resumed rocking with a groan. "Did you fetch the firewood?"

"I didn't," Lillian said. "Mr. Keane is here, and-"

"Oh, is he, now?" *Questions ain't lying, Lord.* "Why ain't you out there with him?"

"He sent me in. He said to stay with you, and-"

"Maybe he could use some help."

"He seems quite capable," Lillian said. "Furthermore, he told me to tell you he'd take care of the matter."

"Take care of …?" *Uh-oh.* Zachariah was fixing to fix her good. In the meantime, Molly figured she'd better make it worth her while. "You might want to keep an eye on him. To make sure he don't hurt himself." *And to see them fine muscles of his.*

Molly shooed Lillian to the window, where Molly had a good view of Lillian, who had a good view of Zachariah rolling up his sleeves and exposing his fine forearms.

He set his hat aside and raised the ax.

~*~

Lillian's jaw dropped as she watched a rugged man, with hair falling about his face, split a log with two blows. Although she knew her facial expression defied her upbringing, for the moment she didn't give a fig. Because there was one thing she knew for certain. *That's him.*

Zachariah Keane. *He* was the man in the frock coat and hat she'd seen from the stagecoach window the day she'd arrived. *He* was the captivating figure of the man building the church. Her elusive cowboy in the moonlight finally had a name.

And a face.

16

Lillian recognized Mr. Keane as one of the two men who had offered her a ride the day she'd broken her shoe. He had a take-charge calmness. Just the sound of his voice had made her feel safe. But when his hat had fallen off...and she got a good look at his face...well, it wasn't what she'd expected.

Were it not for the scar, Mr. Keane would have been handsome—especially because of his serious brown eyes. But on one side of his face, he had a rippled patch of skin that extended from his cheekbone to his jaw. It wasn't exactly hideous, so much as it rendered him—frankly—flawed.

It seemed her epitome of the perfect man—the cowboy in the moonlight with her name in his pocket—turned out to be not so perfect after all. But this was all redundant because her name wasn't in his pocket. It was in Nate's.

The thought of her fiancé sparked a question. Why had Nate tried to frighten her away from Zachariah? Yes, the man was scarred, but he was far from the grotesquely-marred ogre Nate had ascribed him to be. So why had he?

Lillian observed that from this distance—and with his sleeves rolled up—Zachariah had an impressive stature.

She leaned against the windowsill and continued to watch with interest as one log after another succumbed to his strength. Before she was ready for it to end, he set down the ax, collected an armful of wood, and headed toward the house.

~*~

Oh, oh. Molly had her come-to-'ems coming, and she'd better rush Zachariah off before he could give them to her. "Thank you for the wood," she said. "I'll get the fire going myself after I-"

"With that sore back of yours?" Zachariah put a heavy hand on her shoulder, keeping her in the chair. "You just relax. I'll take care of everything."

Which was exactly what Molly was afraid of.

He went out again and returned with some kindling.

"Honest, Zachariah, I can get the fire going." She remembered the excuse that got him here in the first place. "I got something that needs fixing."

"When did it break?"

"This morning."

"Then it can wait until I get this fire going warm and toasty."

Molly didn't like that lingering look he gave her.

~*~

A half hour later, the fire was going full bore, and the heat that had chased Lillian to stand by the open door was making Molly feel like Joan of Arc.

"How's that doing for those sore joints of yours?" Zachariah asked.

They felt like boiling soup bones. "Feels good."

Molly tried to finalize things with a "Thank you," but he wasn't done yet.

"Here, Molly. I want you to have the full benefit of the fire." He picked her up, chair and all, and set her down next to the hearth.

She felt as if she were in an oven. "Yup. Them bones are sure feeling toasty." The quiver in her voice was trying to tell him that any more heat, and she'd start melting.

Zachariah was enjoying this. "Ain't you got anything better than that old, shabby shawl? Here." He found a wool blanket and wrapped it around her. He tucked it in nice and snug. "Now ain't that better?"

Sweat poured down her temples as Molly glared at him. When Zachariah reached for the quilt on the back of the sofa, Molly had met her limit. "Ain't you going to fix what I need fixing?" she growled.

He gave her a look that indicated he'd already done it. He then grabbed the bucket, tilted his hat to Lillian as he passed her, and went outside. He came back in hauling some water. "I reckon your chill's gone now?" he asked Molly.

"It is," she returned in a small voice. It was her way of crying uncle.

He threw the water onto the fire, and doused it. "Now," he said, "what needs fixing?"

"This here shelf," Molly said to Zachariah, after he'd followed her to the pantry. "It broke."

He looked at a plank that was six feet wide, eight inches deep, and two inches thick. It was split in half.

"I reckon termites must have done it."

He rubbed his jaw. "Termites, huh?"

"Hungry termites," she added.

He spied the handle of something stashed behind

the Dutch ovens.

"You didn't give those termites any help now, did you?"

"Course not."

He pulled out a sledge hammer.

Molly feigned a surprised look. "Why, what's that doing in the pantry?"

He let his gaze linger on her. "I reckon the hungry termites brought it in from the shed."

She snatched the hammer from him. "Don't make no never mind how that shelf broke. I got myself four women to feed, and I need this here shelf to put my dishes on."

It was so far gone Zachariah replaced it altogether with a board he borrowed from his wagon. "That ought to do you. Unless the termites get a hold of the ax." He walked out the door and tilted his hat to Miss Rauling as he passed her. "Ma'am," he said and headed toward his wagon.

Molly gave chase. "Ain't you going to stay and listen to Lillian play the piano you donated?"

Donated? He threw Molly a frown as he tossed his tools into the wagon.

Miss Rauling ran up and joined Molly. "Mr. Keane, I wanted to thank you for your generous donation and for allowing me to be the church pianist."

Church pianist? His frown deepened as he climbed onto the wagon bench.

"And I'm sure Lillian here would like to hear you sing," Molly said.

Miss Rauling brightened. "You sing, Mr. Keane?"

Now wait a minute! He stepped down from the wagon. "Molly, I..." He wanted to tell her his singing was personal and he resented her meddling, but he couldn't say much in front of Miss Rauling. Instead, he came up with a good reason for leaving. He climbed back onto the wagon. "That church ain't going to get finished, unless somebody finishes it."

This time it was Miss Rauling who rushed up to him. She laid her hand on his wrist. It was a whisper of a touch, but it held him fast.

He looked into her eyes. They were so blue, it was like looking into eternity.

She drew her hand back.

It took him a moment longer to recover.

"Mr. Keane," she said, "I'd also like to thank you for finishing the church. The men who started it had a special interest, but you…"

"I have an interest," he mumbled. "Keeping Molly happy and out of my hair." He tipped his hat to Miss Rauling again. "Ma'am." And then to Molly—though sometimes it was easy to forget she was also a lady. Then he snapped the reins and headed off to the church.

~*~

Lillian watched Zachariah as he headed off, and then asked an odd question. "What does he do for a living?"

Molly hesitated.

Lillian looked over at her.

"Zachariah, there? Why, he's a cowboy." Zachariah was no fancy college man like Nate, but he wasn't *just* a cowboy, either. He was a gentleman and a hero, and Molly wanted to make sure Lillian knew exactly what he was. "I go on cattle drives with him, 'cause I do his cooking," she said. "I remember one time in particular when he went after a cougar that had been sneaking up on the herd, nerving them up. Just as Zachariah disappeared from my sight, five thieving cattle rustlers came out of nowhere and captured me. And then what do I look up to find, but the whole hilltop lined with Injuns. Suddenly, they come a-whooping and a-charging down on us, like it were Armageddon. I couldn't do a thing, because them rustlers had me tied up. It was all up to Zachariah."

Lillian put a hand to her heart. "My goodness. What did Mr. Keane do?"

"First he roped the cougar and hog-tied it. Then he had a shootout with them rustlers. One of their bullets grazed Zachariah's forehead, just above the eye, and the blood half blinded him. But he's such a fine rifleman he shot every one of them dead. And that's using just one arm mind you, 'cause the cougar clawed up the other. Then he had a powwow with them Injuns, and he made a treaty with them. They were scared after what they'd seen him do singlehanded to the rustlers, so they named him 'Mighty White Bear.'"

Lillian's eyes grew wide. "Mr. Keane did all that?"

"Sure did."

Well, maybe Molly was stretching a five-foot-tall tale to ten feet. Or more like a two-foot-tall tale to twenty. All these incidents had happened. Just not all at the same time. And he didn't exactly hog-tie the cougar. He scared it off by ricocheting a bullet off a rock. As for the renegade Injuns, they were looking for a toll for the right to cross their land, since their buffalo herds had been depleted and food was scarce. Zachariah gave them four cows. But the name they gave him was real—Mighty White Bear—on account of he was so tall.

As for the story about the cattle rustlers, now that made up for the rest of it, because there was something Molly had held back. They didn't just tie her up. Those devils were aiming to have their wicked way with her. She remembered how scared she'd been when they'd threatened to shoot off her yapping jaw first.

But Zachariah did kill them. Every last one. Molly was there when he turned himself in to the Sheriff. The Sheriff turned around and deputized him. He gave Zachariah a pat on the back, and said, *"You know, I've had this hankering to move on. Maybe try my hand at farming, but I won't leave Ramsden without a good sheriff. Wouldn't happen to be interested in the job, now, would you?"*

"He's a cowboy, all right." Molly added with pride, "The best I ever did see."

~*~

Somehow, Lillian already knew Mr. Keane was a cowboy. But after hearing Molly's story, she found him intriguing. So much so, that the scar that had initially taken her aback began to add character to him. The man had tangled with terrible things and overcome them. But something else made him even more fascinating.

He sings.

Of course, no man could sing as well as her papa. She was privileged to have listened to such a brilliant voice. She imagined for a moment the reverent hymn, *Holy, Holy, Holy*, which her father had performed in several cathedrals, sung in Mr. Keane's charming drawl and peppered with words like *that there* and *I reckon.* The thought was so humorous she feigned a cough to cover her smirk.

She arched her neck as she watched Mr. Keane disappear down the road. Still, there was something about his speaking voice. Something in it that was as tranquil as a father hugging a distraught little girl— and showing her a rainbow. Something that pressed her to say, with genuine sincerity, "I should very much like to hear him sing."

17

"Where'd you get the money for this food, you wretched old bum? You spend every penny you have now, and I'll tell you one thing you won't have later. Me. I want china on the table…"

"You can't go spitting around my patients, Aggie. And the neckline on your dresses…"

"Eat up, Prudence. You got to put more meat on your bones and a roar in your voice. Farming's hard work, and with all them children you'll be caring for…"

Kate's Eatery had just opened up in the outdoors behind the general store. It offered beef stew, blueberry pie, and a place to eat other than the saloon.

Lillian sat quietly across from Nate, listening to the disagreements in the other couples and thinking she and he were even less compatible. They finally received their meals, and she was happy for something to do besides avoid his gaze.

"Where were you yesterday?" he finally asked. "I thought we were to meet."

"Did Rosie fail to convey my regret to you, Mr. Powell?"

"She conveyed it." He speared a piece of beef.

Lillian folded her hands. "Won't you thank the Lord for his provision before partaking thereof?"

"If the Lord offered to pay the bill, I'd be happy to thank him for it. But seeing he hasn't…" With a satirical look on his face, Nate took the bite.

Lillian quietly said a word of thanks before taking up her fork.

Nate speared another chunk of beef. "You don't spend much time with me. Considering."

"Is that so?" She thought he was the one guilty of failing to nurture the relationship. "If you were working on the church, I'd be there daily with refreshments. It seems you're the one too busy for me."

"That church again. You've been spending too much time with Molly."

Lillian poked at the pieces of carrots, potatoes, and meat in a puddle of broth in her dish. They provided more entertainment than her present company. "I was a Christian before I met her, so don't blame that on Molly."

"You weren't so holy the day you got off the stagecoach. You were ready to come home with me that same day."

She paused to look at him and to stress, "I arrived from England. Where else was I to go?" She cut a large piece of potato in half. "It's fortunate some people care enough about others to intervene. It was considerate of Molly to require a church—and *very* considerate of Mr. Keane to set out to finish it."

"You mean Zachariah?" He spoke the name more like a growl than a word.

She hesitated. Had she stirred some rivalry from the perfect Nate Powell? She brought the potato toward her lips, and sardonically asked before eating it, "Is there another Mr. Keane I should be aware of?" She chewed and swallowed the bite, all the while studying Nate for some reaction. The look in his eyes suggested she'd gained his attention to the fullest.

Good. This was an opportunity to pit her husband-to-be against a better man, and she intended to utilize that feminine ploy to its fullest.

"The church won't get finished," he said. "One man can't do all the work by himself."

"I would agree, had I not gotten a good look at Mr. Keane. He seems—quite capable." She forked another piece of potato. "And not only has he continued the work on the church, he has also been kind enough to donate a piano."

Nate intently fished for chunks of beef. "You make him sound like he's some sort of hero."

"I think the gentleman is to be commended."

"Gentleman?" His face reddened.

Obviously, he perceived himself to be everything a woman wanted, and he wasn't accustomed to competition. So of course, she continued. "He *is* finishing what everyone else so eagerly initiated and abruptly abandoned." She looked over her fork at him. "And others didn't bother to work on at all." She punctuated her statement by eating the potato bit.

"Maybe you didn't notice his scar." After pointing out Zachariah's most obvious flaw, Nate emphasized his only asset by leaning his face toward hers.

Apparently the tactics he employed were as subtle and devious as her own were becoming. He did *not* bring out the best in her. She cut a carrot. "I noticed his face." After answering matter-of-factly, she calmly ate the vegetable.

The conversation took an unexpected turn when Nate slammed his fork on the table. "Do you know how he got that scar?"

His gesture startled her, but she wouldn't let him see that. She took her time to chew, and when she finished, she responded, "No, Mr. Powell, I don't know how Mr. Keane got his-"

"The man killed my sister, that's how." The arrogance in his eyes gave way to a glare that alarmed her as he came to his feet. "He let her burn to death. So much for your so-called hero."

His abrupt departure left Lillian alone at the table, with *killed my sister* echoing in her mind.

~*~

"Pour me one, Hattie."

Nate sat at his usual table in a shadowed corner of the saloon. He felt Hattie's warm hands leave his shoulders as she complied.

She returned with a whiskey.

He belted it down as he stared into the past. There he saw a brisk winter morning when he and Sally set off to school on a path worn by their footsteps. He was limping.

"I'm going to marry that boy."

Sally was sixteen and silly over Zachariah. She skipped circles around Nate, indifferent to the effort with which he walked. His whole body smarted. But what smarted most was the way she acted. The two ribbons at the ends of her yellow braids bounced on her back, and her coat swirled around her ankles. Her behavior was unladylike. All on account of some two-bit worker. But she fluctuated between a childish girl and a headstrong woman, and there was no telling Sally Powell how a Powell ought to act, although he tried.

"It's not fitting for a rancher's daughter to marry a hired hand."

Zachariah was just one of the hands, but their father

showed him off like he was some kind of trophy. It seemed Marcus Powell deemed a man's worth was based on his ability to rope and ride, and Nate had just tried to earn that respect the day before. He had worked himself to sore muscles and bruises trying to rope a cow, and when he finally did, his father wasn't even looking. He was too busy applauding Zachariah for breaking in Thunderbolt. Everyone else had tried, and, Nate figured, by the time Zachariah got to it, the horse was just plain too tired to buck him off.

"Hurry up, you slow poke." Sally tugged at his hand. "We're going to be late."

"How you doing, Nate?"

The sound of Hattie's voice brought him back to the saloon. Everything about her was a feast to his senses. The breeze of her breath. The fragrance of her perfume. The curves of her body.

There was also a confidence in the way she handled men. She could tame the drunkest and roughest of them. The saloon could get pretty rowdy, and Nate was sure it was more Hattie and that mesmerizing touch of hers than Boss and his gun who kept the customers from tearing up the place.

There were times Nate would find himself feeling jealous when she touched the shoulder of another man and acted friendly toward him. Hattie was a salve to Nate's wounds and everything he thought a woman ought to be. "I'm doing," he said to her. "Get me another."

The moment the glass tapped the table, he picked it up. His throat was numb to its burning contents as he stared into that morning five years ago.

"What's your hurry?" Nate asked Sally. It was the responsibility of the older boys to light the woodstove, and that day it was Zachariah's turn.

"Hurry up," she insisted.

Every bone in his body felt broken, and Nate was in no mood for rushing. He yanked his hand away from hers. "Go on without me."

She ran on ahead, until she was out of sight.

Another mile down the path, Nate met up with Zachariah and Hattie. Zachariah's widowed mother had died, so he lived in the bunkhouse on the Powell ranch. Nate's father had one stipulation for Zachariah, that he finish school. Zachariah had left earlier that morning to get the fire started, or so Nate had thought. It looked as though Zachariah had wandered over to get Hattie instead.

If Zachariah was lollygagging on his way to the schoolhouse and taking his sweet time getting the fire going, it wasn't Nate's problem. He wouldn't mind seeing Zachariah get the switch. Not today.

"Where's Sally?" Hattie asked.

An inkling drew Nate's gaze toward the schoolhouse. That's when he spotted it.

"Another one, Nate?" Hattie, who stood by his side, started toward the bar.

He caught her wrist. "Give me the whole bottle."

With a sigh, she did so.

Smoke poured into the sky from a source much larger than a stove.

Nate looked at Zachariah, and vice versa. They knew what each other was thinking—Zachariah had taken so long, that Sally had gone ahead and lit the fire to keep him out of trouble.

The next thing Nate knew, he'd ignored the pain in his body to hightail to the schoolhouse. Flames flickered in the windows.

Zachariah had gotten there first and Nate met him at the door. It took their combined strength to ram it open. But the doorway was hotter than blazes.

Nate put his arm over his face to try to press through, but the heat shoved him back. He heard his sister scream. "I'm coming, Sally!" he shouted to her.

He ran to the side of the building. The heat blew out the glass in a window, and he ducked just in time to avoid the shards and daggers the fire hurled at him. A flash of yellow pushed him away as he tried to climb in. Another scream. "I'm coming, Sally!" he cried. The flames, however, lashed out at him and kept him away.

He ran around to the other side of the building. That window was also filled with flames that insisted on holding him at bay. The fire seemed to have a mind of its own, and it didn't want him getting to his little sister.

The moments that followed as he kept trying to save her were just a blur.

Nate picked up the bottle and poured some of its contents down his throat. The burn of the whiskey didn't bother him. Cutting off his arm couldn't hurt more than the thing he remembered next. And *that* he remembered with perfect clarity.

Sally lay limp in Nate's arms. Her long yellow braids had been charred to nubs, and her skin was black and blistered. He fell to his knees and hugged her. He wept as he rocked her. "I'm sorry, Sally. I'm sorry."

As Nate sobbed in the chair, Hattie put her hand on his shoulder. "Come on. Let me take you up to bed."

"I'm going to get him, Sally," he wept. "I'm going to get that murdering Zachariah."

18

Lillian said nothing when she returned to Molly's house that evening.

Molly thought it was odd that Lillian had left with Nate, but had returned with the other women. And she thought something else was odd. Late that night when the women were camped out on the floor and Molly's sore back was keeping her awake, she heard Lillian stir in her sleep. It sounded as if she were having one whopper of a nightmare.

Lillian's silence continued on to the next day. While the other women complained about the food and their husbands-to-be, Lillian remained quieter than usual. After the other women left to do whatever they did with whomever they did it with, Lillian quietly helped Molly clean up.

When she finally sat down to play piano, Molly didn't recognize the songs she played. But she did notice they were slow and somber. Finally, she sat beside Lillian on the piano bench. "You keep playing them dirges, and you'll make me feel as sad as you look."

"I'm sorry."

"Ain't no need to be sorry." Molly then asked a question hoping to hear "yes" as the answer. "Did Nate go and break off the engagement?"

"No," Lillian said, "he didn't."

Shucks. "Then what's the matter?"

Lillian walked to a window. "Mr. Powell said Mr. Keane killed his sister." She turned to Molly. "Is that true?"

Molly took a deep breath. "The story goes like this. Sally Powell, Nate, and Zachariah all used to walk to school together. One day when it was Zachariah's turn to get the stove going, she ran on ahead and did it for him. She accidentally set the schoolhouse on fire, and it killed her. Simple as that. Nate accused Zachariah of lollygagging, but I think Sally beat him to it on account of she was trying to impress him.

"Everyone in town agreed it was an accident. But Nate took the matter to a judge. Nate told his side of the story, and Zachariah never said but two words. They were 'Yes, sir,' after the judge asked if he agreed with Nate's account. Then, just like everyone else, the judge ruled it was Sally's decision to start the fire that wound up killing her. He'd determined by the burns Zachariah got out of it he'd made a good effort to try and save her. Even Marcus, Sally's pa, laid the matter to rest. But Nate never did. He still blames Zachariah to this very day, and calls the scar on Zachariah's face the 'mark of Cain.' Says it kept him from getting hanged, like he should have been."

Lillian looked out the window and murmured her recollection of the Biblical story. "Cain killed Abel, and so God cast him out to be a fugitive. But so no one would kill Cain, God put a protective mark on him."

"That's how Nate sees it, anyway," Molly said. "Though nobody else does." She made that point clear. While they were on the subject of the two men, Molly had something else to say on Zachariah's behalf. "I'll tell you one thing about the two men. Nate may have the prettier face, with his blue eyes and that blond hair of his. The boy looks more like his ma than he does his pa. But Zachariah, now, he's tall and strong, and looks more like what a man ought to look like." *With or without the scar.*

Lillian didn't respond. She didn't say a word, she didn't even nod. She just continued to stare out the window in a peculiar way that made Molly wish she could read her mind.

19

Molly paced a path around the kitchen floor.

Lillian played the piano. The dirges had worsened into slow funereal hymns.

Molly didn't pursue Lillian's sadness further. She had other things to worry about.

Nate had dealt a powerful blow to Zachariah by telling Lillian he'd killed Sally. And though Clayton still had no word about a preacher being interested in the job, Zachariah was still working on the church. Each nail he hammered sealed his fate to never marry Lillian.

Molly was frustrated.

Lillian was heading toward a wedding with Nate, when it should be Zachariah.

Molly was having a tough time getting these two together, let alone getting them to fall in love. So she paced to and fro, and fro and to, until...*maybe something could use fixing*.

No. Zachariah was on to that one.

What ain't I never tried before? She needed something new. But what? To and fro again. Then Molly stopped dead in her tracks. *What we need is more money to buy the pews and such for the church.* In other words, she needed a reason for a Molly-conjured-up fundraiser.

~*~

"All right, ladies. What you're to do is cook up some chow and put it in a picnic basket."

Everything in Molly's pantry was laid out on the kitchen worktable. All the women wore aprons, including Molly. "We're going to have a picnic. We're going to auction off the basket, and the lady goes with it."

The instructions given, the cooking began.

Molly made sure she worked next to Lillian.

"You're going to make a basket also?" Lillian asked Molly.

"I'm a single woman, ain't I?"

While the other women went to work, hogging up the preserves and the relishes, Lillian just stood there with a question on her face. Apparently, she'd never cooked a meal in her life.

Molly helped her along by cutting in flour, shortening, and water for the beginning of a perfect flaky crust. Molly then offered the excuse she'd made too much, and cut the ball of pie dough in half. She plopped the other half in front of Lillian.

Lillian looked at it as though it came from the moon.

How much do I have to help this gal along?

Molly floured the counter for both of them, and took up a rolling pin. While Lillian watched with keen interest, Molly skillfully rolled out a ball of dough, and lined a pie plate with it. She then offered the rolling pin to Lillian.

Lillian held it more like a sword than a kitchen utensil. "That doesn't look difficult." Then she rolled out the dough into an oval with ragged edges. It tore as she picked it up, so she balled it up and started over again.

Knowing all too well the less handling of pie dough the better, Molly cringed as Lillian worked and reworked the delicate dough, treating it more like hearty bread dough, which required kneading to work in the yeast. Apparently, the girl didn't know the difference, and Molly cringed at the thought of keeping it in her hands any longer. Lillian's pie crust would come out leathery. But Molly hung in there. When everything was said and done, she'd have to improvise.

After giving the pie dough a good workout, lining the pan with it, and giving it several patches, Lillian finally looked for something to fill her pie with. She picked up a jar of what Molly fathomed Lillian might have mistaken for dried blueberries.

"This looks interesting."

It was the only thing the other women hadn't touched, and Lillian filled her pie to the brim with it.

Whole peppercorns.

Molly stared with distress at the pie as Lillian went through the same procedure with the upper crust as she had with the lower one. *One bite of that,* Molly thought, *and Zachariah's going to feel like a fire-breathing dragon.* That's *if* his teeth managed to break through the crust. It would serve him right after the firewood incident, but that wasn't Molly's goal. *Yup, I definitely have to do some improvising.* "Tell you what," Molly said to Lillian. "Why don't you go outside and kill a chicken?"

Lillian looked at her wide-eyed.

"Ain't nothing to it," Molly said. "All you do is hold the chicken down on the chopping block, and chop off its head. Just make sure you keep a good hold on the body, so it don't get away from you."

Lillian fainted.

By the time Lillian came to, Molly had gotten the chicken herself. While the other women had whipped up a mess—and Lillian had fixed a meal a man would never forget—Molly had prepared a meal fit for a king. Chicken pie, baked potatoes, and peach pie. Zachariah's favorites.

When Molly set out the baskets, she made sure to set aside for herself a dainty little basket decorated with a pretty blue ribbon, and a big, old plain basket for Lillian.

Lillian gave her basket an odd look.

"It don't matter what it looks like," Molly said. "What matters is what's inside." *And yours is going to pack one wallop of a surprise.*

The women filled their baskets with what they'd prepared, and while the others brought their baskets out to the wagon, Molly asked Lillian to fetch her shawl. While Lillian did so, Molly quickly did her improvising.

Molly and the women reached the church grounds.

The men were already there so they could see which woman came with which basket, and know which basket to bid on.

Molly handed each woman their proper belongings, but when she came to Lillian's basket she said, "You can't carry that big old thing way over yonder. Here. You carry mine." Molly handed Lillian the dainty basket with the pretty blue ribbon, while she hauled Lillian's bulky basket. But before Molly walked over to the auction, she intentionally left her shawl in the wagon.

With Lillian's basket in hand, and vise versa, Molly made it a point to prance herself and Lillian around Nate, and then Zachariah before putting the baskets with the auctioneer. She set them at the far end of the pile, to make sure their baskets went last.

And then the bidding began.

The auctioneer picked up Aggie's basket. "What do we have in here?" He inspected the contents. "Some bread. Some chicken soup–and by the looks of it, a little too watered down, I'd say. But there're a couple of cherry tarts in here big enough to feed the town. Who's going to start the bid?"

"Fifty cents," Dr. Hinkle said, not doing much to claim the company of his future wife, or raise money for the church.

Brawley jumped right in there. "I raise two bits."

Dr. Hinkle went quiet.

"Going once," the auctioneer said, "going twice–"

Molly leaped to her feet. "Doc Hinkle bids two dollars."

Doc Hinkle leaped to his feet. "No I don't."

"You can't quit so easy," Molly said. "Aggie's your gal."

"All right," Doc Hinkle surrendered. "I bid two dollars."

"Going once, going twice–"

Brawley had no more fight left in his pockets.

"-going thrice to the doc for two dollars."

And that left four unhappy people–Aggie, Doc Hinkle, Brawley, and Prudence–but Molly was happy, and that's what mattered. "That scientific matchmaker paired you up for a reason." She gave a quick nod of her head, but something hit her.

Why was she fixing the proper woman with the proper man when everyone thought Nate and Lillian belonged together?

So for the next basket, Molly decided to hold her tongue, to let the chips fall wherever they wanted to, rather than where they were supposed to. However, the auctioneer barely touched Rosie's basket, when Malachi bid twenty dollars. This got a rise from Rosie.

"Why are you spending all your money on one meal, you old bum?"

"This ain't just a meal, Sugar Blossom, it's the privilege of being in the company of the loveliest lady alive."

"Then you'd better savor every bite, because it's probably the last thing you'll be eating."

"It'll be worth every penny, Sweet Honeysuckle."

When the auctioneer picked up Lillian's big clumsy basket, Molly abruptly asked her to do something.

"Will you go fetch my shawl? I left it in the wagon."

Lillian looked at her. "Now?"

"Them old bones," Molly said. "Now hurry up before I catch a chill. You can run faster than me."

So while Lillian was off to the wagon and out of earshot, the auctioneer rattled off the contents of Molly's basket, and Zachariah was the only one to bid on it.

Molly smirked. *I sure am a master of timing.* "Be there in a minute," she called to Zachariah.

Lillian returned just in time to hear Nate win a twenty-five dollar bid on Molly's basket.

Molly cocked her head. The girl was too innocent to be savvy to the scheming tactics of her well-experienced elder. So while Molly left to give Nate a surprise he deserved—Molly's company and Lillian's culinary fireworks—Lillian joined the man who'd won the bid on her basket.

20

Relief swept over Lillian when she discovered she'd be picnicking with someone other than Nate. She was in no mood to be with him, and particularly so today, because she was exhausted from lack of sleep. The nightmares she'd been having since she'd left England had become fewer as the distance between her and what she'd fled had become greater. But three words Nate had said when she'd last dined with him had rekindled her nightmares—and with a fury.

"Killed my sister."

Every night since he'd said those words, something had disturbed her sleep. More than once, she'd awoken with a start, and had also woken Molly.

"You doing all right?" Molly had asked.

"I will be fine." Lillian had said, even though she wasn't. She feared she'd never know peace again. Even now, the word *killed* wedged in her mind, and she couldn't dislodge it. She thought she'd scream if she had to listen to another word about how quaint the town was or how lovely she looked in Prudence's clothes. Though it was highly unexpected, she was grateful Zachariah Keane had purchased her basket.

She walked up to him from behind and found he'd already laid out a blanket, and had started to pull out the contents of her basket. Without looking up at her, he said, "You're lucky I'm hungrier than a starving hog. Are these baked potatoes or cow patties?"

She frowned. That wasn't exactly what she'd expected to hear regarding her cooking. Despite the insult, she sat on the large portion of blanket behind him.

"And pie, too," Mr. Keane continued as he dug into the basket. "Too bad Dusty ain't here. She'd have herself a whopping time burying it."

Lillian's face grew warm. Apparently, Mr. Keane was a fussy eater, and she could only guess who this even fussier Dusty was.

Mr. Keane spread the food on the blanket, and then removed his hat. "Since you're more long-winded than me," he said, "you ought to say grace. I reckon this grub could use a good hour or two." He put his hat to his chest.

A good hour or two? Perhaps the man was no gentleman after all. "Is that so, Mr. Keane?"

"Huh?" He abruptly turned his head and scrambled to his feet. "Begging your pardon, ma'am." He put his hat back on and touched the brim in greeting. He'd tugged the hat forward, low over his face. "What are you doing here?" he asked.

"You won the bid on my basket."

"This ain't the one you carried in."

"Molly thought mine was too heavy, and…" It dawned on her that it wasn't the basket the men had bid on, but the woman carrying it.

With the brim of his hat tilted toward Lillian, Mr. Keane took a long look in the direction of Molly.

Lillian looked down at the food spread out on the blanket, and realized something else. "These aren't the things I'd made."

A yelp split the air.

Nate, bulging eyes streaming tears and his face fiery red, ran to the horse trough and plunged his head into it.

Mr. Keane cleared his throat. "Things must have gotten mixed up, ma'am."

"Yes," she said. "Things must have gotten mixed up." She almost accused Molly of doing it on purpose, but for what reason?

"My apologies, ma'am," Mr. Keane said. "I'd be obliged to set things straight and see you off with Nate."

"No, Mr. Keane," Lillian rushed in. "Please don't."

That was last thing Zachariah expected. But it wasn't the words that grabbed him so much as the pleading in her gaze.

"I mean, I'm afraid I won't be good company for Mr. Powell," she said. "I-I didn't sleep well last night."

He nodded, and then offered her an excuse. "I've slept out under the stars with Molly plenty of times. That woman can snore up a storm."

"Yes. Yes, she can."

He gave her a long look. There was more going on. "But that ain't what kept you awake."

Her gaze connected with his, and she abruptly looked away. "Will you oblige me by saying grace, Mr. Keane?"

That cut the subject short, and he knew well enough to leave it alone. But it left him with another predicament to deal with. His. He was uncomfortable praying with anyone but Molly, and he was especially uncomfortable with the thought of Miss Rauling staring at his face while he ate.

But there she was sitting straight and proper, like the fine lady she was, on that old, itchy horse blanket. She was bound and determined to stay and eat with him.

Bound and determined. Those weren't exactly words a man wanted to use to describe how a woman was keeping his company. Or avoiding another man's company. But she'd settled in, so he hesitantly removed his hat and accommodated her request. "We thank Thee, Lord, for giving us so generously of Thy bounty. Please bless this food, and may it nourish us to do Thy will. Amen."

Miss Rauling echoed his amen and raised her gaze. The woman seemed like a proper Christian, and he liked that. With hands too dainty to hand out dingy tin dishes, she offered him a plate.

He accepted it from her hand. Since it seemed like the polite thing to do, he kept his hat off while they ate. It was just his luck the scarred side of his face was toward her. Vanity needled him to shift on the blanket and turn his good side to her, but he didn't listen to it. He was who he was, and he imagined she was glad she was getting married to Nate instead. Zachariah suddenly felt a pang of suspicion. *If those really are Nate's intentions.* Since Sally's death, there was no telling what Nate might be up to. For the time being, Zachariah decided it was best to disregard the issue concerning Nate. Thinking of Miss Rauling's comforts, he offered, "Ma'am, I know I ain't comely to look at. You're not obligated to eat with me."

She ignored his statement. "Molly tells me you're a cowboy. It must be dangerous, with cougars and thieves and renegade Indians."

Renegade…? Zachariah frowned. Apparently, Molly had said a word or ten about him to Miss Rauling. Yes, there were Injuns out there, but they'd never caused him any grief. All they wanted was a toll to cross their land. Seemed fair enough, since all the buffalo had been killed off, and their people were starving. Still, Zachariah found it surprising a genteel lady should be curious about the life of a working man.

Despite that tired look in her eyes, she had an inflection in her voice that suggested she might genuinely be interested.

So he chewed on his answer for a moment. *What's it really like?* "Cowboying has its problems," he said thoughtfully. "Longhorn can be mighty cranky. And you want to stay clear of those horns. They could be as wide as four feet across. Furthermore, there are rustlers and other dangers. But you know what the greatest hazard is?"

"What is it, Mr. Keane?" she asked.

"It's falling off your horse." He grinned because the notion sounded ridiculous, considering. But the grin faded from his face because he'd seen it happen. Back when he'd worked for Marcus, he'd even seen a man get trampled to death by cattle. Miss Rauling didn't need to know those details.

"But cowboying also has its privileges," he continued, and he elaborated more than he'd expected. "When I'm standing on a hilltop, somewhere between earth and heaven, it's like standing in the palm of God's hand. Below me, the cows low peaceful, like they're singing a hymn. Above me, the stars light up the sky like a thousand angels holding candles. And beside me the Almighty leans down his ear and listens to my prayers."

"What do you pray for, Mr. Keane?"

He'd taken a bite, and stopped chewing. *That's a mighty personal thing to ask a man.* But something in her voice sounded like a little child who'd gotten lost. Miss Rauling was a long way from home, and she wasn't the type of woman he fancied seeing a matchmaker, let alone a scientific one. Maybe she wasn't prying into him so much as she was prying into herself. He finished chewing, put down his plate, and took in a breath for thought.

He had a list, and went over it in his head. He'd pray that Molly would get her church, that Nate would forgive him for what happened to Sally, and that Hattie would find her way out of the saloon. But that was other folks' business, and nothing suitable to tell Miss Rauling about.

There was one prayer in particular he always added at the end of his list, but it was so personal to him that the Lord was the only one Zachariah had ever told that one to. So he thought a minute longer, and came up with, "I pray God will tell me what he created me for so I can get to work doing it. I feel like a tool waiting for a task and just rusting on the shelf." There. That was personal enough, and a proper thing to pray for.

"I pray for someone who will love me more than skin deep," she said softly.

That was intimate and unexpected.

He turned the patch of rippled skin away from her because he was too well aware of his own skin. He pretended to study the unfinished church structure. "I'd like to think I do more thanking than asking," he said. "I got lots of things to be thankful for. I lost my folks when I was a boy, but Molly and her late husband took a hankering to me, and Nate's father taught me a trade. And the good Lord, well, He's been helping me build a herd." That sounded more to Zachariah like yapping than talking.

The next thing that came—rather, spewed—out of Miss Rauling's mouth was, "Nate hates you."

Zachariah looked at her. She looked right back at him, and for a moment they were gaze to gaze, until he blinked away. He rested his fork in his dish. The food had tasted pretty good until that statement came up.

"Did he tell you why, ma'am?"

"He said you killed his sister. Is that true?"

He lost his appetite. It looked as though the Good Lord wouldn't let him off the hook so easy.

"If Sally hadn't died, we'd probably be married today." He solemnly added, "And I wouldn't be branded with this reminder."

He and Sally had slipped off several times to be alone. She'd tease him about how shy he was, and he'd tease her about her outgoingness. But they both liked what they teased each other about. Zachariah's so-called mark of Cain wasn't just a reminder of Sally's untimely death, it was a reminder of how things had left him. Lonely.

That fatal day was filled with regrets. If only he'd gotten to the schoolhouse sooner. If only he'd pressed harder to save her. That's what brought him to the conclusion it did. "I did kill her, ma'am."

Miss Rauling looked down. He knew from the pallor in her face something was troubling her, and it wasn't his role in what happened to Sally.

Rosie let out a laugh.

Miss Rauling threw a sideways glance. She was well aware of the presence of the others.

"That was some fine food, ma'am. Why, it was just as good as Molly's," Zachariah said facetiously. "I reckon I could use a walk. Would you care to join me?"

She answered just as he thought she might.

"Yes, Mr. Keane, I would."

~*~

Lillian walked by Mr. Keane's side. He was tall and rugged, and she felt delicate beside him. When she discovered she was dining with him, something in her had hoped their conversation might lead to this. But something else in her had hoped it would not.

Apparently the distance she'd put between her and England wasn't enough. It would never be enough. Not when words like *killed my sister* made the proverbial wolf from which she'd thought she'd escaped feel as if it had found her, and was once again slathering and snapping at her heels. She tried to subtly rub the thought away by brushing back a stray strand of hair. Which reminded her. That was either a safe place to start—or turn back from.

"The thought of a scientific matchmaker sounds like a ridiculous notion, doesn't it, Mr. Keane?" She became well aware of her walking companion's every movement.

He spoke without turning. "I don't take you for someone who'd be gullible enough to believe that a man can learn about a person's temperament, likes, and dislikes by a strand of hair, if that's what you mean."

The sideways glance he shot her made the match-making method seem even more foolish. She also realized in Mr. Keane's intonation he was insightful enough to know there was more to her story.

"Thank you for regarding my intelligence." She waited for him to inquire as to what exactly brought her here, but he didn't. His patience put her at ease. She stole a glance at the brand on his face. She had a similar one on her soul.

"I didn't sign up with the matchmaker to find a husband," she said. "I signed up to escape the authorities." She took a deep breath. "You and I have something in common, Mr. Keane."

"And that is…?"

She stopped walking. This was her last chance to back out. "I killed a man."

He also stopped short.

She felt her face go pale and wished to heaven she hadn't said it. Mr. Keane had been acquitted, she hadn't. For a moment she feared he might drag her back to the Sheriff, and rightly so.

But he just nodded and started walking again. "I'm wearing comfortable boots, ma'am."

21

I killed a man. This was the first time Lillian had ever said those words out loud. She felt detached from her voice. The words that followed were just as frightful and foreign. "The man I killed was my former employer in England. His name was Mr. Drummond." She paused.

Mr. Keane nodded. "I'm listening, ma'am."

She was keenly aware of the even inflection in his voice. It maintained the same calmness it had a moment earlier, before she'd spoken those ugly words. "I didn't...I should have known, but I..." She put her hands over her eyes. Everything was suddenly a jumbled mess with no chronological order. "I don't know where to begin."

"Maybe you ought to start before it happened," he said. "Sometimes that's a good place to collect your thoughts."

"Yes." She removed her hands from her face. "Before the incident." *Incident* was an easier word to manage than *murder*. Where was she before it happened? The boardinghouse. Yes. She was at the boardinghouse when she'd seen the posting placed by the Drummonds. "I was seeking employment and I responded to an advertisement for a governess. Thus far, I'd had several interviews, but no success. I'd become desperate." Lillian stared across the field. "But the Drummonds, they were a peculiar lot…"

~*~

"I think she's absolutely charming, Alexander," Mrs. Drummond had said. "Don't you?"

Mr. and Mrs. Drummond were complete opposites. She was twenty some-odd years of age, blonde, vibrant, and stunning in her red dress with décolletage. She spoke easily, and was—unlike Lillian's previous five interviewers—unthreatened by the notion of an attractive governess.

He, on the other hand, was an ogre. He was at least fifty years of age, and had bulbous eyes that seemed to scheme rather than consider. His black suit was too elegant for those calculating eyes, and he looked like a man wearing stolen clothes.

He approached Lillian until his face was just inches from hers. He remained in this uncomfortable proximity for what seemed like eons. The hairs on the back of her neck stood on end as his bulging eyes analyzed her.

I need this job, she repeated to herself as she braved his intrusion. She looked past him at the velvet drapes on the floor-to-ceiling windows of their palace-like parlor. She looked past him at Mrs. Drummond sitting comfortably on a damask settee chatting away as though nothing out of the ordinary was happening. She looked past him at a painting of a bull staring down a matador, and she noted with a dry throat how the bulky black creature bore a strange resemblance to the dark-haired, heavy-set Mr. Drummond.

What his wife was saying was indistinguishable, until she came to her feet. "Alexander, will you make this an all day affair? Either you want her, or you don't."

"She'll do," he said at last. He walked away, allowing Lillian to release her breath.

"Wonderful," Mrs. Drummond said in her easygoing manner. "Can you start tomorrow?"

~*~

"I wish it was you who was going away, and not my mother."

The next morning, Lillian arrived at her new job with suitcases in hand. She had barely been introduced to seven-year-old Isabelle, when Mrs. Drummond, also bearing suitcases, told the child to be good, and kissed her good-bye.

Mr. Drummond, however, had not packed his bags.

Mrs. Drummond left. But the house was full of servants, and all day long, it bustled with activity. They dusted, cooked, and complained about their chores.

Lillian busied herself with trying to keep a child with yellow curls, pink ribbons, and an acrid disposition from inflicting another smarting kick to her throbbing shins. Whoever said little girls were sugar and spice had not met this one. She was vinegar.

"I hate you!"

At long last, Isabelle sat next to Lillian on the piano bench. It was after dinner, and for nine grueling hours the child had ranted, raged, and ripped pages from the day's lesson books. Although Lillian had to continue supervising the child, schooling time was over, and the Drummonds, as did all people of their class, had a piano. That's where Lillian retreated, albeit with the child in tow.

In a life set adrift in the turbulence of being orphaned, music was Lillian's only anchor. Her home had always been filled with the sound of the piano being played by herself or her mother, or her father's beautiful tenor voice. No matter where life had displaced her since, God had always provided her with a piano. There was one at the dwelling of her aunt and that disturbing uncle who'd shown young Lillian an unsettling kind of attention by always touching her. There was the piano at the boarding school to which she had abruptly been shipped. In that cheerless place of unsympathetic, black-clad inhabitants, she would close her eyes and play, and the music would take her back home for a little while.

And now Lillian barely heard the whines as she thumbed through the sheet music and stopped at Mozart's Fantasy in D Minor. *That ought to get the child sleepy and calm my nerves.* She started playing, and the cheerful music indeed tamed the shrew.

Isabelle sat quietly by Lillian's side until Lillian finished the piece.

"Play it again, or I'll tell my father." Isabelle didn't realize the impact of her statement. Or perhaps the little conniver did.

Lillian's gaze slipped past the sheet music and through the doorway. Stillness had settled upon the house. The bustling servants who'd given her a sense of security had disappeared. They'd retired to the servants' quarters. In their stead was the darkness creeping in. The thought of Mr. Drummond's bulging eyes watching her from the shadows suddenly gave Lillian chills.

She got up from the piano bench. The room was supplied with gaslights, but she had an uneasy fear of them. Instead, she lit the candles on the piano candelabra and set it upon the mantel in front of a mirror for more light.

"Play it again, or—"

It didn't take another threat from Isabelle for Lillian to press her fingers to the keys. Her hands were clumsy, and the chord she'd stumbled upon came out flat and unsettling. The room felt as though it were ogling her.

She tried to play *Fantasy* again, but her hands refused to cooperate with the lightness of the song. The music came out slow and uncertain. Her fingers became stiff and heavy as the full brunt of her circumstances settled upon her. *Tonight I'm going to sleep in the west wing with only a child…*and the dreadfully quiet Mr. Drummond.

All day long, the notion had been nudging her. All day long, she'd been shoving it back by asking herself, *Where else am I to stay?* But now that night had fallen, the emptiness and the darkness added so much weight that it had become a dread too heavy to budge.

A yawning Isabelle failed to protest as Lillian left her side and walked to the candelabra. In the mirror, she thought she saw the reflection of a stocky shape in the doorway. She whirled around.

There was no one standing there.

Suspicious silliness, she scolded herself. Mr. Drummond had said earlier he was retiring to the library. He was likely sitting in one of the winged chairs engrossed in a book or at the desk tending his business accounts at this very moment. Besides, Mrs. Drummond was so lovely, why would he have interest in any other woman?

Enough of this nonsense. Lillian had a job and every reason to be grateful.

Being attractive had been an impediment to her employment, but here it didn't matter to Mrs. Drummond. During Lillian's prior interviews, every prospective female employer had done nothing but scowl while Lillian tried to persuade them with her credentials. *"My English is impeccable, and I speak French fluently. I play the piano-"* *"Yes, I realize that is expected of any governess, but I possess an advantage in that-"* And *that* was when they'd loosen their tight lips. *"I'm sorry, you won't do."* Lillian never had a chance to add, *"I have an extraordinary love of music that will inspire your children."*

"I'm tired." Isabelle sat at the piano and listlessly pecked at the keys.

"I suppose it's time for bed." Lillian blew out all but one candle, which she plucked from the candelabra.

By its light, she took a detour and led Isabelle past the library, where the door was closed as expected. But the lack of light in the crack beneath indicated Mr. Drummond was not where he said he'd be.

There's no need to panic, she told herself. *He probably went outside to the stables, or who knows where else.* There were sixty-two rooms in the mansion.

The journey toward Isabelle's bedroom seemed never-ending. At last, Lillian reached her destination, and the child was easily freed of hair ribbons, dressed in night clothes, and put away for the night in a bed large enough for five children.

Lillian took up her candle, and closed the door behind her. She was now alone. The feeling she'd had of gaping eyes intensified a hundredfold. She lifted the candle to see the hallway around her. She'd come this way earlier that day, when she was shown to her room. She'd seen the paintings that lined the hall. They were of a matador and that Mr. Drummond-like bull. But what she hadn't noticed before was the sequence they were in.

The first painting was of a humped-back bull pawing the ground. The next was of a matador waving a red cape. The one after was of the beast charging toward the matador. After that was a gruesome depiction of the bull goring its challenger. Yes, there was an order. The final one in the series, not one she could yet see in the weak candlelight, but one she remembered, wasn't a painting, but a gold statuette.

This trophy, of a sort for the bull, was set on an ivory pedestal. The beast was the size of a heavy, hunched-back bobcat. It had disproportionately long horns that came to sharp, shining points. Lillian remembered it vividly because it was a dangerous thing to have around a child, and an accident waiting to happen. She had expressed her concern to the Drummonds.

Though they had agreed with her, she thought it peculiar that they hadn't realized this hazard before. When Lillian reached the pedestal, she saw in the candlelight that the bull had been removed. Instead of relief, however, she felt irritated.

Why is my room so far from Isabelle's? When she was first taken to her room, she'd asked why this was so.

The servant answered, *"Because the missus' rooms are next to Miss Isabelle's."*

Mrs. Drummond required a sitting room, a dressing room, a privy, and a breakfast room, as well as a bedroom the size of a hall. These rooms lined the left side of the wing. To the right was an outside wall.

Lillian had impulsively asked where the master's bedroom was.

"He sleeps there." The servant had pointed to a door at the far end.

Lillian's room was halfway between Isabelle's and his.

All the doors that lined the hall were closed.

Lillian had already passed by Isabelle's room and two others. As she approached the next, a fear in the pit of her stomach rose to the surface. *What if Mr. Drummond is lurking behind one of those doors?* She stopped. Her heart pounded in her throat. She recalled what little she'd seen of him earlier that day.

He had breakfast on the veranda at ten o'clock. Occasionally she'd spot him between scuttling servants. He'd taken dinner with Isabelle at seven, after which he'd said he'd be in the library. So if he wasn't where he'd said he'd be, then where on earth was he?

Perhaps he'd simply retired early. After waking up so late? *The man's wife is lovely. Why would he be interested in a governess?* And who said he was interested? He'd simply said, "She'll do."

Why did the sound of that make her skin crawl?

She raised the candle to eye level. The tiny flame barely lighted up her next footstep. The sensation of animal eyes glaring at her from the darkness beyond grew overwhelming. She slid her room key from her pocket.

Though the carefree Mrs. Drummond had laughed and said it was unnecessary to lock the door, Lillian had insisted she have the key to her room.

The Drummonds complied so far as to give her the maid's key as well. Now Lillian was grateful she'd been so firm, because her room had become a safe haven. The moment she reached her sanctuary, she would throw herself in, lock the door behind her, and be secure from staring eyes.

Her footsteps were silent on the rug as she quickened her pace. All the while, she held the key like a weapon, ready to gouge if necessary. Just before she reached the next door, she stopped. This was where the feeling of leering eyes felt strongest. It only led to reason that if Mr. Drummond were to spring out, it would be from this room. It was the room before hers.

She crossed to the other side of the hall. Her back pressed against the wall, she proceeded as though walking on a ledge. Shadow and candlelight flickered ominously across the shiny mahogany door. Her every sense was alert. Her ears for the click of a latch, her nose for the musky smell of his cologne. Even the fine hairs on her arms waited on the slightest breeze of a door opening. The key quivered in her hand. Midway past the fiendishly still door, the key fell.

She stooped and quickly panned the rug with candlelight. *There.* She plucked the key from the carpet and rushed to her room. It took five pokes before she jabbed the key into the lock. The click resounded. The knob turned. She threw herself inside, slammed the door, and used the same key to secure herself within. Safe at last, she leaned against the door and closed her eyes.

Ouch! A drop of melted wax had burned her thumb. She brought the wound to her mouth, and soothed it with her tongue. Absolutely nothing had happened to have warranted her suspicions, and how ridiculously she had acted. She looked at her sore thumb. *Serves me right.*

She let out a snort of mild self-vilification as she set the key on the table in the shadows by the door, beneath what she remembered to be a vase of fresh-cut flowers. They had welcomed her that morning with their pastel colors and fragrance. But as she drew her hand away from the key, something struck her as odd. *Why can't I smell the flowers?*

She brought the candle toward the table. Her breath caught in her throat when the candlelight glistened off a surface not of milk glass, but of gold.

"Hello, Lillian."

A heavy shape was sitting in a chair.

How did you...? The answer came faster than her voice–by the room's other door. One wall-to-ceiling drape on an inside wall, which she'd initially thought simply decorative, was slightly askew, hung up on a doorknob. She didn't know what was strongest, her fear or her regret. How could she be so stupid as to fail to inspect the room and overlook this alternative entry? But when they surrendered both keys, who would have thought...?

"We have lights." The shape heaved its weight off the chair and lit on a gaslight. Light flooded the room, and Mr. Drummond's bulbous eyes appeared, reminding her of a picture of the heavy-browed, gleaming-eyed ogre in a fairytale that had frightened her as a child.

He sauntered toward her, and she stumbled back into the locked door. He found it humorous. "Come now." His grin exposed crooked, pointed eyeteeth. "You're not naïve enough to think my wife wished to hire you for Isabelle's sake. And I'm sure you believe as much as I that she's off to see her sick mother."

What happened next was a flurry of motion. He drew near. She threw the candle at him. With a yelp, he fell against the table. The table broke. He and the gold bull plummeted to the floor. There was a crash, a cry, and then silence. He lay sprawled on the floor, his torso hidden behind the capsized tabletop.

She stood with her back pressed against the door, waiting for him to get up, but hoping he wouldn't.

They both remained motionless for a long time.

So long, that after a while she stepped forward and craned her neck to peer behind the table. She brought a quivering hand to her lips as she saw his bloodstained jacket and a sharp gold horn jutting out of his chest. His bulging eyes had a horror in them that she would never forget. They stared past this life and into the damnation of the next.

She spotted the key on the floor, freed herself from the room—and ran.

22

Zachariah realized he was a long ways from the church grounds, and in the company of a sobbing woman.

Miss Rauling looked like a broken doll as she crumpled to her knees. "I didn't mean to kill him."

Had she been Molly, he'd have held her, as he'd done when Molly's husband passed on. But Miss Rauling was different. Not knowing what else to do, he knelt in front of her. He thought about putting his hand on her shoulder, but couldn't bring himself to even do that. Instead, he sat back on his heels, where he towered over her.

She was delicate and frail, and in this condition, even more so.

He had to do something. "Look at me, ma'am," he said.

She shook her head.

"I know I ain't pretty to look at, but I'd appreciate if you'd look me in the face." His honest humor earned her glassy gaze upward. "In the eyes, ma'am." They were the mirror of the soul.

She looked at him eye to eye, and he'd never seen a soul that looked more frightened.

Being a deputy sheriff, he had his responsibilities, but he was convinced she hadn't murdered the man. However, there was someone else who needed to be convinced.

"So tell me," he said. "With God as your witness, did you intentionally kill that man?"

She gave a quick shake of her head.

"I want an answer from your mouth."

"I-I was retreating to my room, Mr. Keane. It was the last place I thought he'd be. When I saw the statue of the bull...it was an accident waiting to happen. I threw the candle at him only to keep him away. I swear I didn't..."

"No, you didn't." He felt indignation rise in him. A man's obligation was to use his strength to protect a woman, not to use it against her. If Zachariah had been there that night, Mr. Drummond might have fared even worse. "Maybe it was an angel of mercy. Maybe it was dumb luck. Either way, the man got what he deserved."

Her jaw dropped. Her gaze shifted from his right eye to his left. She brought her hands to her mouth, and her shoulders trembled as she cried out the rest of her guilt. She dabbed away the last tears.

"It might not be a good idea to tell other folks about this matter," he said. "Around here, rumors start faster than you can strike a match."

"Thank you, Mr. Keane, I'll tell no one else."

He got up, and his duty as a gentleman dictated he help her to her feet as well. As he did so, her delicate hand felt good in his. A little too good. "I reckon we ought to get back to the picnic grounds," he said.

"Yes, Mr. Keane. We should."

He was still holding her hand, and he abruptly let it go.

They started walking.

The silence made him feel even more awkward. He wished she'd say something to ease things, but after having had such a hard talk, he figured it was up to him to lighten things up before they returned to the others. "If you please, ma'am. Calling me Mr. Keane makes me feel as if I'm as old as the hills. The name's Zachariah."

"How old are you, if I may...?"

He didn't consider his age personal. "Twenty-two, ma'am."

"Is that so?" she asked.

"It is." He looked at her.

She got a hint of mischief in her eyes that suggested she'd also taken to lightening the mood. "Well." She crossed her arms and looked determined and dainty doing so. "I'm barely nineteen, and being called 'ma'am' makes me feel like an old maid."

He half grinned. "So what do you reckon I should call you?"

"I *reckon* you should call me Lillian."

"Miss-"

"No. Just plain Lillian."

He thought about it for a moment. There was something about the name that didn't fit her quite right. But he knew what name did. "Mind if I just call you Lilly?"

The prettiest smile he'd ever seen spread across her face. "Lilly will be just fine...Zachariah."

~*~

I'll get back at that Molly. Trying to cool the fire in his mouth, Nate had knelt in front of the horse trough, and kept dunking his face in the water. He knew Molly had had a part in rigging the auction so that Zachariah would end up with Lillian. Initially Nate wasn't too concerned they'd ended up together—until the flames were quenched, and he looked up to discover Zachariah and Lillian from afar walking toward the grounds. Nate forgot about paying back Molly. Instead, his face became as hot as his mouth had been when he'd first taken the bite of peppercorn pie. He forced calm as he walked up to the couple. "Where have you been?" He demanded of Lillian.

She was speechless as her gaze swept across his wet hair.

Zachariah answered. "We just went for a walk. Nothing more."

"I asked her."

"We went for a walk," she replied.

"I don't want you keeping company with a killer." Nate yanked her away.

Zachariah started. He obviously didn't like the way Nate was handling her.

Lillian sensed the trouble brewing. "It's fine, Zachariah."

Nate further put him at bay with a glare that conveyed that—unless Zachariah was willing to admit he'd sent for her—she was Nate's woman.

~*~

Nate's woman. There was no doubt in Nate's mind that Lillian was beautiful, but as far as a *real* woman was concerned, he knew of only one.

"Pour me one, Hattie."

That night he was sitting in his usual corner of the saloon, watching her from behind as Hattie walked away from him toward the bar. Her waist was long, and there was a spellbinding rhythm in the way she swayed her hips. Her dress was low on her back, and it showed off her silky, light brown skin. He was captivated by her, and always would be. Hattie was the epitome of everything a woman should be. But keeping men happy and drunk was how she made her living, though oftentimes he found it hard to tolerate the sight of her acting friendly toward some stranger.

When she returned with his whiskey, he paid her for the drink and any more drinks he might have. He made it a point to cover his expenses up front, and then some, while he was still sober. He also insisted on generously compensating her for the disproportionate amount of time she'd spend with him.

Having learned to take the money without an argument, Hattie tucked it in her corset, and then rested her hand softly on his shoulder. Her company was worth every penny.

She'd bought herself a new dress, and he commented on how fine she looked in it. Every movement she made was sensual. Even the way she breathed. But she was giving him that motherly look again. He read the accusation in her eyes. However, his reason for coming this time wasn't to get stone-drunk. He had some thinking to do.

So he nursed his drink, he thought, and absorbed Hattie with his eyes, his ears, and that warm flesh on his shoulder where her hand reassured him she'd always be there for him. This was the woman who'd made his life tolerable. This was the woman he'd like to call his and his alone. It wasn't her race or her occupation that kept him from asking her to marry him. He didn't care about other people's opinions. It was Hattie who kept him from proposing.

Tying her down would be like clipping a dove's

wings. Nate nursed his drink some more. Finally, with a smack of his empty glass on the well-worn table, he decided. He grabbed Hattie and kissed her long and sweet, like he'd never kissed her before.

~*~

"We need to talk."

The next day Nate rode up to Molly's to see Lillian. This time he took the surrey, but left behind the driver.

She hesitantly got into the surrey.

He took up the reins, and brought them a ways from Molly's before blurting out the reason for this meeting. "I want you to gather your things. It's time we started living as man and wife."

She stared at him.

His plan had evolved. Pretending to be her fiancé in order to build her hopes, and then dash them by shoving her at that scarred-faced Zachariah, didn't look as though it would have the impact he'd hoped for.

Lillian was supposed to run away from the marred murderer. Not go for a walk with him.

So Nate had decided on another course of action. A cool, well-bred English lady would make a good business partner. With Hattie around, that's all he needed in a wife.

Lillian resisted by offering her usual passive form of protest. "Molly is still looking for a preach-"

"Common-law marriage is acceptable in these parts," he said.

"Common-law marriage may be acceptable to you, but it's unacceptable to me," she returned.

"It seems Molly's got you demanding an elaborate wedding."

"A church wedding is all I require." She spoke with indignation. "If Molly could advertise that we have a church-"

"Why?" He was through playing this verbal tug of war. "You're already my wife."

"Your wife-to-be, Mr. Powell, Paying my expenses doesn't grant you liberty. Our union will require nothing less than a church service performed by a preacher." She was holding her breath.

He'd taken her out into the middle of nowhere. Without an escort, he could consummate the union right here and now. But there was no need for him to force himself on an unwilling woman. It wasn't lust for Lillian he was feeling, it was contempt toward Zachariah. Nate decided the marriage could wait. "You want your church wedding?"

She let out her breath. "Yes, Mr. Powell, I do."

"Then you'll have it. I'll see to it your church is finished, on one condition."

"And that is?"

He stated a stipulation she had little choice but to agree to.

~*~

"How many hands can we spare?" Nate belted out his question as he entered his father's den.

His father was sitting in a tufted leather chair behind a massive mahogany desk that made him look high and mighty. The work Nate had completed was spread out before his father. The books had to balance down to the penny to keep Marcus happy.

However, they did not.

But with Nate being his only living child, and the patriarch wanting to immortalize himself by passing on his business to his heirs, Marcus didn't have much of a choice but to settle for the imperfect.

Nate could just as easily have fixed the books and even robbed his father blind of a lot more than the two dollars and nine cents they were off by.

"We can't spare any hands," Marcus said, not looking up. "I need them to break in some colts."

"Oh, I'm sure we could spare two or three."

Marcus crossed out a number in a not-so-subtle gesture.

Nate interpreted that as Marcus's way of saying that had Nate finished college, the books would have balanced.

"Why do you need some hands?" Marcus asked.

"To build a church," Nate said. "I'm getting married."

That got Marcus's attention. "Rumor says you sent for a wife. I didn't think it was true."

Word got around fast in a small town.

"It is."

"I don't recall you doing that."

You don't recall me doing much of anything, except botching things. Nate walked to the bar and poured himself some brandy. Unlike the glasses in the saloon, these rang when the bottle hit the rim. Crystal, glass; brandy, whisky—as far as Nate was concerned, liquor was liquor. He poured some over his tongue. "Am I required to report to you everything I do?" He glanced at the books and added, "Right down to the penny?" He emptied the glass.

Marcus studied him before answering. "I reckon

you don't."

"Good," Nate said. "Then I *reckon*..." he stressed the word to demean his father. While Marcus picked at Nate's two dollar and nine-cent shortcomings, Nate dug back at his father's deficiency in language skills. "I'll take four hands."

The sooner Nate had this church built, the better. If there was any chance of Lillian finding out he wasn't the one who'd sent for her, he wanted to make sure she found out *after* they were married.

23

"That ought to do you." Zachariah checked Thunderbolt's hooves daily, and this time he found a chip in one of them. He cleaned it out and filed it down with the rasp. The stallion stood calmly, cooperatively. The horse was one of the best gifts, besides learning a trade, that Marcus could have given him.

Zachariah gave the horse some oats before hitching him up to the wagon. He patted Thunderbolt on the flank, and the horse acknowledged the attention by shaking his head. No sooner was the wagon hitched up, but Dusty was in it, wagging her tail and barking. He gave her a scratch behind the ear on his way into the kitchen.

He picked up a sack of flour and glanced at the sagging ceiling. Those warped boards overhead were hard to ignore. He looked at what he was standing on. He'd made some progress there. He'd gotten rid of the old, rusty nails and hammered in new ones. At least he didn't have to worry about stepping on a floorboard and having it swing up into his face.

Spending all his spare money to buy back Molly's piano on account of her meddling had put a damper on his plans to fix up the place. But he wasn't as sore at Molly as he ought to be.

Not after talking with Lilly and things had lightened up. In fact, he was beginning to understand why Molly was so eager to get him a wife. A woman like that could sure make a man's world agreeable. In fact, a woman like that was probably the reason he'd come back to the house and started fixing it up in the first place.

He smiled. "And that accent of hers…" He stopped there.

No matter who'd paid her fees and fare, she belonged to whoever she wanted to—although she seemed content to be with Zachariah the day of the picnic.

Furthermore, he didn't like the way Nate had treated her that day.

But she didn't protest. Why would she? What woman wouldn't prefer Nate over him?

Instead of imagining, he should just plain accept the facts. Who knows? She might even have the healing power to mend Nate's heart after what had happened to Sally. It wasn't pleasant being the object of someone's bitterness, but Zachariah could understand why Nate's torment was even worse than his own. The fire had left each of them with scars inside and out.

He set the sack of flour in the back of the wagon. It was late afternoon, he'd finished with his chores, and he knew that feeding four women was costing Molly an arm and both legs. "Not that she'd complain, Lord," he said with a smirk. He stepped into the wagon, and headed to Molly's place.

Zachariah had the sack of flour over his shoulder and his knuckles ready to rap on the door when it suddenly flew open.

"Zachariah," Molly said as if she hadn't seen him in ages. "What a surprise."

He frowned at her. He'd just told her a few days

ago he'd be by with some more food.

Molly was up to something again.

"Come on in." She sounded as if she'd had a heaping helping of honey, her voice was so sweet.

Which meant he wanted to be in and out before she could dole out any more trouble. He headed toward the pantry with the sack, but stopped dead in his tracks.

Just out of nowhere, the music started.

It was the prettiest sound he'd ever heard. He lowered the sack onto the pantry floor. "Who's playing the piano?"

Molly's horses and wagon were gone, so he had assumed all the women were gone also.

Molly mumbled something about timing being everything.

Zachariah took off his hat and followed the music.

Lilly was sitting at the piano. She was playing *Rock of Ages* so fine, he couldn't help but listen. He'd heard Molly play that old, scuffed-up piano a thousand times, but not like this. Lilly was unaware of his presence, and wrapped up in the music in a way he understood, because that's how he felt when he sang a hymn. Just listening to her play was a pleasure and a privilege, and it made him glad he'd bought back the piano.

When she finished the song, he spoke. "That was mighty beautiful, Lilly."

She turned to him, and her face lighted up into something he wished he could wake up to every morning.

"Thank you, Zachariah," she said. "I can't tell you how much this piano means to me." She smiled. She looked as if she was right where she belonged.

Lilly? Zachariah? Molly froze in her footsteps. *When did those two start calling each other that?* And the way they looked at one another...*if that ain't admiration...*Molly mentally scolded Lillian. *Why ain't you giving him that thank-you kiss like you said you was going to?* Instead Molly said to Zachariah, "Why don't you stay a spell? Maybe we could sing some hymns." *Lillian would fall into your arms once she heard that voice of yours.* "It's been a long time since Sunday gathering." Of course, that wasn't exactly the gathering she had in mind.

That broke the spell Lillian had on Zachariah.

"I got work to do," he said.

"What's more important than singing to the Lord?" That bellow didn't come out with the gentle devoutness Molly had intended. She knew Zachariah was on to her now.

"Yes, Zachariah." Lillian was sweetly naive of Molly's intentions. "I'd love to hear you sing."

Molly offered Lillian a helping hand of coaxing. "You ain't never heard nothing finer." He was shy about his grand voice, and needed to be persuaded. "Come on, Zachariah." Molly tried to yank his hat out of his hands. It was the one thing he wouldn't leave without.

"The church ain't going to get built this way." With a blush on his face, he gave the hat a good tug and Molly a dirty look. He headed out the door.

After he left, Lillian's gaze lingered on the door. Then she started playing the piano again. But this time, it was something glum. "I'm getting married," she said, from out of nowhere.

That ain't news. Molly sighed.

Theoretically, Lillian was getting married before

she'd set sail from England. She just didn't know to whom yet. So why was she playing those dirges again?

Lillian's fingers continued to make the keys whisper in sad, solitary notes. "Mr. Powell has promised me he'd see to it that the church was completed."

Molly didn't like the sound of that. "It don't mean you have to get hitched right after it's finished."

"Actually, it does," Lillian said. "I promised him our wedding would be the first church service."

Molly's gaze shot to the door that had closed behind Zachariah. *And he's hurrying this along?*

24

When Zachariah got to the church, he found a new wall lying on the ground perpendicular to the one he'd finished framing the day before. He scratched his chin. Apparently, someone else had taken an interest in putting up the building. By the looks of the progress, it was a keen interest.

He loosened the horse from the wagon, let Dusty run amok, and got to work. Between him and whoever else was helping, they'd get this job done in no time.

~*~

"What can I do you fellers for?" Hattie asked the four men, who came through the door, hired hands who worked for the Powells.

They sat down at a table in a sour mood, ordered a round of beers in a sour mood, and when Hattie brought over the tray, they were still in a sour mood.

"My thumb's black and blue from smashing it with the hammer," one of them said. "I came here to break-in horses, not put up churches."

Hattie took a glance at herself in the mirror behind the bar. She had her face made up pretty with rice powder and rouge, her hair was done up nice with a thick tendril off the shoulder, and the neckline of her dress was low enough to leave no doubt that she was a woman. So why were they treating her as though she weren't even there? She pounded a mug of foaming beer in front of the first sour face, spilling some of the suds.

That got their attention.

"What are you fellers so sour about?" she asked.

"Ain't you heard?"

Usually Hattie got the town gossip on the third round. This update would come early. With more ease, she placed the second mug in front of the second customer. "I don't get out much." With a boss who was aware he had a good commodity he didn't want to lose, Hattie's social life was restricted to whoever came into the saloon.

"You know about them scientific-matched brides?" one of the hands asked.

She placed the third beer on the table. "Uh-huh." She was well aware. Even though business had suffered since the women arrived, she still had to snicker at the notion. She'd heard about the strand of hair thing, and even plucked one of the few brown ones left from old Malachi's head "for good luck," as he'd put it. She sort of missed him. He was a sweet old man who'd tried over and over again to talk her into marrying him. Apparently, he'd given up. And where he'd gotten the money to send for a bride was beyond her. She guessed it might have been misused charity.

The first hired hand picked up his beer. "Nate's got us building a church." He took a swallow.

Nate? She froze with the fourth mug still in hand. Yes, she'd heard the distant hammering. And yes, she'd even seen from her second story bedroom window a structure going up in the distance. In fact, she could hear some hammering now. She could fathom Zachariah building a church. But Nate? She offered a cool, just-one-of-the-fellows kind of smirk, and finished putting the last foam-capped beer on a worn-smooth table. "Since when has Nate gotten religion?"

The men mumbled and grumbled, but one statement came out clear enough. "Since he got engaged."

Hattie looked up with a start.

"He sent for a bride," another hand said. "And he got the prettiest one in the bunch. He promised her he'd build her a church to get married in."

Hattie lost the cool in her voice. "Not Nate."

He'd never mentioned sending for a bride.

She warily looked at the stairs. Earlier she'd seen Boss retreat to his room above the saloon. She had no contract with him, but he wasn't keen on her being anywhere except inside the building. Sometimes she questioned if she was his employee or his prisoner. "Take care of these men," she whispered to the bartender. Regardless of the risk, today she needed air.

It'd been a long time since Hattie stepped foot outside. As soon as her face met the natural light, she hung her head. Marrying Nate was the only thing she'd ever hoped for. She turned toward the sound of solitary hammering. In the distance she found someone she hadn't spoken to for quite some time, although on occasion she'd watch him from her window.

Braving the chance that Boss might discover her gone, or that Molly Crammer might be around to holler, Hattie headed toward the only person she'd ever trusted. "Can't a body get some peace and quiet around here?"

Zachariah looked up from his hammering to find someone he hadn't spoken to in a while. Not since

Hattie started staying in a place that didn't suit him. Sometimes he'd catch her looking out a window over the saloon, and he'd look up and beckon her with his thoughts to come down. But she'd just turn away. Oftentimes he'd also catch a glimpse of Boss standing behind her, and Zachariah would get an uneasy feeling in his stomach.

Hattie stood at the edge of the church grounds. She was close enough and unclad enough that Zachariah could see the pretty girl he'd known had grown into an exotically beautiful woman he didn't know. With her black hair and brown eyes as pretty as a calf's, Hattie might have been as nice-looking as Sally. Only Hattie couldn't afford the ribbons, the lace, and the fancy dresses. Not until now.

He took off his hat to her. "Howdy, Hattie."

She set her hands on her long waist. "You put that hat back on, Zachariah Keane." There was a choke in her voice. "You know I ain't no lady."

In defiance of her statement, he tossed the hat into the wagon, and walked over to where she stood. "Been a long time," he said.

There was a hard edge in the voice of the woman that hadn't been in the girl. "You're sure making a ruckus out here."

"I reckon I'm making enough noise to wake the dead." He put the hammer down. He knew she wasn't out here just to tell him he was making a lot of noise.

"What are you building?" she asked.

"You know what I'm building. That's why you're standing over there."

Hattie abruptly cast down her gaze.

Apparently his words had come out as blunt as he'd intended. "I could use a rest," he said. "Ain't no reason we can't sit down a spell," and he nodded toward the church staging.

Hattie resisted. "Yes, there is."

"No, Hattie, there ain't."

"Molly says that I'm-"

"Molly ain't pouring her sweat into this here ground." As much as he loved her, sometimes Molly had a pocketful of stones she ought not be throwing. "Here." He offered his hand to Hattie. "If the Lord's going to strike you with lightning, this way he'll get the both of us."

People usually took to his humor, and sure enough, she smiled and took hold of his hand. Her feet were unsure as he led her to the platform. But once they reached it, she slowly sat down by his side.

The church was on a hill, and she looked around. He could tell she experienced a whole new view of the town. She took a long look at the saloon.

"We're an odd pair, you and me," she said. "Of all the men in this lousy town, you're the only one who's the marrying kind, and of all the women, I'm the only one who ain't. And here we are…" She sighed.

He looked out over the town with her. "Ain't meant for us, I reckon." He tried to harness an ache of loneliness from seeping into his voice.

Her demeanor softened. "Did you know Nate's getting married?"

He looked sideways at her, and then back to the view. "Yup. I know."

"Do you know he's getting married as soon as this church is built?"

No, he didn't know that. For some reason, it stung.

"Nate's got some hired hands working on it," she said.

He nodded. At least that solved the mystery as to who was helping him.

"Why did he go and buy a bride when he had me?" The words spilled from her heart, reminding Zachariah of the crush she'd had on Nate. As a girl, that's all she'd ever talked about–to everyone but Nate. "I reckon Molly's right about me," she said.

That last statement drew a scowl from Zachariah. He mumbled, "Molly ain't right about anything lately."

"She's right about me." Hattie brought a hand to her face. "This powder itches my eyes."

"Come here, Hattie."

Just as he'd done back when her mother had left, Zachariah held Hattie. The warmth of her naked shoulders felt uncomfortable against the palms of his hands as she grieved. But it was nothing compared to the heat he'd felt when Lilly had simply touched his wrist.

When Hattie finished sobbing, she stayed in his arms. Her body rested listlessly against his.

"Can I tell you a secret?" He supposed she had a right to know. Besides, this wouldn't be the first secret she'd kept for him.

"What's that?" she said.

"It wasn't Nate who sent for Lilly. It was Molly. She done it for me."

"Lilly," she repeated. It seemed the name made things even more tangible to her.

He told her the whole story.

"So Molly did it because she cares about you."

"She cares about you too, Hattie. She's just got a bothersome way of showing it."

"What Molly offered, back when my ma left? That

was mighty kind of her. But I couldn't live with her when her husband was failing. He got shot, they got robbed...they had enough troubles without adding mine."

"Molly's a stubborn old mule. She'd have found a way." He added with a heavy sigh, "I can attest to that. But things happened as they did, and I reckon Molly got hurt when you declined her. You know how mad people get when they feel refused. But I'm willing to bet if you asked her again, that offer for you to move in would still stand." He couldn't help but add, "Although I hope Molly would help you with less meddling than she helps me."

Hattie continued to lean against him as she would an older brother. She was deep in thought. "If Lilly's yours, then why ain't you with her?"

He looked down at the rippled skin that ran along his forearm. Most people never looked at that scar. It seemed it was there for his sake, in case he forgot about the one on his face. "When I saw her step down from the stagecoach," he said, "she was so pretty and ladylike. All I could think was, how can a woman like that spend her days looking at a man like me?"

Hattie looked up at him. "If I'd had half a brain, I would." She kissed him on the marred cheek.

He felt the light, moist touch of her lips, not intended to be sexual, but healing. He tried to absorb it, but couldn't.

They were both quiet for a while, until she said, "Nate's always been a cold fish. Do you really think he's in love with Lilly?"

"I ain't sure," Zachariah said. "But I can't see him wanting to settle down all of a sudden. I've got this inkling he's aiming to use Lilly to get back at me for what happened to Sally."

Sally.

He and Hattie shared a glance.

"You think Lilly's as darn-fool stupid as me to be in love with him?" Hattie asked.

"It can't be too hard for a lady to fall for a man who's handsome and educated, and whose father owns a spread the size of Marcus's." But something told Zachariah Lilly hadn't fallen for Nate. Something like the way she chose to stay with Zachariah at the picnic. Or the fact she was the only woman who happened to be at Molly's when he came around. Granted, he was sure some of it was Molly's doing. But all in all, it seemed Lilly didn't spend much time with her fiancé. Considering.

Hattie interrupted his thoughts. "You like her, don't you?"

He glanced at Hattie's reddened eyes, and then down at the rough hands of a working man. "I reckon I do."

"Why don't you get her back?"

"Because she wasn't mine in the first place." Lilly had her reasons for marrying Nate, and as much as he wanted to, Zachariah wouldn't stick his big old boots in the way. "Look here, Hattie. Lilly ain't mine, and Nate ain't yours, and we both got to let go of our entitlements." That came out with more irritation than he'd intended. Lilly had crept into his heart where she didn't belong.

Hattie fell quiet. Then she looked back at the saloon. "You know," she said, "many a man has tried to solicit me to take a romp with him. I teased plenty, but I ain't never pleased a one, because it never seemed right to me to give up that much. I just had to tell you that." Her face was tear-streaked and powder-caked. She listlessly snickered. "I guess you can call that Hattie's religion." She touched a frill on the hem of her red dress as though she realized for the first time what she was wearing. "I took a wrong turn, didn't I?"

"I'm here to help you if you want to turn back."

"It ain't in me to be perfect like you," she said.

Perfect? He threw her a glance. Where had she gotten that idea? Just because he didn't cuss and frequent the saloon didn't mean he was perfect. Inside he felt like pure rebellion.

Ever since Sally died and he got scarred in the fire, he'd been bucking the idea that God was testing him to the hilt by condemning him to a lonely life as a bachelor. The bronco in him was just beginning to tame down, and then Lilly came along and roused it up again.

"Only One perfect man has ever walked the face of this earth," he said. "It sure as shooting ain't me."

She gave him a long look and then she modestly covered her naked shoulders with her hands. There was something about the way she stared down at the saloon that suggested she just might pay Molly a visit someday.

25

"Brawley expects me to birth and raise a dozen children, and help him work a farm," Prudence moaned. "He might as well bury me now."

"All Doc does is tell me what to do," Aggie whined. "Or what *not* to do. 'Don't spit on your hand.' 'Don't touch your hair.' 'Don't wear those low-cut dresses.' I want a frisky young man—not some old geezer with a long list of what-not-to-dos."

"At least he's not some old bum with the clothes rotting off his back," Rosie carped. Then she grumbled at the food. "Chicken again. Why can't we have lamb? Why is it always chicken, chicken, chicken?"

The women were gathered at Molly's dining room table, and once again, they'd turned a nice dinner into a griping session.

Molly hung back and ate in the kitchen, where she tried to enjoy her delicious chicken and dumplings, but couldn't. *Why can't we have lamb? Do you see any lambs around here?* There was no pleasing that ain't-so-rosy Rosie. Molly couldn't tell what was louder, the women's bickering or the clanging of their silverware on her good china. She cringed with every clink.

"I'd set a goal," Rosie said, "that by the time I reached the age of forty, I'd have myself a fortune." Then she mumbled, "Is this a dumpling or a lump of flour?"

Molly huffed. *Maybe if you weren't so fussy, you*

wouldn't be so skinny.

"You said you were only thirty-five," Aggie said. "You've got plenty of time."

Thirty-five? Molly doubted that.

Rosie hesitated. "I'm forty-one. And the reason I still ain't in England is because the boss fired me on account of I was too old. Too old," Rosie wailed, and her fork clinked on her dish.

Molly had given the women a treat this evening by using the dishes Danny had bought her for their twenty-fifth anniversary. She swore this was the last time she'd use her fine china for these barbaric women.

"At least Malachi doesn't look at other women," Prudence said. "Brawley can't take his eyes off Aggie, and I'm afraid he'll always wish he had married her instead of me." *Clink!*

"And my man's always looking at Prudence," Aggie said. *Clink!*

"Your doctor is *so* debonair," Prudence said, dreamy-eyed. *Clink!*

"And your Brawley's so handsome," Aggie said with a heavy sigh, and what followed was more of a *Clank!*

That did it. Molly barged into the dining room. No, she wasn't going to swipe the meal away. She just wanted to bring some peace to the table and gentler treatment to her dishes. "So why don't you just switch fellers?" What she said was so preposterous, the room went dead quiet. Molly had even rubbed against her own grain. "Forget about that old matchmaker. What can he tell from a strand of hair, anyway?"

"We can't just forget it," Prudence said, "because of what was in the fine print."

"I don't remember no fine print." Molly defended

herself from the looks she got. "From the fellers, I mean. You women were all they talked about for months."

Prudence explained about the reimbursement and the damages. She concluded, "None of us has the money to buy our way out of our contract. Except Rosie."

"And you can bet I'll do exactly that," Rosie said with a nod. "Soon as the old coot and me are alone. Ain't no reason to humiliate the old bloke."

"But as for the rest of us, we're stuck," Prudence said. "Rosie and Lillian. They're the only lucky ones."

"Of course the little prissy has it made," Aggie mumbled.

Rosie shot to her feet. "Why don't you stop picking on Lillian? Just because she ended up with the finest of the men. Why, she's the prettiest of us all. So what skin is it off your nose if she's also the happiest?"

"I'm not happy," Lillian said to everyone's shock. She hadn't said a word of objection until now. She'd also barely touched what was in her plate. She excused herself from the table, thanked Molly for the meal, and sat at the piano, where she started playing dirges again.

~*~

Lillian played Beethoven's *Moonlight Sonata*. She played from memory, but her fingers seemed to have a mind of their own. They played the piece slower than the score would have indicated, and so a movement that should have been gentle and romantic came out gloomy. She started thinking about Zachariah, and for some reason the music pouring from her lightened.

She wished he had complied with Molly's request to stay and sing the other day. It was adorable how Molly thought so highly of him. *"That grand voice of his."* The thought even drew a smile from Lillian.

Of course, no man had a voice as magnificent as her papa's—he'd been trained by the best opera instructors in Europe. But the thought of a rugged cowboy singing with that drawl of his was utterly enchanting. Especially since it was utterly disenchanting that Nate Powell had no interest whatsoever in music.

She stopped playing to study a wedding picture of Molly and her late husband. They looked happy together, which drew a thought from her. *Mr. Powell, you and I have absolutely nothing in common.* Then she retracted her thought. *I stand corrected, Mr. Powell. You and I do have something in common.* Elocution.

She heaved a sigh, and let her mind wander back to a moonlit night on the ship's deck—and the vision of a silhouette far away on a blue-black horizon aglow with magic. She could see him now, waiting for her on that far-away shore, his tall, slender figure topped with a wide-brimmed hat, and his gaze cast over the ocean.

He had her name tucked in his pocket, and a heart that ached for her as much as hers ached for him. His name and face were a mystery, but his character was not. He was strong, but soft-spoken. Brave, but shy. He would love her tenderly, protect her fiercely, and delight in the children she bore him.

Perhaps it was that small hope of finding him that had brought her here after all. Her noble American cowboy. Hidden in the shadows of pure idealism.

She looked down at the yellowed piano keys. What was it about Zachariah that drew out the woman in her so she could confess and cry? And then moments later, coax the little girl to come out from hiding and play? Her mind flashed back to the first time she'd met him, when she'd slipped from the wagon.

"I got you, ma'am."

It wasn't the statement that had calmed her panic. It was him. She knew he'd hold on, because something more than her hand had clasped him that day. Yes, she knew beyond a doubt he was the cowboy in the moonlight. Or would have been, but for the scar. The rippled blemish didn't make him hideous, but it did mar an otherwise handsome face, rendering him less than perfect. Could she passionately love a man with such a flaw? And what was the whole history behind it that caused Nate Powell to loathe him?

Nate Powell.

The thought of his name drew a huff from her. The words she'd grown to hate rang in her ears. *"You look lovely, Lillian."* That was the depth of his love for her, and it would never proceed further because he didn't care to see past her *lovely* face and into her lonely heart. She suddenly brought her hand to her cheek. *Past my face.*

It seemed of its own accord her index finger started playing the solitary notes from the song she'd learned long ago.

Did she want to be seen for what lay inside, but wasn't willing to do the same? She stopped there. There was no need to delve further into her duplicity. Not when Nate Powell was the man with her fate sealed in his pocket.

26

The next day Molly went to the Telegraph Office, this time to make sure a preacher *hadn't* answered their ad yet. She found the furniture crowded in the back of the room, and Clayton hammering wainscoting to the wall. He turned to her.

"I figured I'd used a nice dark shade of varnish." He nodded toward two new lamps. "I'm going to put one by the door, and the other on the wall by the desk. What do you think?"

The wainscoting covered the cracked walls and peeling paint, and the new twin oil lamps, with their frosted glass chimneys and shiny brass bases and collars, were particularly fancy.

"It'll look real nice for the ladies," Molly said. "I'll whip you up a pair of curtains to finish it off."

He offered her money for the material, but she argued that fixing up the place was her idea in the first place. She cut the discussion short by asking, "Any word on the preacher?"

Clayton put down the hammer. "Sorry, Molly." On a note that was meant to cheer her, he added, "But the church is going up quickly, and Nate's ordered some pews and a stained glass window. He's also paying to advertise for a preacher in every newspaper from here to Missouri. It's bound to happen. It's just a matter of time."

"Yup," Molly said. "It's just a matter of time."

Nate's crew and Zachariah had been putting in a lot of hours working on the church. It was just a matter of time before the nicest woman Molly had ever met would marry the rottenest man she knew.

Nate had everything a man could want—a fancy house, a rich pa who gave him a cushy job, and he had that wanton woman Hattie. *Why can't he marry her?*

Life wasn't fair. Nate hadn't even finished college like his father wanted him to. Marcus had sent him off to school, Molly supposed, because Nate couldn't handle cattle worth a can of beans. *But sure as shooting, he'll inherit his pa's ranch.* It was Zachariah who deserved it, because it was Zachariah who'd set his mind to work hard and pay his dues learning the skills. *How can Marcus hand everything over to that lazy, good-for-nothing son of his?*

And how could Zachariah hand over Lillian?

Lord, can't you give Zachariah just a teaspoon of happiness? He's already had a heap of troubles.

Life had been hard on Zachariah since the day she'd met him. He was eight years old, new in town, and he'd knocked on her door to ask if she had some chores he could do. When Danny found out the boy was a widow's son trying to provide for his mother, he respected the boy. Although Danny was handy, he hired Zachariah on for one job after another. Danny taught him how to fix leaky roofs, replace rotting boards, and he even made Zachariah a tool box. Then, as if life wasn't hard enough on the boy, his mother died. Zachariah was only eleven, but he was already a man. Danny would have taken him in, but Marcus had already taken him on as a hired hand.

Life just plain wasn't fair, and that irked Molly.

She stepped out of the Telegraph Office and climbed onto her wagon to head home, when she spotted something else that irked her.

~*~

Hattie had been watching Molly from the saloon, until she got enough gumption to go outside. She was just about to ask Molly to take her away from the saloon, when the look in Molly's eyes stopped Hattie short.

Hattie self-consciously crossed her arms over her shoulders, all too aware of the red dress cut low on her shapely figure and hemmed up to her knees. It contrasted with the bland calico garment that covered Molly's lanky figure from toe to neck. Hattie wished she could have gone up to her room for her shawl, but if Boss had caught her…

Hattie was only yards away from Molly's wagon and escaping Boss. But the look that had crossed Molly's face turned those few yards into a ravine. Hattie knew what Molly was thinking. *You ain't got enough business in there, you got to bring it out here? Can't you see there's a church going up? Least you can do is hide yourself so decent folk don't have to look at you, you hellbound harlot.* Hattie knew if she hesitated too long, Boss was bound to find her gone. And sure enough, he did.

"Get back in here, Hattie."

From the corner of her eye, she saw him standing in front of the saloon. He was so big, he blocked the doorway.

The longing in Hattie's heart frosted over. Breaking free of the saloon was hopeless. *Zachariah, you made it sound so easy.* No, she wouldn't cry. Crying was a sign of weakness. If she was hopeless, if she was hell-bound, at least she could be hopeless and hell-bound with dignity.

After Boss beat the dickens out of her.

Hattie turned and walked back to the saloon.

Boss moved aside to let her pass.

She was just about to go through the door when somebody else stepped between her and Boss.

The sight of that somebody caused Molly to leap out of her wagon. "Zachariah, you come along with me." She grabbed hold of his arm and tried to yank him away from Hattie. "You leave my Zachariah alone, you hear? He's a good and decent man…"

Molly was right. He was as decent as they come, and he had no business being there.

But the man wouldn't budge.

"Get back to your wagon," Zachariah commanded Molly. He repeated himself again louder, and she obeyed.

"I'll have a talk with you, Hattie," Boss said. He glared her down over Zachariah's shoulder.

She didn't want more trouble. "Get out of my way, Zachariah."

But he stood fast. "Molly don't mean what she said." He defiantly crossed his arms. "And Boss don't own you."

But Hattie knew better. Molly *did* mean what she'd said, which is why it felt like Boss *did* own her. She brushed past Zachariah and forced herself to go inside to deal with Boss.

"Get on up there." Boss nodded toward the stairs. "So we can have that talk."

Hattie went quietly to her room, and he followed close on her heels, and shut the door behind them.

Mustering every pound of courage, she turned to face him. It wasn't the talking she was afraid of. It was the beating that came between words.

"Take off that dress. I don't want it torn."

She reluctantly stripped down to her petticoat.

"What'd I tell you about leaving?" He unbuckled his belt.

She turned and braced herself against the bedpost. Boss was "kind enough" to strike her on the small of her back, where it didn't show. The problem was, he'd hit her in the same spot, until it got so tender sore, she could barely move. Depending on how mad she'd gotten him, he'd likely hit her between five and ten times. Except once, after spending a whole evening giving all her attention to Nate, and failing to keep the mirror from getting busted, she'd counted seventeen whippings before she passed out.

"This is where you belong, Hattie."

She shut her eyes tight and waited for that buckle to smack into her flesh. Sure enough, she heard the metal whip the air and felt the blow like a branding iron. The pain rippled through her, but she wouldn't satisfy Boss by crying out.

"You ain't never leaving this place again, you hear?"

By the sound of his voice today, she had a feeling he'd surpass that seventeen. She hung her head. She wanted to give up and die.

"If I ever catch you leaving…"

Again, she heard the whoosh of flying metal. It made a loud cracking sound. But this time she didn't feel the sting.

"If you ever catch her leaving again, you'll do what?"

She turned around to find the only man in town big enough to put Boss in his place.

Zachariah had caught the buckle in his palm. He yanked the belt out of Boss's hand. "I ought to give you a whipping with this. Tenfold. But I'll give you this instead." Zachariah's fist crashed into Boss's jaw and sent him spiraling over the bed and crashing into the dresser. The lamp, the hair brushes, and the perfume bottles spilled on top of him. "You whip her again," Zachariah said, "and you'll reckon with me." His eyes were filled with fury as he turned to Hattie. "Let's go."

Boss slouched on the floor with a look on his face as if he were wondering what had hit him.

For a moment, anything seemed possible. She grabbed her shawl to leave, but froze when she heard a shrill voice outside.

"Zachariah you get on out here! You don't belong in there with them!"

Hattie let her shawl slip from her hand. *Go. Go where?* To the home of the woman who rightly accused her of being one of *them*? Maybe Hattie could escape the saloon, but she couldn't escape what she'd become. "I can't."

He held his hand out to her. "Yes, you can." He looked like a saint standing there upright and virtuous.

She suddenly became aware that he was in her bedroom, and all she had on was a petticoat. She turned her back to him, and tried not to let her voice crack. "Go away, Zachariah. Just go away."

He was too much of a gentleman to force her. "I'll be here," he said instead. "Whenever you're ready to leave, Hattie, I'll be here."

~*~

Molly didn't care that she was kneeling in the muck. She was fervently praying for Zachariah, when she felt someone seize her around the middle. Zachariah picked her up and set her down in her wagon.

Molly was relieved to see he was still the man she knew. "How could you go in there?" she scolded him. "That woman might have led you to the grave alongside her."

"Or that woman," Zachariah said, "might have been on her way to finally take you up on that offer you made her years ago."

That shut Molly up for a moment. "But strutting around in a dress with less than three yards of fabric..." Suddenly Molly realized. "It's all she's got, ain't it?"

"That's right," Zachariah said. "It's all she's got."

Molly heaved a repentant sigh. "I reckon I dealt a nasty blow to the Lord's good work, didn't I?"

He didn't say a word. The answer was obvious.

She looked at the saloon door as though it were the last place she wanted to enter. "I reckon I ought to go in there and apologize."

"I reckon you ought to leave her be for now." He huffed. "None of us is perfect, Molly."

"You mean my fibs?" she meekly volunteered. "They're just little ones. I don't mean nobody harm."

"Molly, you got a heart as big as all outdoors, but you got to stop sticking your big toe where it don't belong. You're meddling with things you ought not to be meddling with."

Which reminded Molly. She got down from the

wagon, and looked over at the almost-completed church.

"I got myself some help," he said.

"I reckon you do." Her mind wandered off to thinking of some way to sabotage their efforts. Since setting fire to a church wasn't exactly a righteous thing to do, she thought she could sit down in the middle of it and wail something about having leprosy or some other plague that would cause Doc Hinkle to quarantine the place. *That ought to stall the work for a while longer-*

"Molly...?"

Zachariah broke her out of her scheming.

"What did I tell you about meddling?"

She planted her hands on her bony hips. "How can you tell?"

"Oh, I don't know. Maybe it's that half smile that gives you away, the way it spreads across your face when you're staring down at the ground, and there ain't anything there to smile about except horse manure."

"And you don't want to hear no more fibbing from me, not after what just happened with Hattie," Molly offered. Her shoulders sagged. *Hattie.* She'd finally taken a step out of the saloon, and Molly had shoved her back in. What would she have to do to get Hattie to finally come to the house? As if four women didn't crowd the place up enough. But now it seemed empty without Hattie. And what could Molly do to break up Lillian and Nate? *Maybe I could feign-*

"Molly...?" It was Zachariah's soft but stern voice again.

Her eyes focused. *Humph.* He was right. *Those foul-smelling horse droppings ain't nothing to smile about.*

27

"Mr. Powell. Mrs. Powell." Lillian finally met her future in-laws.

Their greeting was hesitant, and both seemed taken aback.

Were they not expecting her?

The sire was a head taller and twice the bulk of his offspring.

Nate Powell obviously took after his mother, who was almost as petite as Lillian. Mrs. Powell had fair skin, blonde hair, and appeared too young to have a son in his twenties. She took on her duty to be a hospitable hostess and escorted Lillian to the dining room. "Please sit down."

Amidst candles and flowers were four place settings situated on a polished mahogany table too large to accommodate merely two couples. Lillian realized it had been some time since she'd dined with people of wealth. The arrangement now impressed her as too formal to be friendly.

Dinner started off with the creamiest mashed potatoes, buttery corn, and the most tender steak Lillian had ever eaten.

The flavor, however, was rendered bland by the strained atmosphere and lack of conversation. The only vocal exchanges were the instructions and "Yes ma'ams" that transpired between Mrs. Powell and the servant.

Lillian avoided eye contact by looking around the room as she ate. There was one thing in particular that caught her interest. Mounted above the scrolled mahogany mantel of a stone fireplace was a life-size painting of a beautiful young lady with mischievous eyes and golden-yellow hair.

So this was Zachariah's would-be wife.

"What do you think of my parents, Lillian?"

The question stirred her from the painting and put her in a prickly spot. Fortunately, she had food in her mouth, and she avoided answering by emphasizing the motions of her masticating jaw.

It was Mr. Powell, the elder, who put down his fork and took up the task of doing the assessing. "So Nate." Mr. Powell had the same curly blond hair as his son, but with white at the temples of his wiser, weathered face. "What made you decide to send for a wife all of a sudden? No offense meant, Lillian, but I don't fancy Nate wanting to settle down just yet." Though he addressed Lillian, his gaze bored into his son. The manner in which he added, "I reckon he has a few more oats to sow," was not an afterthought, but an accusation.

"I've *done* sown my *oats*, and I *reckon* Lillian and I are *itching to get hitched*. Isn't that so, Lillian?" Young Mr. Powell smirked. He was mocking his father's dialect.

Lillian thought it rude rather than humorous.

The father, however, wasn't thwarted. "Matchmaking's for the desperate, especially when it's done by some fool who matches hair rather than folks. If you don't mind me saying, Lillian, you look about as desperate and gullible as my son here."

"Marcus." Mrs. Powell cast her husband a

beseeching glance and unwarily rescued Lillian from trying to fabricate a history as to what brought her here.

The man's language skills may have been dull, but his discerning skills were sharp. He'd spoken the precise question that needled Lillian concerning Nate.

She cast her fiancé a sideways glance, just as he cast her one.

~*~

Molly sat by herself in her rocking chair. She hemmed the curtains she'd promised Clayton and smiled.

Three women yakked away at the dinner table in the next room.

Between all the women and their belongings, Molly felt as if she was living in a mess up to her eyeballs, with no end to it in sight. But she did see an end to one thing. She knew that end would happen as soon as that fussy Rosie got a taste of the dessert Molly had just set on the table. Molly had finally made the apple pie Rosie had been hankering for.

The women bickered about how to carve a pie into five equal shares, to include Molly's, and later Lillian's, portions.

"You can't cut it in half, and then in half again," Rosie said.

I should have cut it myself. Finally, things settled down, and there was a moment of quiet when Molly surmised they'd figured it out, and Rosie was now scooping up a forkful of savory delight. Molly could envision Rosie's long jaw biting down with indifference. But the moment her taste buds got hold of the sugar, cinnamon, and tenderly-cooked apples, her eyes would light up and she'd say, *"Why, if this ain't the best pie I ever ate."* Molly listened up for her sweet moment of triumph. And then it came.

"The apples are too tart."

What! That wiped the grin off Molly's face. *There ain't no pleasing that ain't so-rosy-Rosie.* She slammed down the curtains and mumbled, "I got enough going on without catering to that hussy." She had the curtains to finish, a wedding to stop, and a houseful of women to cook and clean for.

And she had to listen to them bicker about the men they got stuck with and the food she was serving them. There was no one to help her clean up tonight, because Lillian had gone off with Nate.

Why the others couldn't help out a sixty-eight year old woman was beyond Molly. To top things off, she felt bad about what she'd done to Hattie. She barged into the dining room, stormed up to Rosie, and snatched her plate.

Rosie was dumbfounded.

Molly noticed the slice was half gone. "Seems you ain't having no trouble eating my 'too tart' apple pie," Molly said. "If it ain't good enough for you, you can go without. I'm tired of listening to you complain about everything. I'm tired of listening to the whole lot of you complain. I got myself some complaints, too. You think your fellers are bad? Wait until they get a taste of how lazy and fussy you women are."

And whether or not the women were finished eating, Molly collected the dishes and dumped them in the kitchen. She leaned against the counter and heaved a sigh to calm her nerves.

28

"Well Lord, I reckon that ought to do it."

Zachariah stood in the church, paint brush in hand, and looked at the finished project. The pews were in, the stained glass window depicting The Marriage of the Lamb, which Nate's men had done a sloppy job installing, was fixed proper, and the walls were as white as the pearly gates. All that was left to do was find a preacher.

He looked at the piano. Clayton had helped him move it from Molly's place, and they'd set it to the right of the pulpit.

Zachariah could picture Miss Rauling sitting behind the keys, eyes closed dream-like—as they were that day at Molly's when she'd played *Rock of Ages*. She made the old, scarred-up thing sound like a grand piano. The contented smile on her face made it worth every penny to buy it back, and then every minute to paint it up fresh for her. With a smirk, Zachariah caught himself in error, and he corrected himself. It wasn't Miss Rauling. It was Lilly.

"If you please, ma'am. Mr. Keane makes me feel like I'm as old as the hills. The name's Zachariah."

"Is that so?" She looked playful and dainty the way she boldly crossed those little arms. "I'm barely nineteen, and being called ma'am makes me feel like an old maid. I reckon you should call me Lillian."

Her eyebrows arched when she said reckon, *and he*

thought the word sounded endearing in that accent of hers. Although she was refined on the outside, he had a hunch she was a high-spirited filly inside. As for the name, Lillian just plain sounded too fancy coming from his lips. That's why he asked, "Mind if I call you Lilly?"

A smile crossed her face again. He'd never seen anything prettier.

"Lilly will be just fine...Zachariah."

Zachariah stared at the stained glass image of a man dressed in royal purple robes and his bride dressed in a pure white gown. Then, it hit him.

She's marrying Nate.

The thought sapped his strength so that he sat in a pew and hung his head. It was obvious he and Lilly had everything it took to be friends. But husband and wife? What could a beautiful, genteel lady and a scarred cowboy have in common?

"Molly tells me you're a cowboy. What's it like? It must be dangerous, with cougars and thieves and Indians." Lilly sounded like a fascinated little girl asking a question to an adventurer.

There was only one way he could describe it. "When I'm standing on a hill, half way between heaven and earth, I feel as if I'm standing in the palm of God's hand. The cattle below bawl peaceful, as if they're singing a hymn; the sky above is lit up with stars that look like a thousand angels holding candles; and God's ear is leaning down, listening to my prayers."

"What do you pray about?"

At the time, he'd thought her question was intrusive. Now he wondered if he was that transparent. *You, Lilly. I pray about marrying someone like you.*

The night was cool. He'd laid his hat and coat on

the pews earlier, and took them up to leave. He said, without looking back towards the pulpit, "I reckon you got some unfinished business with Hattie, Lord. I'll make sure I'm at your disposal." Now that the church was finished, he could hang around town for a few hours each day in case Hattie decided to come out again. "Don't take no offense toward Molly. She meant well." He wasn't only referring to what Molly had done to Hattie, but also for the state her meddling had left him in.

He made his way to the door, and hesitated with his hand on the knob. Despite the way both women had practically canonized him, he knew one thing for sure. "I ain't no better than Molly or Hattie." It had been a battle for him to accept the fact that what he wanted and what God decided he would get were in stark contrast. But why add Lilly to the turmoil? Still, Zachariah merely prayed, "Thanks for bearing with me." Before he closed the door behind him, he was compelled to add one more thing. "It's been years since I've prayed inside a church." He paused to look around at the white walls and ceiling that boxed him in. "You look small in here."

He stepped outside where the evening air was cool and the sky never-ending. *That's more like it.* He put on his hat, and then tossed on his coat.

Dusty saw him and jumped inside the wagon, ready to head home.

But Zachariah paused a little longer to take in a deep breath. He unconsciously tucked his hands in his pockets, and he found a piece of paper he'd forgotten about. He pulled it out.

Lillian Rauling.

A thought intruded upon him as he stared at the

name. This was evidence. Evidence she belonged to *him*. Evidence he had a legal claim to Lilly and a right to stop her marriage to Nate. All Zachariah had to do was shove that piece of paper in her face and show her who'd really paid for her. That would obligate her to marry him—a man with a scar she'd have to look at every day for the rest of her years.

He couldn't force that on her.

If he was ever to get married, it had to be to a woman who saw something just as comely in him as he saw in her. And since he had a scar right smack on his face, it seemed that stipulation was impossible to meet with Lilly. He folded the piece of paper and tucked it deep into his pocket.

That's where it'd been all this time. That's where it would stay.

~*~

"Is there a problem, Lillian?"

Aside from the fact she hadn't seen Nate Powell in over a week and hadn't missed him in the least, yes, there was a problem.

He had boasted that he'd sent away for something for her, and here it was. He made a big to-do over it, and even intruded upon her by coming to Molly's house at eight o'clock in the morning. The house was in shambles, and some of the women were still in their night clothes, so Lillian met him outside.

She didn't take the box from him because she already dreaded what was inside. So he untied the ribbon, he took off the cover, and Lillian simply looked at the folded wedding dress.

"You could at least take it out of the box," he said.

Yes, she could, but she wanted to leave it in there, put the cover back on, and send it back, along with him, to wherever it came from. However, she complied with her fiancé's wishes and responded with an insincere, "It's lovely."

"That's all you can say?" he said. "This dress cost a fortune."

Yes, a fortune in damages.

The dream of throwing herself into her beloved's arms and kissing him over and over was buried under a pile of debt. This dress simply added to the heap.

"It'll need altering, but I'm sure Molly would be happy to do it for you," he said.

"Yes. I'm sure she'd be thrilled." Lillian had figured out Molly wasn't fond of him. Wishing to stir some feelings for him herself, Lillian reviewed Nate Powell's good qualities. He was polite, he was well-off, and he had a pleasant face to look at. If those were points for which to be grateful, then why wasn't she?

Because the problem lay not in what he was, but in what he wasn't. He wasn't joyful. He wasn't interested in music. He wasn't the least bit passionate. He just *was*.

"And I have an even bigger surprise." Even his surprises were spoken in his matter-of-fact, business-like voice. "I found a preacher who's willing to preacher the church. He'll be here Friday."

Friday? It came as a shock rather than a surprise, because that meant...

"I've built your church, found your preacher, and employed Kate's Eatery to give you the finest wedding this town has seen. And that wedding," he concluded, "will be this Saturday."

29

Molly was right. Everything I play lately does sound like a dirge. Thursday afternoon Lillian was alone in the church playing *Sealed with a Rainbow* on the piano.

The preacher would arrive tomorrow, and unless something drastic happened, by Saturday she'd be Nate Powell's bride.

Her despair ebbed from her fingertips into the music. Mr. Powell had no understanding of her or her love of music, nor did he even care to try. But she knew who did understand. For the umpteenth time, her gaze caressed the new finish on the piano, and she felt a spark of joy ignite in her heart. And for the umpteenth time, despair snuffed it out.

Life with Nate Powell and his parents would be no better than her stifled existence had been as a governess. She'd be as a ghost wondering about in someone else's home. Her wedding would be a funeral, and with the dress he'd purchased, the services he'd employed, and the arbor with the satin bow that stood outside, Nate had heaped upon her shovelful after shovelful of so-called damages. Already she felt the weight of being six feet under.

The music poured, and drops of hope trickled down her cheeks leaving what felt like permanent stains on her face. She couldn't bear to live the rest of her life with him. But what were her alternatives? She should have escaped when she'd had the chance.

If only she could tell Zachariah. But if she indeed vanished, and Nate Powell discovered the man he'd accused of killing his sister was involved in the disappearance of his bought-and-paid-for wife… whatever Lillian decided to do, she'd have to do alone. And she had determined to do something. But what?

Her fingers played on as she pondered her options. *Prison. Wandering alone in the wilderness. Marriage to a man who doesn't give a fig about me.* What was the least of the three evils? She let out a soft snort as something occurred to her.

Prison. What a strange twist in fate. Avoiding prison was what drove her into this quandary in the first place.

She paused to listen to the song her hands knew so well they automatically played it, and to wonder how the well-loved daughter of a well-to-do opera singer had come to this wretched crossroads in her life.

She stopped playing. Feelings of being cheated over and over again goaded her to accuse God of breaking His promises.

Why had her parents died? Why had Mr. Drummond slipped into her bedroom? Why had she gotten matched with Nate Powell? Why was her life one storm after another, with no end in sight? What had a child done to offend God so that He hated her so much?

Lillian's eyes blurred, but this time it wasn't hope leaving her body. It was liquid anger welling up in her eyes. *Why?* She got up to stand by the window and stared out. But the sky wasn't stormy at all. Rather, it was a calm expanse of blue—with two white puffs drifting closer to one another.

~*~

"You stay here and watch the place."

Zachariah finished saddling Thunderbolt, and he gave Dusty a see-you-later pat on the head. He'd done enough work on the place for today. He'd gutted out the upstairs of the house, and found some boards good enough to fix up the barn.

With a "giddy up," he was off to pay vigil to Hattie, as he'd promised. There was a better chance of finding her in the daylight than in the night time, when the saloon was at its busiest. But there was something else he wanted to do first.

Word was the preacher was due in tomorrow, so Zachariah figured he ought to make a final check on the church to make sure everything was in fine array.

When he reached the church, he found it was in finer array than he'd anticipated.

He dismounted Thunderbolt.

What he'd been told was coming to pass, in fact, was. Some tables and chairs had already been set out on the church grounds. There was also a fancy arbor with a big white bow. It appeared Nate wasn't even allowing the preacher to hang his hat before putting him to work.

Zachariah passed by the matrimonial plans in progress as he would through a row of tombstones.

Lilly and Nate were getting married. Up until now, it had seemed like those were just words.

As he drew closer to the building, he heard music. He opened the church door and hesitated in the doorway.

Lilly was sitting at the piano playing.

His mother used to play this very same sonata

back before his family moved to Texas fourteen years ago. He quietly closed the door and sat in the back pew.

Lilly's eyes were closed, her brow furrowed. She was so deep into the music the sound seemed to come from her rather than the piano. Before she reached the end of the sonata, her fingers stopped playing and came to rest on the keys, until the sound disappeared. Her eyes remained closed, as if the silence was part of the song, and she was absorbing it.

Zachariah thought it best he should leave before she opened her eyes, but an ache in his chest wouldn't let him go until he said something. Not knowing what else to say, he said something trivial. "*Moonlight Sonata.* It's a pretty song."

Her eyelids popped open. Her startled gaze swept the church until it landed on him. "Molly says it sounds like a dirge when I play it," she responded, "but the sonata is supposed to be played slowly."

"As I recall," he said, "it should be played adagio."

She stared at him for a long moment, and then looked away. She started playing the sonata again at her slower-than-adagio pace. "You're a man of mystery, Zachariah."

Mystery? That wasn't a word he'd have used to describe himself. "How so?"

"How do you know this sonata?"

He'd known easier times. "My mother played it back when we lived in Michigan."

"You lived up north?" She looked down at her slowly-moving fingers. "Another mystery."

"Is it?"

He'd lived his first eight years as the son of the Chief Constable back in Negaunee, Michigan. It was a town that mined iron ore, and then shipped it over the frigid waters of Lake Superior. In a world of long winters, his family spent a lot of time indoors, where his mother would play piano, and his father would read the newspaper.

Until one day, his father commented about the unruly West. *"I could bring order to one of those towns."* An advertisement for a sheriff in Texas gave him the chance. However, three days short of reaching his destination, as Zachariah's father was helping to push an overloaded wagon up an incline, it rolled back and killed him.

The truth of the matter was, if Zachariah set his mind to it, he could talk almost as well as Nate. But circumstances molded him into what he was, and what he reasoned he'd always be—even if he could no longer drive cattle. What Zachariah Keane had become entailed more than just making a living. It defined how a man lived, beginning with the fact that a workingman didn't put on fancy airs. "I'm just a cowboy," he said at last. "There's no mystery about that."

"Yes," she said. "A cowboy." As though that was the greatest mystery about him.

They both fell quiet.

She continued to play the familiar sonata, and the sight of her face and the sound of the music began to stir in him images of nightfall on a newborn earth and the first man awakening from a deep sleep. Zachariah closed his eyes and imagined how it went.

Adam blinked open his eyes and saw in the moonlit sky above, the silhouettes of two whippoorwills flying from fern to fern in the canopy overhead. Their dance in flight was graceful, and should have been pleasant to watch, but for one thing.

Just days earlier, God had presented to him all the creatures that inhabited his paradise garden home in order for Adam to give them names. There were flying things which Adam gave names to, such as magpie, osprey, and nighthawk; swimming things he called manatee, marlin, and dolphin; and creatures that, like him, walked upon the land. He gave them names such as ox, cougar, and badger. Adam laughed out loud at the seemingly endless varieties, until he had seen them all. It was at this moment a realization stabbed his laughter. He was the only one of his kind.

The thrill of watching a twelve-point buck raise his head, or the spray of sweetness in his mouth as Adam sank his teeth into the flesh of a ripened peach turned to blandness. There was no one to share these with.

Adam lay on his back for a moment longer as he watched the two whippoorwills playing. He started to raise to sit, but a pain throbbed in his side.

What had he done to hurt himself? He could not remember, and he did not wonder about it long, because this pain was shallow. It was the prick of a thorn compared to the impalement of loneliness.

"Adam."

The voice of his Maker brought Adam to his feet, and Adam answered, "Here I am, Lord."

"There is one final creature whom you should name."

Adam heard the whisper as a twig snapped. He turned, and his gaze landed on something so exquisite, he could not move.

Zachariah felt paralyzed as he watched Lillian. He watched her as she looked down at the slim fingers waltzing so slowly across the keys that the beautiful song she played did, in fact, sound like a dirge. He watched as her black eyelashes swept across her porcelain cheeks. He watched as her cherry lips parted as if in a kiss. It was at this moment Zachariah realized God had created man to please Himself, but he had created woman to please man. She was, in fact, the most beautiful thing in the world.

The creature's eyes were as stunning as a dove's. Its hair flowed long and elegant as a mare's tail. Moonlight glistened upon its skin, across the curve of its hip, and adorned its form with veils of moon shadow.

Adam and the creature stood face to entrancing face, captured in the illuminating gaze of the watchful eye above. Adam was drawn to this creature by a force more powerful than the attraction of the tide to the bright moon overhead. A force that overtook him and unlocked his limbs. A force that compelled him to take a step forward. And then another. The closer he got, the more he wanted it. No. Needed it. Finally, he stretched out his trembling hand, and the instant his fingertips touched the silk of the creature's cheek, the puncture of loneliness healed. This creature was more than simply one of his kind.

"This is now bone of my bones, and flesh of my flesh," Adam said. *"She shall be called woman."*

"Did you see the preparations outside?" Lilly asked, stirring Zachariah from the daydream, but not the desire it had roused. "Mr. Powell has made all the arrangements himself."

"I saw them." The question as well as the answer was redundant. She knew he didn't miss them. He also noted that she was getting married in two days and still calling her husband-to-be Mr. Powell.

She rested her right hand in her lap, and started playing the sonata with her left hand only, note by solitary note. It made the piece sound even lonelier, as if Adam, in the garden of Eden, had awoken to find he was still alone. She played the song even slower yet as she looked down at the keys. "Have you ever been disappointed in God?" she asked.

Zachariah looked at her sitting there, doing nothing about her circumstances except expressing self pity in her music. It made him angry. He wasn't disappointed in God, he was disappointed in her.

She'd poured out her heart to him, but was giving the rest of herself to Nate.

But did Zachariah have the courage to ask her how she could do that? Time was running out. It was now, or forever hold his peace. He decided if he didn't ask, he'd be as disappointed in himself as he was in her. "I can't say I always understand God," he answered. "But there's something else I understand even less."

Her eyebrows arched with mild curiosity, although her gaze remained on her left hand, which moved so slowly, it was almost still. "What's that?"

"Why all these women are marrying one man when they're in love with another. All because some crazy matchmaker looked at a shaft of hair and said this one goes with that one. Each man and each woman has had plenty of time to take a good look at the whole person. Can't they see for themselves the pairings are all wrong? Especially you, Lilly. You never swallowed that hogwash."

He put his hand deep into his pocket. Yes, that piece of paper that entitled him to her was still there. He wished she'd look at him and start playing that sonata with the same awe Adam had felt for Eve. With the same passion Zachariah was feeling for her now.

But she wouldn't even lift her gaze.

"The women are saying nothing, because if one reneges," Lilly answered matter-of-factly, "she must reimburse the man all fees, all fares, and all related expenses he's incurred."

"And you, Lilly?" he asked. "Is that why you're marrying Nate?" He held his breath and inwardly pleaded, *Please look at me.*

"What woman could resist a man like Mr. Powell?"

He kept looking at a woman who wouldn't look back. If her answer was sincere, then he had one question. "Then why are you playing that song like that?"

It took a while for her to answer this time. "Perhaps it's because I feel more like a commodity than a person."

Is that it? Zachariah closed his fist upon the small piece of paper, crumbling it. *Because you don't want to feel like Nate bought you?*

The woman who wanted to be loved more than skin deep had mighty shallow eyesight. Apparently, he'd been right about her from the moment she'd stepped off the carriage. A beautiful woman wanted a man who was just as good-looking as herself, and she'd never find anything handsome about a man who possessed the mark of Cain right smack on his face.

But did she smile for Nate the way she smiled for him? Did she ever confide and cry in front of Nate? Most of all, could she ever be to Nate a playful whirlwind blowing through the scorched prairie of his life?

No.

Given what she'd said about the contract, Zachariah had no doubt the piece of paper in his fist–the evidence bearing his name and hers in Clayton's handwriting–gave him the power to seize her from

Nate. Once she saw it, she'd have no choice. She'd have to leave Nate and marry the man who wanted her. The man who needed her.

Zachariah was tired of being lonely. He was tired of feeling like the only creature of his kind. Never before had he wanted something more than he wanted Lilly. It was no longer blood pumping through his veins, but desire. It drugged his senses, took possession of his hand, and slowly withdrew the piece of entitlement from his pocket.

She kept her gaze on the keys, playing the sonata and luring him from the pew. The heels of his boots tapped against the wooden floor, the rhythm contrary to her song. It was the rhythm of desire pounding through his heart and brain. Yes, he could spend his days exchanging with her playful banter. Yes, he could spend his nights holding her in his arms and kissing away her nightmares. And yes, he could listen to her play piano for the rest of his life.

Those feelings of being so close to a man's yearning he could have it snared him in its gravity. He was a feather floating from the sky, and she was the ground. He couldn't stop his feet from closing the distance between them. The "click, click, click" of his heels was a perpetual, steady motion beyond his will.

Finally, the clicking stopped. Only one thing sounded and resounded through his mind as he stood close enough to touch her face. *This is now flesh of my flesh.* He stretched out his hand.

His trembling fingers were within inches of stroking the ivory cheek of Eve, when she turned her face away.

His feeling of feather-like floating became that of lead glass crashing against rock and shattering into oblivion. He pulled his hand back.

Nate had dragged Lilly into their war, and won.

She needed the freedom to choose, and Zachariah needed to be chosen. Though her actions had suggested contrary, her words dictated she had chosen Nate.

Zachariah looked at the piece of paper, now crumpled, in the palm of his hand. It could get him the most beautiful creature he'd ever laid eyes on, but it couldn't do what he needed most. It couldn't make her fall in love with him.

But it could do what she needed most. It could release her from feeling like a commodity bought by Nate at a high price.

If Zachariah couldn't love her as his wife, he could at least love her as a human being. He could give her back her worth.

"I release you from all recompenses, Lilly," he said, *including the incalculable damages you've done to my heart.* With her face still turned away, he placed the paper on the piano, and walked out of the church.

30

When Lillian heard the door close behind her, she let go of the tears she'd been harnessing.

Zachariah was gone. The calmness of his voice still resonated in her mind. *"I release you from all recompenses, Lilly."*

She wondered what he meant. But there was one thing she knew for certain. She cared about him. Her tears were proof of it. Zachariah was the man in the moonlight. The fact his face was imperfect was irrelevant; however, the fact her name wasn't in his pocket was. It was a cruel twist of fate—the thorny twine of which the last five years of her life had been woven.

Though Zachariah had made the solution to the contract stipulations sound so simple, if she dragged him into her breach of contract with Nate Powell, Nate would retaliate against him with a vengeance. She didn't know the details about Sally's death, but she knew Zachariah.

He was no murderer. Whatever happened was an accident, and Zachariah was as much a victim to the misfortune as was Sally. How Nate could blame a good man and deride him so was sheer cruelty.

She felt her face heat up. Maybe it was yet another impulsive, barbed decision, but she couldn't be yoked to a husband who treated a kindly man with such contempt.

She continued to nourish her anger, feeding it sticks of Nate's derogatory statements, until her anger began to nourish her. It straightened her back, raised her chin, and rejuvenated her energy. She felt empowered to walk out the church, and to keep walking until either she reached the other side of the continent or she collapsed from exhaustion. At the moment, it seemed she would see the Atlantic Ocean first.

She rose from the piano bench. She was more than decided, she was in motion. The momentum would have carried her out into the wilderness that very evening—had she not found a crumpled piece of paper.

31

Lillian's first reaction upon seeing the piece of paper was the shock of discovering exactly what Zachariah meant when he'd said, *"I release you from all recompenses."* Her second reaction was the pure rage that Nate had taken advantage of her.

Instead of taking her into the wilderness, Lillian's momentum carried her out the church, past the arbor—where she tore off the ribbon—and over to Kate's Eatery, where Prudence had left Molly's wagon. Lillian confiscated the wagon and careened it to the Powell ranch. The butler left her in the den, where Nate sat behind the desk.

When he stood to greet her, she shoved the ribbon at him. He was too stumped to understand, so she asked him outright. "How could you trick me into marrying you?"

"Trick you?" The snake still acted innocent. "You mean, offer to properly wed you after you attempted to come home with me the very day you arrived?"

She was mortified silent. What else could she expect from him but to twist things around? "I mean, claim me as your wife when you hadn't sent for a wife at all." She waved the crumbled piece of paper in his face.

He snatched it, read it, and then dismissed her evidence. Instead, he countered with an accusation of his own. "Oh, yes. The Love Doctor's match, which was based on the qualities of a hair shaft—and a science in which you believe as much as I. We both know no self-respecting lady would offer herself over to such a harebrained scheme. What were you running from, Lillian? The scandal of an affair?"

She was about to slap him, but he caught her wrist. He looked squarely into her face. "Judging by that fear in your eyes, it was more than just a scandal. What did you do? Rob someone? The dress you wore the day you arrived looked to be a bit expensive, don't you think?"

She tried to pull her hand away, only to ensnare herself more in his grip. He turned her so her back was against him, and he crossed her arms over her chest. His hold on her was iron. "It doesn't matter what brought you here. I did you a favor."

"By trying to heap insurmountable damages over my head?"

"By sparing you from marrying that scarred-faced murderer."

She was trembling, but forced out what she instinctively knew. "Zachariah is *not* a murderer."

Nate turned her to face him. The crazed look in his eyes evinced he'd read more into her statement than what was intended. His grip on her wrists tightened, and her hands tingled with numbness. "You're in love with him."

She could neither confirm nor deny it, and so Nate took her silence as confirmation. He shoved her, and her head smacked against the floor. She almost lost consciousness.

The blood drained from her face as she looked up at him. Had he gone mad with his hatred toward Zachariah?

Perhaps if he could see past his anger…if he could see the situation from another perspective, particularly the perspective Molly had told her…perhaps if someone could gently lead him to the truth. Since circumstances dictated Lillian had to intercede in the volatile matter, she picked her words carefully.

"Your dear sister was a lovely girl," she began. "I couldn't help but notice her portrait in the dining room. I've never seen a prettier young lady. Any brother would be proud to have such an angel for a sister. I offer my sincerest condolences for her bitter loss."

Judging by the calm that fell over Nate, she'd chosen her beginning words wisely. But there were less comforting words he needed to hear.

"Her loss must have been devastating to you." She added cautiously, "As well as to Zachariah."

His eyes flashed. But other than that, he didn't stir.

"Zachariah loved her as much as you did," Lillian continued. Was Nate at last beginning to see reason? "Had he been given the choice that day, I know he would have received his lashings ten times over, before risking any harm to her. Indeed, he has received his punishment a thousand times over, on his own flesh—and in his heart.

"Her passing was an accident," Lillian said, grateful for the calm settling on Nate. "She should have allowed Zachariah to reap the repercussions of his tardiness, but she also loved him. Stepping in for him so he wouldn't get chastened was how she had expressed her love. How noble of her. Your sister loved deeply. But how heartrending that her good intentions led to such tragedy." Lillian fell quiet, and let the words soak in.

Nate stared at the wall for a moment, a moment during which he seemed to absorb, and to study the perilous course of those long-ago events. A moment during which his eyes began to grow tender. But for whatever reason, that moment was cut short.

His gaze landed decidedly on Lillian's face. "No. That lying murderer isn't going to be rewarded with a wife." He walked to the door and locked it. "It looks like the wedding can't wait until Saturday." He peeled off his coat, and she realized his intentions.

"Nate." She backed away from him. "Don't."

He stopped short. "That's the first time you've called me by my Christian name."

Lillian realized calling him that at this time was a grave mistake in light of the fact she'd informally referred to Zachariah by his given name. She read that much in the glare of Nate's eyes.

And of all the impulsive decisions she'd ever made, Lillian knew coming here would be the one she'd regret the most.

~*~

As far as Nate was concerned, nothing would keep him from claiming his due. Not even his father who banged at the door, yelling at him to open up. Not even the spray of splinters as the bolt burst through the frame. Or the crash of the door against the wall. Not even the rifle in his father's hands.

"Let her go, son."

"Get out," Nate said. "She's my wife, and this is none of your concern."

Marcus cocked the rifle and did the unexpected.

He fired a hole through one of his accounting books. There weren't many things more important to him than that. He cocked the rifle again, and aimed it at Nate. He meant business. "I said, let her go."

Lillian slipped out of the room.

All Nate could do was watch, because his own father held him at bay. Nate glared at the patriarchal traitor. "Zachariah murdered your daughter, and you still favor him over your own blood."

"What's Zachariah's belongs to Zachariah. You got enough. You got everything I own."

Marcus kept half an eye on him, and half an eye on Lillian through the window. She climbed into the wagon, and Marcus waited until she was long gone before he relaxed his guard. He carried the rifle with him as he walked over to the book he'd shot. He assessed the damage not only to the book, but to the desk and chair as well. "Now finish up what you were doing before this ruckus started," Marcus ordered.

Nate snatched the weapon and swung the butt of the rifle onto Marcus's skull. "I *got* everything you own, huh?" Nate mocked. "You know what I *don't got*? I *don't got* a sister."

Marcus stumbled, and then fell to the floor, his eyes closed.

Nate fled with the rifle, to finally take care of long overdue business.

32

Lillian had to warn Zachariah that she had instigated Nate's fury against him, but didn't know where to begin to look. She returned to Molly's house to ask her where Zachariah lived, and found Molly in her rocking chair, up to her neck in sewing. Lillian blurted out her question, and was shocked by Molly's response.

It was the incomprehensibly slurred speech of a drunkard.

Lillian had thought Molly was a woman of strong constitution, but she supposed taking care of four unhappy women would drive anyone to take a nip. Or, in Molly's case, more like ten. Lillian got down on her knees and again asked Molly, "Where does Zachariah live? Molly, it's imperative that I-"

"It ain't what you think." Rosie appeared in the doorway with a cup of tea. She somberly walked up to Molly, and then tested the temperature of tea against her own lips, before touching it to Molly's. "She acts like she's been drinking, but she ain't had a drop. She's been like this since early this afternoon, and she's getting worse." Apparently, Rosie had been keeping an eye on Molly.

"What's wrong with her?" Lillian asked.

"I think it was my doing," Rosie said. "I complained about her cooking, and she stomped off in a huff and sat in the rocker. She started sewing like tomorrow ain't never going to come, and mumbling about how she had to finish the curtains for the telegraph office. She finished those off and started working on your dress, but out of nowhere, she stopped. And she's been just sitting there like this ever since."

Rosie's eyes grew glassy. "I didn't mean to upset her. I mean, all that carping about the food? It's how I'd always kept my weight down. The better it tasted, the more I complained." She touched Molly's arm. "That's my way of talking myself out of eating. Everything you cooked was fit for a king. I just wanted to keep...trim. You understand?"

But Molly didn't seem to understand. She uttered something garbled.

Lillian noticed the wedding dress draped over her lap. She snatched the dreaded thing and threw it aside. "I don't need this anymore. Nate and I aren't getting married."

Molly, however, seemed to understand that. She offered Lillian a smile in which only half her mouth cooperated. The other side drooped.

Lillian couldn't fathom what was happening to her, but since rest was the prescription for everything, she took Molly by the hand. "Let me help you to bed."

Molly didn't budge. She seemed stubborn and obstinate, until Lillian dropped Molly's hand. It fell limp onto her lap.

She can't even move her arm. Lillian suddenly realized the horror Molly was in. Zachariah was in danger, but so was Molly. And without Molly's help..."We've got to get the doctor." Lillian turned to leave.

Molly grabbed her wrist with the other hand in a

death grip.

It convinced Lillian all the more Molly needed help

Molly spoke again.

Lillian couldn't understand the garbled words. But she did see the pair of finished curtains that were so important. "Yes, Molly. I'll take the curtains to the telegraph office. I promise." Whether or not she did so immediately was irrelevant. Lillian just wanted to keep Molly calm.

Prudence followed her to the wagon. "I'll go with you."

Lillian didn't argue as the more capable woman took the reins.

~*~

Rosie managed to get Molly into bed. "If I ate my fill of your cooking," Rosie lightly confessed, "I'd be plump as a pumpkin. Yours is the best cooking I ever ate. Matter of fact, you ain't just a cook, mind you, you're as good as those fine Parisian chefs." Rosie repentantly rambled on, until Molly tapped her wrist. "What do you want, dearie?"

Molly pointed to the dresser.

"You want me to get something out of the drawer?"

Molly nodded and then moved her good hand in slow, circular motions.

"You want me to write something down?"

Again, Molly nodded.

Rosie realized she was going to write Molly's will.

~*~

Nate had his father's rifle and his fastest horse as he rode up to Zachariah's house. He barged through the door.

"Where are you, Zachariah?"

Silence met him.

After a good look around the house, Nate ran out to the barn. Zachariah's horse was gone, but his dog wasn't. The animal barked, and instead of putting a bullet through Zachariah, Nate put three into the dog. He went back into the house and fired more shots into the windows, until the rifle was empty. He reloaded his rifle with a box of bullets he found on the floor. He got back on his horse and headed toward town. He figured he'd probably find Zachariah at the church.

~*~

"Sounds like Molly's having an apoplexy," Dr. Hinkle said to Lillian and Prudence. He scrambled for his coat and medical bag.

"Is it serious?" Prudence asked.

The doctor paused, and then turned to Lillian. "You'd better get Zachariah in case either needs to say their piece." Then he rushed to saddle his horse.

Prudence got into the wagon and called him over to it. "This will be faster," Prudence said as she started turning the horse around.

"Where does Zachariah live?" Lillian almost implored of the doctor.

"Seven, maybe eight miles from town. Clayton should still be at the telegraph office. Ask him to take you."

"You promised Molly you'd bring those curtains

to Clayton, and since you'll be going there…" Prudence took off with the doctor, leaving Lillian with Molly's curtains, and about a mile away from Clayton's office.

~*~

Nate used the butt of the rifle he was carrying to knock over the tables and chairs that had been set up for his wedding reception as he headed into the church. He kicked open the door.

"Where are you, Zachariah? Come out and face me, you murdering coward."

He aimed the rifle toward every crevice and corner. Maybe Zachariah was hiding in the pews. He fired a round to scare him out.

Nothing.

Nate fired a round into the stained glass picture of the Marriage of the Lamb, shattering it. He barged out. The next place on his list was the telegraph office where Zachariah sometimes hung out with Clayton.

He found Zachariah settled across from the saloon on a bench in front of the Sheriff's office with his heels perched on the horse rail.

Nate took a detour, and led his horse between the buildings. He tied the animal behind the general store. He slid his way around the building, and raised the barrel of his rifle, until he had Zachariah dead center in his sight.

"I've got you now." He slowly squeezed the trigger.

33

"Put that rifle down." The voice startled him.

Nate turned to find his father walking up behind him.

His head was still bleeding, but the man gave Nate a belt that knocked the rifle out of his hands and landed him on the ground.

"You want to get your neck stretched?" Marcus asked as he poured the bullets from Nate's rifle onto the ground.

Nate came to his feet and touched a sore spot on his lip. He looked at the blood on the back of his knuckles. "It's about time one of us stood up as a man and did something about Sally. Since you're too stupid-"

Marcus grabbed his son by the throat and held him against the building. "You ain't killing Zachariah." Marcus held Nate long enough to choke the strength out of him, and to give him a hint of what a hanging felt like. Marcus let go, and Nate slid to the ground. "Now get on home."

Nate got up and stumbled toward his horse. He led it toward his father. "Sure. I'll 'get on home,'" he mocked. Then he smacked the horse in the rump so that it reared into Marcus. Nate took off to find Zachariah again.

Without the rifle Nate wasn't sure how he was going to kill him, but he swore to Sally that her killer would get justice, and he would get it before the day ended. She'd waited long enough.

Something distracted Nate from his quest to kill Zachariah.

Someone of particular interest rushed into Clayton's office.

Nate ran toward the building and hid outside the door to listen.

~*~

Lillian was breathless as she threw herself into the telegraph office. If Molly was dying, then Zachariah had little time to say his good-byes.

"Be with you in a minute." Clayton was installing a brass wall bracket for an oil lamp. The furniture had been pushed against the far wall, and against the back door. The office reeked of a harsh, chemical smell. "Molly's been nagging me to do something about this place since you ladies arrived," he explained as he worked. "Don't touch the walls. I just varnished them. And whatever you do," he looked at the oil lamp by the door, "don't light that. Even striking a match could make this place go up like a torch."

The oil lamp was just inches away from her. The wainscoted wall behind it was shiny with dampness, and there was a handy box of matches placed on the chair rail. She backed away. She'd once had an experience with gaslights she'd never forget.

Clayton looked up from screwing the hardware on the wall. "What's that you got in your hands?"

She'd forgotten about the curtains she was clutching. "These. Molly made them for you. Clayton, you've got to take me to see Zachariah. Molly may be dying, and-" and she also had to warn Zachariah about Nate.

Clayton abruptly stopped. "Dying?"

"The doctor said she's had an apoplexy."

He put the screwdriver down. "I'll get my horse."

"What shall I do with these?" She indicated the curtains. "Molly made me promise…."

"That Molly," he said with a shake of his head. "Put them over on the desk."

They passed each other, Clayton to get his horse, and Lillian to the far side of the office to leave the curtains where he'd indicated.

~*~

Nate stepped away from the door as Clayton emerged.

"If you need anything you'll have to come back tomorrow," Clayton told him. "I've got an emergency."

"Just moseying on down to the saloon." Nate mocked the local colloquialism, and feigned that he was going to see Hattie. After Clayton disappeared into the livery, Nate peered into the office.

Lillian stood at the far end, her back to him, and he realized he had an opportunity that just might even the score. *You want some religion, Zachariah?* He found the matches and snatched them off the chair rail. *How about an eye for an eye?* He struck a match, and held it to the wall.

The flare that followed sent his mind reeling back five years.

~*~

Hattie noticed it first. "The schoolhouse! It's on fire!"

Seventeen-year-old Nate instantly broke into a run. He reached the schoolhouse and, with Zachariah's help, threw open the door. The heat inside drove him back. He dashed to the window and banged on it with his fists. "Sally!" He could see her figure in the smoke.

"Help me, Nate! Help me!"

He'd never seen his bold little sister so terrified.

"I'm coming! I'll get you out!"

He circled the building looking for a way in and cursing Zachariah at the same time. If Zachariah hadn't dragged his feet and made Sally do his chore...well, Zachariah knew how hard-headed she was. Although she'd seen Nate light the stove a dozen times before, she'd never done it by herself. If anything should happen to her, he'd never forgive Zachariah.

~*~

Zachariah sat across from the saloon, paying vigil to Hattie, when he smelled something unpleasantly familiar. He came to his feet and looked around. Then he spotted the smoke. Clayton's office was on fire. The combustible varnish he'd just painted the walls with...Zachariah ran. He skidded to a stop.

Clayton was coming out of the livery on his horse.

Relief flooded Zacheriah's soul.

When Clayton saw the fire, he yanked the reins on the horse so hard the horse almost reared him off.

Zachariah ran over to him.

"Lillian is still in there!" Clayton yelled.

And then she screamed.

"She can't get out the back door," Clayton frantic. "I pushed all the furniture against it."

Nate was running around the building, yelling for Sally, as if his mind was gone. Not only had Nate lost his sister, he was now at risk of losing his wife.

The Sheriff, the local business owners, and everyone who was in the saloon, including Hattie, came out.

The men formed a bucket brigade, but at the pace the fire was spreading, their efforts weren't going to help Lilly. She was trapped inside, and there was only one chance she had to come out alive.

Zacheriah threw off his coat, dunked it in the horse trough, and tossed it over himself. He barged through the fiery doorway. "Lilly!"

~*~

Lillian was fourteen years old again. Her parents had just installed gaslights with pretty milk glass sconces throughout the house. It was evening, and she was in the sitting room while her parents were by the door.

Although it was too early to get the full effect, Papa couldn't wait to try the new lights. "Now, for the moment of truth." He was humorously turning a simple to-do into a grand ceremony.

Lillian and her mother were laughing at his overly-exaggerated ritual.

"Let there be..." He lighted the gaslight.

Instead of a delightful glow, there was a hiss. An instant later, the wallpaper was ablaze.

~*~

"Zachariah! Is that you? Zachariah!"
Sally's screams tore at Zachariah's heart. He loved her,

and his responsibility to protect her drove him through a doorway as hot as the gateway to Hades. "Sally, it's me. I'm coming, and I'm going to get you out."

But the fire had a mind of its own, and one which wasn't in agreement with Zachariah's goal. It was a carnivorous beast, Sally was its next meal, and it wouldn't let him near her. He could hear its roar, feel its hot breath, and see the tongues from its many heads striking out at him, tasting another morsel as he tried to plow his way through to her.

Claws of flames lashed at him as he tried to whisk away the thick gray wall that stood between him and the young woman he wanted to spend the rest of his life with. Blinded by the choking smoke, he crashed into a desk, and toppled over a chair. It sent him plummeting with a smarting crack to his knees.

"Zachariah!" she coughed. "Zach-" She coughed some more.

From his hands and knees, he glanced behind. Down here, the smoke was thinner. The path to the door that would enable him to save his own life was still passable, but flames were quickly closing it off. Ahead, there was no path. Only a labyrinth of the legs of chairs and desks, and flickers of red and yellow pain.

And Sally.

Her shouts turned to coughs.

"Hold on!" Zachariah cried out to her. "I'm coming!"

He crawled toward the sound of Sally's coughs, which deteriorated to chokes. He shoved aside everything that was between him and her, as he charged on all fours like a bull. His knees were two bruises that throbbed each time they pounded the floor. Nails and slivers stabbed the heels of his hands. Finally, he reached the place where he thought she'd be. But Sally wasn't there.

"Sally! Where are you? Talk to me!"

He spotted something on the floor, and squinted at it through the smoke. What was it? A mound of blankets that had ignited?

Sally had stopped coughing.

There was no sound.

He leaped to his feet and crashed through the smoke, shoving aside the desks and chairs, everything that kept him away from her, until he reached her. He threw his coat over her and smothered the fire. He picked her up and hugged her to his heart. "You're safe now. I've got you."

With his love now in his arms, Zachariah paced. He was like a confused animal trapped in a rapidly shrinking cage with bars of fire. His nostrils and lungs burned with hot ash. From where he now stood, the blaze had grown more furious, the smoke blacker, and together they barricaded the door. One thing he knew for certain, he couldn't stay where he was. The way out was just a direction, and he threw himself and Sally toward it.

Those twenty feet in the flames and smoke were like twenty miles in a gauntlet with demons slicing his flesh with razor-sharp whips. His eyes stung. His lungs burned. He choked. He stumbled. From somewhere in the chaos, a blazing beam came hurtling at him. He shielded Sally from it and received its full burning brunt to his face and forearm.

He staggered, almost senseless with pain, but he wouldn't let go of Sally. He was determined he would get her out.

Or die in there with her.

~*~

"Papa!"

A second gaslight exploded, and Lilly's mother

screamed.

Somewhere behind the smoke and flames, Papa ordered Mama to meet them in front of the house. Then he demanded, "Lilly, tell me where you are. I can't see you."

"I'm here. Behind the sofa. Help me, Papa! I'm frightened!"

At last, her Papa reached her. He tore off his jacket and wrapped it around her. He picked her up. "You're safe, Lilly. I've got you." He hugged her.

The fire would take his life before he let it take hers. But there was no need to worry, because Papa was strong and invincible. Wrapped in his jacket, she could see nothing. But she could hear Papa choke. She could feel him hesitate and jolt. But she could also feel in him a determination in the way he clutched onto her that he would get them out. And sure enough, he did.

But once they were outside, he couldn't find Lilly's mother. "Elaine! Where are you?" He raced back and forth across the garden, stomping the flowers she'd so diligently cared for. "I told her to wait for us here. He paced some more, until he decided, "Lilly stay right where you are. Don't move an inch."

Why her mother wasn't already outside was something Lilly could only speculate. Perhaps her mother had also entered the burning room to try to save her daughter. Or perhaps she ran upstairs to salvage the music box Papa had gotten for their anniversary. It was so dear to her. But Papa went back in for Mama, and Lilly didn't move an inch. She waited right where she was told.

She waited as the flames feasted and grew furiously strong. She waited as the flares flickered high, lighting up the night sky. She waited as the raging roar began to weaken to a hiss. She waited until daybreak revealed a mound of charred beams where a house had once stood.

She waited until relatives tore her away.

~*~

Hattie's heart throbbed in her throat as the tragedy that had turned two youths into enemies unfolded once again—just as it had done on that winter morning a half decade earlier.

The building was filled with red and yellow fury. Black smoke billowed into the sky.

Nate was running around like a crazy man crying out his sister's name.

Though this time there was a brigade hauling bucket after bucket from the horse trough to the fire, their efforts proved useless. Flames continued to consume the wooden structure, and Hattie couldn't help but fear Lilly would meet the same fate as Sally. In fact, this fire was so intense, Hattie was even more afraid Zachariah would meet the fate he'd somehow been spared that day.

Moments passed as the fire rapidly increased in size and rage. Still no Zachariah.

Hattie could feel its incinerating heat from as far back as she stood. She couldn't help but think how strange it was that Zachariah, who was too shy to confess to the woman he loved how he felt about her, might die trying to save her. And wind up spending eternity with her.

You done this before. You knew better than to try it again, she mentally scolded him. But she had to admit she admired the man more than ever. In fact, so much so, that she actually sputtered a prayer for him. *You know I ain't been no angel, and I ain't pretending to be one now. I just want to ask if You'll bring Zachariah and Lilly safely out of that there fire.* That was her request, plain and simple, and she applied an *Amen.* Would God actually listen to a fallen woman?

Despite the chaos and the confusion, despite what Hattie was witnessing, and despite the fact that she was just a no-good saloon girl who'd been abandoned once by her father, and then again by her mother and deserved a good whipping now and then from Boss, for the first time in her life, Hattie felt a strange sense of hope.

If Zachariah's God was anything like Zachariah, then just maybe...just maybe she'd see Zachariah running out of the smoke, limping, coughing, and holding Lilly in his arms, just as Hattie was seeing now. She laughed and cried at the same time.

As he'd done once before with a girl, Zachariah surrendered his beloved Lilly over to Nate.

And once again, Hattie could see Zachariah had gotten hurt as he limped out of sight.

As for Lilly...unlike Sally, she threw off Zachariah's coat and pushed away from Nate.

Nate, however, was still stuck in the past as he withered to the ground, his hands still spread out in front of him, holding the ghost of his sister. "I'm sorry, Sally," he said. "I'm sorry."

Lilly cautiously stepped back from him as he grieved over the apparition.

Hattie didn't comfort him this time. *"It's not your fault,"* she'd said back then, and he'd taken that to mean it was all Zachariah's doing.

It was time Nate finally faced the truth.

It wasn't Zachariah's turn to start the woodstove that day.

34

By the time the flames were put out, dusk was well underway.

The fire had done its damage not only to the telegraph office but to the general store beside it.

The crowd that had collected started to disburse. Most of the folks headed into the saloon to have a drink and to talk for the next few hours about the event.

Hattie'd better get back to work before Boss missed her, but her feet wouldn't move in that direction. Instead, she stayed put and watched the rest of the town try to pull itself back together.

"But I've got to tell Zachariah," Lilly said to Clayton. The quiver in her voice conveyed the pretty little thing was still recovering from her brush with death, but she had a mission to accomplish. What was so important to make Lilly disregard everything that had just happened?

"I'll tell you what you got to do," Clayton said to Lilly. "You got to go back to Molly's and get yourself some rest. It's what Zachariah would have me tell you to do, considering..."

"But-"

"Ain't no buts about it, ma'am," Clayton insisted. "I'll take you to his place tomorrow, but I'm taking you back to Molly's tonight."

What Lilly had felt was so important to tell

Zachariah, when she was Nate's fiancée, was something Hattie could only guess. Did Lilly even know Zachariah had rescued her?

The woman appeared as pure as the flower that was her namesake, and although Hattie had a tinge of jealousy, she could understand why Clayton would want to protect her, Zachariah would want to love her, and Nate would want to marry her.

Clayton and Lilly rode off, the business owners locked up, and the streets emptied, except for Hattie and two men.

One knelt in the manure-mixed mud, and the other stood behind him.

Marcus put his hand on Nate's shoulder. "It was the fire that killed Sally. Now let it go, son."

Hattie shook her head. Zachariah had made her swear to secrecy, but she realized then and there, by the somberness in his voice, Marcus knew all along what had happened. And he still let Nate treat Zachariah like soot.

Hattie's and Marcus's gazes connected, and with a long look, she conveyed to him her disappointment. *All that misery to Zachariah just to keep your precious Nate happy so he'd take over a fine business he'll never appreciate.* Then she started feeling the same disappointment in herself.

But that got cut short by a familiar phrase in a familiar voice. "Get on back to work, Hattie." Boss went back into the saloon.

But Hattie didn't follow. Instead, she closed her eyes to feel the whisper of a breeze. It felt good to be out in the cool night air, rather than crammed in some smoky saloon with a bunch of sweaty, burping, foul-smelling men. Even the horse droppings smelled better than them. The breeze was long and soothing, and it sure felt good. So good it made her wonder what it would be like to be free as the wind. When she opened her eyes, she saw Nate's horse.

Zachariah had taught her a thing or two about riding when they were children, but that was on his mother's old nag. She'd always wondered what it would be like to ride a creature as fast as that.

"Hattie." Boss appeared in front of the saloon again. "I said get on back here."

She looked at Boss. He wasn't much to look at, just an eyeful of big and burly and mean scribbled all over his face. She looked at the horse.

It was one fine-looking animal, chestnut and sinewy, and fast, she was willing to bet. She walked over to the animal and stroked its muzzle. "Yup, you're a fine horse, ain't you?" And before she knew it, she had one foot in the stirrup.

"Who's going to take care of you, Hattie?" Boss belted out.

One foot in the stirrup. That's the way things had been for Hattie all of her life. Because she couldn't get the other foot off the ground. She looked over at the man who'd been taking care of her for years. Taking care of her by beating her black and blue, where it didn't show, of course. But nonetheless, taking care of her.

Hard-as-steel Hattie Brown. That's what the regulars called her, because she had the guts to grab the pistol away from the rowdiest and roughest of men. But nobody knew she was scared to death of being alone. Nobody, that is, except Boss.

One foot in the stirrup, the other on the ground.

Not even a month had passed since her mother

left, when Hattie had given in to her fear and gone to him. He'd been hounding her to work for him. Sure, Molly had asked if she wanted to stay with her, but Hattie couldn't. Not after Danny got shot up and took to his death bed. Molly had all she could do to tend to him.

"Who's going to take care of you, Hattie?" Those were the same words she'd asked herself the day she stood in the doorway of an old shack, crying.

Her mother, all dressed in her best clothes, had said, "You're all growed up now." Then she headed back home to Georgia.

Who would take care of a woman who was never good enough for a father, and whose own mother was ashamed of her? Who would take care of a woman who'd been propositioned by most of the men in this town, and was ashamed of herself?

The breeze continued to pour over her face and shoulders. It was like the stroke of a man's fingers brushing against her skin in a non-sexual way. It was the way she wished Nate would have touched her every now and then. It was the way Zachariah had held her back when she'd grieved her mother's leaving, and then again, when she'd learned that she'd lost Nate to Lilly. Hattie's heart felt like a rope caught up in a game of tug of war, with freedom tugging on one end, and fear yanking on the other. Half of her wanting, the other half settling.

One foot in the stirrup, the other on the ground.

She stared out into the darkness. She could ride the horse, for a while. And then…w*ho would take care of Hattie Brown?* There was plenty to ride to, but nowhere to go. Her foot slipped out of the stirrup.

"That's right," Boss said. "You know where you

belong."

She looked at him and cocked her head. There was something about Boss standing there with that worried look on his face that suddenly struck her funny. Maybe he needed her more than she needed him. Maybe he was also scared. And if Boss was scared, then maybe everyone was scared, even just a little. She gave a snort. *I know where I belong, huh?* And suddenly she knew where she *didn't* belong. In one motion, she put her foot back in the stirrup and swung the other leg over.

She imagined she was quite a sight, wearing that fancy red dress of hers and sitting high on a thoroughbred horse. But from this perspective, it was nice to look down at the strong and mighty. It was even nicer to talk down at them. "I don't need your kind of care no more." There was something else she didn't need, and she looked over at it. Nate was a pathetic sight, sobbing over outstretched, empty arms. What had she ever seen in him, beyond pity?

Marcus stood over him, and he acknowledged with a nod that she could take the animal. It seemed he knew where she was headed even before she did.

Good riddance, she bid to her old life. Then she kicked the horse's flanks.

35

By the time Clayton got Lillian to Molly's house, it was nightfall.

Lillian entered just as the doctor gathered his medical tools into his bag.

Rosie and the other women were quiet for the first time since they'd arrived.

"The only thing we can do for her now is to keep her comfortable," Dr. Hinkle said before he passed Lillian on his way out.

Rosie offered to pay for his services, but he refused, saying that Molly had helped the town out more than enough.

Prudence expressed the women's gratitude and paid their hospitalities by seeing the doctor home.

Clayton stood by the door and took off his hat.

Lillian rushed to Molly's bedside. By the light of a kerosene lamp Molly was lying on her back, staring blindly at the ceiling. She was motionless, but for the shallow rise and fall of her chest. The ageless woman who'd been so strong and determined yesterday looked weak and defeated tonight.

Lillian knew it wouldn't be long, and for all Molly had done for her, she'd failed her in the most important task of all. "I'm so sorry, Molly. I tried to bring Zachariah back, but things happened so wrong tonight. I brought the curtains to Clayton as I promised, and-"

"And they look right pretty hanging in the window." Clayton took a step into the room. "I'd just finished varnishing the walls nice and shiny, and hanging up those fancy lamps, and now the place is suiting for the Queen of England herself."

Lillian met Clayton's gaze. There was no need to tell Molly about the fire that had destroyed her efforts as well as Clayton's business. Lillian could see the sacrifice in his eyes, and although Molly's eyes were dull, Lillian knew Molly was imagining Clayton's new office clear as day.

"Well, Molly." Clayton cleared his throat. "I reckon I ought to be going. Thank you for the curtains." He hesitated at the door, his back to her. "Thank you for a lot of things." Clayton left

Tears gathered in Lillian's eyes. She held Molly's hand between her own, kissed it, and gazed into her thin, wrinkled face. It had become so familiar.

Molly had eased her way into Lillian's heart and had become the caring aunt she'd always wished she had. Molly had done so much for all the women by taking them into her home. But by demanding a church be built so they could have a respectable wedding, she'd done the most for Lillian. Molly had inadvertently stalled Lillian's marriage to Nate long enough for the truth to come out.

But something crossed Lillian's mind. There was suddenly something odd in all of this.

The sharp gaze that had once occupied those eyes was not that of an unwary woman. In fact, perhaps all those haphazard meetings with Zachariah were not so haphazard at all. A chance meeting with Zachariah when Molly had sent Lillian to chop wood? The switched picnic baskets? Molly's remark about "that grand voice" of Zachariah's—which Lillian had yet to hear? Molly had made many accolades about Zachariah, including the piano he'd donated.

Molly had been trying to get Lillian to see it was Zachariah who'd sent for her. How could he possibly claim Lillian when the rest of the couples were so poorly matched—and Nate, that opportunist, was just waiting to vex him? Especially after Zachariah had been taken in by that silly scheme.

Which in turn stumped Lillian.

If Zachariah didn't believe in the Love Doctor's twaddle, why did he send for me?

Furthermore, why the other ladies and gents who'd been engaged to this one and adoring that one failed to mutter one word to the opposite sex about it— contract or no contract—was beyond Lillian. How could they be so blind? How could all of them be so blind? Then something occurred to Lillian. *How could I be so blind?*

Her gaze slipped through the doorway and she really saw it for the first time.

An empty space.

It was the place in which the piano had been situated before it was moved to the church. Coincidently, that nook was precisely the same size as the piano—as though the space had been built to accommodate it. She took a long look at Molly.

It wasn't Zachariah who had sent for her at all.

A smile broke through Lillian's grief like the rainbow song. "Molly, you certainly know a good man when you see one." Lillian kissed her sponsor on the forehead, and Molly offered a weak smile in return.

Then Molly's chest rose and fell, and failed to rise again.

36

"Lillian."

She'd fallen asleep sobbing by Molly's beside, and it was morning when the sound of her name woke her.

Rosie stood in the bedroom with a folded piece of paper in her hands. "Clayton's here to take you to see Zachariah," Rosie said. "That wouldn't happen to be a Zachariah Keane, now would it?"

"Yes, it is," Lillian said, awed at such a question coming from Rosie.

"I couldn't make out much of what Molly said last night," Rosie said, "but there're two things Molly took great pains to get across. She wanted to remind this Zachariah Keane of some promise he'd made her, and she wanted someone named Hattie to have this." Rosie surrendered what she was holding to Lillian. "Molly said Zachariah would know who the woman is."

Lillian looked down at the folded piece of paper which she'd been commissioned to deliver. It was now the property of a woman Zachariah knew named Hattie.

Hattie? Lillian wasn't as curious to the nature of the paper, as she was to the identity of the woman to whom it now belonged. With a raised brow, she regarded the written name of this unknown woman, until she figured this Hattie might simply be another elderly widow like Molly whom he had befriended. So she thought nothing more of the matter. She did, however, inquire into Zachariah's promise. "Did Molly say what the promise was?"

"No," Rosie said. "But it seemed very important to her. Do you think Zachariah will know what his promise was?"

When Clayton and Lillian reached Zachariah's home, Lillian noted it was being repaired, with the barn being in better condition than the house. Zachariah struck her as the kind of man who took care of the needs of others, even those of animals, before seeing to his own comforts.

The grounds were neat, and every tool seemed to have a place where it belonged. Given the care rendered to the property, she was surprised to find a window broken and glass sprayed on the ground. And given Zachariah's character, she was particularly surprised when a woman wearing a red dress answered the door. Lillian turned to Clayton, who had remained in the wagon.

He looked as shocked as she.

Hoping to receive a negative answer, Lillian inquired, "Is this the home of Mr. Keane?"

"You must be Lilly." Although the woman knew her by name, her response failed to put Lillian at ease. The woman was exotically beautiful, with large brown eyes, and high cheek bones, but she had an edge to her voice. She pulled a blanket she wore as a shawl tight across her shoulders. The dress underneath came to her knees, and was unmistakably the attire of a woman who made her living entertaining the kind of men whom Lillian thought, above all things, Zachariah was not.

The woman eyed Lillian, but addressed Clayton in a way that made Lillian feel shunned. "Zachariah left last night, and I reckon he ain't going to be back for some time." She looked back and forth from Lillian to Clayton. This time she addressed no one in particular. "What's going on here?"

That's exactly what Lillian wanted to know. Zachariah? Involved with a woman of ill repute? She had to collect her thoughts before she could get on with her mission in coming. "I need to tell Mr. Keane something. It concerns Molly."

The woman's voice got an even sharper edge to it. "And that is?"

"She's—passed on."

The woman's eyes blinked open, and the news took the edge out of her voice. "Poor Zachariah." Her whole demeanor softened, and she now averted her gaze from Lillian's. "In case you're wondering, that choirboy never laid a hand on me. But it's about time you knew that Nate ain't the kind of man a gal like you should be marrying."

"Then what are you doing here?"

"What am I doing here?" The woman snorted. "I came to look after Zachariah after he got hurt, that's what I'm doing here. Who do you think risked his life running into that burning building to save your pretty neck?"

Lillian thought it was the very spirit of her father who had rescued her. How outright thick-skulled of her to fail to recognize whose strong arms carried her out of that fire. And how thick-skulled of her to fail to recognize something else.

The woman proceeded to give Lillian a well-deserved tongue-lashing. "If you think you're too pretty or too fancy for Zachariah, let me tell you a thing or two. What difference does it make which scars he got trying to save Sally and which scars he got saving you? What some prissy little hen like you thinks is some ugly old scar, ain't nothing less than a badge of courage."

As the woman spoke, Lillian thought back to the day she was speaking to Zachariah in the church, and she now realized the *full* meaning of his statement, *"I release you from all recompenses, Lilly."*

He could have forced her to marry him, but he looked beyond what others had described as her *soft-as-mink hair* and *eyes of a blue-eyed doe*—and saw a person. She felt weak and wished there was a place to sit, because she realized she was suddenly beginning to see with the eyes of her heart.

"This time, he got burned on his shoulder," the woman continued, making Lillian feel even more ashamed of her shallowness. "I patched him best I could, and told him to rest. But his place had been shot up, and-"

The statement snapped Lillian out of her remorse. "Oh, my goodness. I told Nate I wasn't going to marry him. He blamed Zachariah, and-"

"And Nate's already paid him a visit," the woman said. "God must have been watching over Zachariah because he wasn't here. But he found that dog of his dead, and he felt real bad. He barely gave me time to bandage him up before he hitched the wagon. He put his dog in it, and headed off."

"Zachariah's gone to bury Dusty," Clayton said.

"Where?" Lillian asked.

"Some place special out there." Clayton looked into the vastness. "Zachariah loved that dog of his."

Lillian took some steps toward the openness. She was willing to run after him, if need be, to warn him.

"What if Nate goes after him?"

"After what happened last night?" the woman said. "Zachariah don't have to worry about Nate no more." It was obvious she knew more than she'd said but had, by her briefness, determined what she'd offered was sufficient. "Is that for Zachariah?" She nodded toward Lillian's hands.

Lillian looked down, suddenly remembering the paper she'd held on to all along. "No," she said. "It's for someone else. Someone named Hattie Brown."

The woman frowned. "I'm Hattie Brown."

That came as a surprise, and it took Lillian a moment to proffer the paper. "Molly wanted you to have this."

Hattie pushed it back. "I don't think she's got anything for me."

"Molly was clear about two things," Lillian said. "The first being that you should have this. See? She wrote your name on it."

"You mean, she scribbled my name."

"Molly could barely move." Lillian insisted, "She took great pains to write this."

Hattie's frown deepened with perplexity as she unfolded the paper. What she read took her by surprise. "Why–it's the deed to her house." Hattie fell against the doorway and it was clear that whatever peace needed to be made between the two women, indeed had been made.

But there was another matter that needed to be resolved before Molly could be laid to rest. Perhaps Hattie knew about it.

"Molly also wanted to remind Zachariah of a promise he'd made her."

"A promise to do what?" Hattie asked.

That answered that.

"We don't know. But it was very important to her, and Zachariah was so close to her. He needs to say his good-byes before they bury her." She looked toward the wilderness. "But how am I going to find him out there?"

"You ain't." Clayton scratched his jaw. "But I know somebody who might."

~*~

"I had a feeling I'd find you here."

Marcus approached Zachariah, who was on one knee beside a mound of dirt on a hilltop along the cattle route. It overlooked a river that calmly flowed through a valley dotted with wildflowers. Marcus thought it was the prettiest place on earth, and reckoned Zachariah did also. It was quiet without the bawling cattle. The way Zachariah stared off into the valley, Marcus imagined he could still see that long-furred canine running through the herd.

"She was good help," Zachariah said, looking afar. "All she required was Molly's leftovers and a scratch behind the ear now and then."

"I'm sorry about your dog." Given it was his own son who'd killed it instead of killing Zachariah, Marcus felt particularly out of place. Though he had intended to offer it, he now judged that monetary compensation for the animal would be petty.

Zachariah came to his feet and crossed his arms, as if he'd grown tired of all Marcus's petty comments and finally started locking them out.

"Folks are worried about you," Marcus said. "They're wondering how you were faring after the fire."

"I'm faring." Zachariah was blunt.

Marcus didn't blame him. They both had some unspoken pact concerning Nate – Marcus as a father and Zachariah as a man of honor. That agreement left Marcus with a bandage around his head and Zachariah with patches of burnt skin, shot up windows, and that dog of his six feet under. Zachariah was quiet as always, but Marcus was uncomfortable with the way Zachariah avoided looking at him.

"I worked hard all my life," Marcus reasoned. "I wanted to pass on the work of my hands to my kin."

Again, Zachariah wouldn't look at him. He simply responded with a twitch of a scarred cheek he'd gotten while trying to save Marcus's daughter.

It seemed everything Marcus had to say was petty.

Marcus was talking to the wrong man about hard work. Zachariah was a gangly eleven-year-old when he'd come to Marcus asking for a job. The boy had just lost his widowed mother, and Marcus felt bad for him. Still, Marcus thought he should be at least fourteen to start cowboying, but wished Nate, who was the same age, had had the same ambition. Marcus's respect for the boy ended up getting the best of him, so he hired him on. He started Zachariah off like he did every other hired hand, riding drag, eating dust, hoping to discourage him.

But the boy worked hard. Earned his way up to swing, and flank, and by thirteen, he was good enough to ride point. The boy was a natural, and rode a horse as if he had four legs. When Zachariah turned eighteen Marcus hired him on as trail boss and sent Nate off to college. He wished Nate would have stayed there.

"I reckon Nate ain't going to bother you no more."

Marcus cleared his throat. "I sent him off to an asylum." That second sentence was hard to spit out.

"I'm sorry," Zachariah said.

"I'm the one who should be apologizing."

Sooner or later Nate had to face the truth about what had happened to Sally. It'd been up to Marcus all along to tell him.

Zachariah had done more than his share, offering himself as the whipping boy for Nate's guilt. Zachariah had never said a word about what really happened to anybody.

Meanwhile, Marcus had hoped time would heal Nate's wounds. Unfortunately, Nate's displaced bitterness, like nitroglycerin, never got stale. Marcus tried sending him off to college with the hopes distance would compound the healing power of time, but he didn't stay long enough. After that, Marcus let things go altogether, figuring Nate had Hattie to take the steam out of his engine. It worked fine for a spell.

Until Lillian came along.

Putting off that meeting between Nate and the youth who'd accidently caused his sister's death only made that foe harder to face. And when Nate finally did face him, it left him crying in the corner of some locked room, stuck in the past, and saying over and over again, *"I'm sorry, Sally. I'm sorry, Sally."*

Marcus had lost two children that day.

"Nate wasn't right in the head after Sally died because it was his own lollygagging that caused it. Yup, Zachariah. I knew it was Nate's turn to get the stove going that day. He'd been complaining about it all morning. Thought that being a Powell made him too high and mighty, and that the chore ought to go to a hired hand." Marcus's glance at Zachariah indicated who in particular.

Zachariah rendered him a wounded look Marcus knew he misinterpreted as, *So are you so thick-headed you're just figuring things out now?* No. But with glazed eyes, Marcus was finally willing to admit it. What had scared him into doing something about it wasn't just the thought of his son hanging from a noose for killing a man. It was the thought of his son hanging from a noose for killing a man who'd shown Nate more integrity than his own father.

Marcus looked out over the river below. Now it was he who couldn't look at Zachariah. "That river down there looks mighty peaceful and inviting, don't it?" Marcus said. "But it sure is a bear to cross during a storm." He had that feeling in his gut like he'd ignored the signs and had the bad sense to cross during a tempest. He let the choking in his throat settle before saying more. "You done right by me and my kin. You always done right by me, Zachariah. That's why I'm offering you a job as trail boss. I'll pay you half of the profits." It was a generous offer, and Marcus had his reasons. One of them being, "I'm getting too old to sit in a saddle all day." The other reason was it was about time he did something right. Maybe blood was thicker than water, but he'd determined integrity was even thicker than blood.

Zachariah looked into the blue and shook his head. "I can make it on my own."

"I know you can," Marcus said. "But I'd surmise your share of the profits from the next drive will fetch you enough money to fix up that place of yours, and then some. Lillian will be needing a suiting place to live."

That hooked Zachariah's attention.

"For a refined lady, she sure can kick like a filly. She plum bucked Nate clear off the saddle."

Zachariah looked as though he didn't understand what Marcus had said, but Marcus knew the man would figure it out once he returned to town. "Now I said my piece," Marcus said, "and I hope you'll take me up on my job offer. It'll do us both some good. But though this talk was long due, it ain't the reason I come out here to find you." Marcus hesitated. After all that, and standing beside the grave of his dog, how do you tell a man his best friend had died? He sighed heavily. "Molly's passed on. I'm sorry, son. She died of an apoplexy the night of the fire."

Zachariah abruptly hung his head.

"Passed on peaceful, I'm told, with Lillian by her side. Molly had two last wishes, one was that Hattie got the house–and she's there right now. But there's something else. There's a promise you'd made that was important to Molly, and she's calling in her due. Do you know what she's talking about?"

His head still bowed, Zachariah nodded.

"Funeral's tomorrow. Wouldn't be right if you weren't there."

37

Lillian sat at the piano, as ready as could be expected for this particular first church service. Malachi had told Lillian that Molly had once mentioned to him she'd get everyone in town to go to church, even if it was over her dead body. She had fulfilled her words. Her casket rested in front of the pulpit, and the townspeople poured in.

The preacher was a young, scholarly-looking man, with eyeglasses and the Good Book in hand. He'd inevitably prepared to celebrate this first service with a wedding, and had been abruptly commissioned to perform a funeral. Still he looked comfortable with his station, and greeted everyone as though the church had always been there and the town was occupied by saints.

"How do you do, Sister Rosie. I'm Reverend Everton…a pleasure to meet you, Sister Aggie." Judging by their pauses, he was younger than what they'd expected, but that didn't seem to faze him. "Yes, a pleasure to meet you, Dr. Hinkle." He greeted all of Molly's women, as they'd come to be known, as well as the husbands-to-be who escorted them. And even the Reverend cocked a brow at the mismatches.

After the saints were greeted, they hesitated before venturing further into the House of God. Their wide-eyed looks suggested they feared the roof might cave in or lightning might strike. But the increasing volume of people behind forced the ones in front to find a seat, and so they populated the pews from the back of the church forward.

Lillian sat at the piano watching this with humor, but she kept an eye open for one face in particular.

"A pleasure to meet you, Reverend."

"The pleasure is mine, Mr. and Mrs. Powell."

Marcus entered with his wife, and Lillian was happy to see that Nate wasn't with them.

Apparently, the town gossip was true. Word had circulated that Marcus had sent Nate off with a one-way train ticket to live with an aunt in Iowa. The story went that Marcus had put his foot down and insisted Nate finish his education, no matter how long it took.

Clayton came in and nodded confirmation to Lillian that Zachariah had, in fact, been found. He looked around in expectation, and his puzzled face relayed the same question Lillian asked herself.

So where is he?

The crowd meandering in thinned, until the pews were packed with every face in town, except the one for which Lillian was looking.

The Reverend waited at the door and raised her hopes that a latecomer might be Zachariah. Instead it was Hattie, who, by the way the Reverend greeted her with a *"Very* pleased to meet you Sister Hattie" had piqued his interests.

Hattie had moved in with the women and exercised her right to the ownership of Molly's house, as well as her wardrobe, the very day Lillian had given her the deed. Donned in one of the bonnets she'd inherited and one of Molly's old-fashioned, high-neck calico dresses, the unescorted and unsuspecting Hattie looked like a suitable prospect for an eligible preacher.

Hattie, however, wouldn't meet his gaze, and so she was innocent of the spark she'd lit in his eye. She hung her head and walked shamed-faced, and the more she practiced her humbleness, the more she provoked his interest.

Lillian was the only one in the church with a view of them and she covered her amusement with a hanky to her mouth.

The Reverend watched Hattie walk between the aisles and self-consciously shift her gaze as she looked for a place in the pews to disappear. Then he smiled when circumstances forced her to sit in the front pew.

Hattie settled across from Lillian, and Lillian could just imagine what was going on in Hattie's mind. A sinner who knew she was a sinner. In a church? How absurd. But after watching Hattie try for the back pew and timidly inch her way to the front, Lillian was reminded of the proverb Jesus had told of who would sit at the head of His table.

Lillian and Hattie exchanged glances.

Lillian's was warm.

Hattie's was ill at ease

Lillian whispered, "Welcome."

Hattie returned the greeting with half a smile. Then she mouthed, "Where's Zachariah?"

Lillian responded with a shake of her head.

It seemed nobody knew.

Finally, the Reverend closed the door, and then came to stand beside Hattie's pew. His nod signaled Malachi, who stood behind Lillian with his fiddle in hand.

Malachi raised it to his chin. With long, smooth stokes of the bow, he started playing the first verse of a hymn Molly had once told Lillian she liked. It was too bad that all Molly had ever heard Malachi play was that "knee-slapping ruckus," as she'd put it, because the man could play.

Lillian wished Molly could hear him now, because he played even lovelier than when they'd rehearsed.

And as they'd rehearsed, Lillian would eventually join in with the piano, and finally with a voice too soft to fill even this small church. But someone had to sing, and since there were no hymn books, and no one else knew all the lyrics, the task had fallen upon her.

The sweet tune arising from Malachi's so-called fiddle had hushed the gathering, and filled the church like a prayer. It was as if no other sound emanated from the town at that moment other than the soft, sweet mourning of the bow upon the string.

Lillian wished Molly could see everything—the new Reverend standing to the side with the Bible to his heart, the entire town gathered to pay her homage, and, indeed, Malachi playing so sweetly. Everything would have been perfect, but for her weak voice she feared would diminish the music—and the most important thing. Lillian cast one last hopeful glance at the door.

And that's when it softly opened.

A tall man wearing a black frock coat and a cowboy hat low on his face appeared in the doorway. He carried a bouquet of wildflowers, and looked exactly as he had the first time she'd first seen him from the stagecoach window. Zachariah Keane. The man with her name in his pocket. He removed his hat like a gentleman.

Accompanied by the weeping of a solo violinist, he made his way to Molly's casket. There he paused and rested the flowers upon it. He continued walking, but instead of stopping at the front pew and sitting beside Hattie, to Lillian's surprise, he continued to the front of the church, and stood beside her.

Her cue to begin playing drew her attention to the piano. She found the proper keys, and pressed the chord.

Zachariah turned to the congregation. He held his hat in front of him, and fixed his gaze on Molly's coffin. He looked ill at ease standing in front of everyone, but as always, he was steadfast. He began to sing in a voice as soothing and serene as a Texas breeze.

> When peace, like a river, attendeth my way,
> When sorrows like sea billows roll;
> Whatever my lot, Thou has taught me to say,
> It is well, it is well, with my soul.
> It is well, with my soul,
> It is well, it is well, with my soul.

Malachi echoed the refrain on his "fiddle." His face was filled with concentration as he made his violin sing like a heavenly instrument.

Rosie's gaze was fastened on "the old bloke." But instead of the stony expression Rosie always wore when she looked at him, her face had given way to a smile of pride.

Zachariah's gaze hadn't budged from Molly's casket. Perhaps he had gotten used to standing there. Or perhaps he was inspired by the beauty of the music. Either way, the second verse seemed to give him more confidence.

His voice was so unexpectedly fine that it began to stir in Lillian memories of her playing piano while her father sang. As the lyrics flowed from Zachariah's lips, her passion for music began to stir until her eyelids floated shut, and she played not as the sheet music dictated, but as the awakening life within moved her fingers.

~*~

Though Zachariah sang words of serene assurance, there was an upheaval inside him. He felt like a scarred spectacle standing in front of everyone, while his grief reared and kicked like a wild bronco against the fence of his heart. He tried to tame it with humor.

You always did have a talent for putting me on the spot, Molly Crammer. He kept his gaze fixed on her casket as the words to a hymn that had characterized her life poured from his mouth. *And you done it right down to the end by wangling me into a promise, and then getting yourself a church, and packing it with the entire town.*

The day she'd wrangled him was a day when they were out on a cattle drive. He'd sang that song on a hilltop, while she'd looked up at him, smiling as usual. But when he rode down, she walked over to him. *"I want you to sing that hymn when its time for me to wake up on the wrong side of the grass,"* she said.

Her statement made him realize the iron-willed woman whose cackling kept him from despairing was, in fact, made of flesh. He came back with, *"I reckon the Lord won't want you for quite some time yet, 'cause he's hoping you'll get all your nagging out on me."*

But she set aside all bantering and insisted, until Zachariah nodded his promise.

"And don't leave me out here in the middle of nowhere,

neither," she'd said. *"I want you to bring me back home and plant me next to my Danny."*

My Danny. Before he passed on, Molly had always referred to her husband as *that Mr. Crammer*.

Zachariah had a feeling henceforth, he'd be referring to *that Molly* as *my Molly*.

Despite the difference in their ages, Zachariah had always hoped the day would never come when he'd be singing this song. Not without his Molly looking up at him from afar.

That troublesome old woman had kept a lonely man going with her perseverance, her strength, and her peach pies made with a pinch of cinnamon and a peck of caring. But the day had arrived, and instead of looking at her smiling face, he stared at a box she was in.

From his peripheral vision, he could see the box *he* was in. It was just a bigger box. A box packed with bachelors and brides-to-be, Clayton, the Powells, and all the other locals. And Lilly. All staring at his scarred face as his obligation to Molly forced him to share with them something very sacred and very personal.

His singing.

Churches, he thought to God in an effort to distract himself, rather than a complaint. *Don't folks know they can't stuff You in a box?* He'd sang in Molly's house before. It was never like singing on a hilltop, in the wide open. How did that scripture go? *"The heaven is my throne, and the earth is my footstool: where is the house that ye build unto me?"* God wasn't one to be all cooped up, and neither was Zachariah.

But his boots were nailed to the church floorboards with a promise, and his gaze was just as nailed on Molly's casket as he sang. Though the glaze in his eyes made things blurry. So blurry that the walls and the spectators faded away. So blurry that a glimpse he caught through a window of cobalt sky seeped in and spread wide. So blurry that the bundle of wildflowers he'd placed on the casket resembled the wildflowers growing on a hillside. Until Zachariah's vision became so blurry, that things became crystal clear.

He could feel God's eyes looking down on him in the warmth of the sun. He could sense God's divine touch in the breeze tousling his hair. Zachariah could even swear he could hear the far-away sound of Dusty barking.

It was as if he could see through walls and back through time to a place where he stood between heaven and earth. To a place where he was once again in the palm of God's hand. This was a place where Zachariah could lift his scarred face to his Maker—and let his voice break free.

Above him, Zachariah could see nothing but bright blue eternity. Below him lay tranquil creation. The sparkling, stone-bottomed river wound its way from east to west. The cattle were scattered over the river valley lowing and grazing on the plush, green grass. Dusty was zigzagging through the herd, doing what she loved to do best.

Then Zachariah's gaze landed on the most beautiful sight of them all. Just beyond a patch of pretty bluebonnets was Molly's weathered face smiling up at him.

Zachariah always finished a hymn with a grand ending, the way his heart said it should be sung. His finales would make Molly hold her shoulders, shake her head, and smile even broader, as if she hadn't a care in the world. This time her smile was more peaceful than he'd ever seen it before, and he looked down at her with more love than he'd ever felt for her.

That old frame of hers looked mighty rickety. But it sure was one good solid foundation to lean on.

As he sang the final words, something amazing began to happen. Molly's back began to straighten, and the wrinkles began to clear from her weathered face. Her silver hair got darker, and her grey eyes got bluer. Until it was no longer Molly who stood there smiling at him—but Lilly.

His mind returned to the church, where he found himself looking at Lilly, and her looking right back at him as if she'd never looked at him before.

38

The majestic beauty that had poured from Zachariah held Lillian in such awe the scar on his face disappeared completely, leaving the most poised and handsome man she'd ever seen standing there looking back at her.

Molly had once commented about *"that grand voice of his,"* but Lillian had no inkling a cowboy's voice could be this grand. In fact, as she recalled, she had even smirked when Molly had made the statement.

Lillian wasn't smirking now.

She was stunned silent at the magnificence displayed in the humble man. His voice had taken her breath away. It had far outshined the performance of a talented violinist and an accomplished pianist. *Grand voice of his, indeed.* She now deemed Molly's remark an understatement—because Zachariah's voice was even statelier than that of Lillian's own father who'd sang for royalty. She shook her head with wonder, until she realized something.

While her father sang for kings, Zachariah Keane sang for the King of kings.

~*~

Malachi was just about to lay down his fiddle and find a seat, when the Reverend dashed over to the pulpit and, without giving the musicians time to sit down, commenced with his preaching. "Dearly beloved, we are gathered here today to pay homage to our dear sister Molly Crammer, who…"

And that left Malachi stumped and still standing in front of the church, fiddle and bow by his sides, not knowing what to do. He turned to Miss Lillian to see what she was doing about it, and he discovered what had made the Reverend rush to the pulpit.

Miss Lillian was looking at Zachariah, and Zachariah was looking right back at her as if there were nobody else in the world but them. In fact, the romance brewing between the two was so blatantly obvious, that the fragrance of love filled the church more so than the fragrance of the flowers on the casket.

"Our dear sister," the Reverend continued in an even louder voice as he tried to draw everyone's attention away from the starry-eyed lovers, "has passed from the toils of this life, and through the pearly gates…"

Malachi scratched his head. Even he was distracted. Why, no sooner had Nate Powell left, but she was already fluttering to another man.

"We are comforted to know…" By now the Reverend downright bellowed in the booming voice of Divine judgment, "…that our dear sister Molly Crammer now walks upon the golden streets of…" But his shouting was to no avail, because nobody paid much attention to him.

The event going on behind him was much more interesting. So interesting that it caused a chain of events, starting when Brawley Wilson came to his feet.

"I object," Brawley said.

"Object?" The Reverend stopped short and fired back. "Object to what? This is a funeral, not a wedding."

"But in a few short weeks it will be," Brawley returned, "and I got some 'fessing up to do." He looked at his wife-to-be, who sat beside him. "No offence, Prudence, but I can't marry you." Then he turned to Doc's fiancée and blurted out, "Not when my heart's a-yearning for Aggie."

Miss Aggie rose from the pew and looked all dreamy-eyed at Brawley, and he looked right back at her in the same manner, so that before the congregation knew it, it wasn't just Miss Lillian and Zachariah casting eyes at one another, but Miss Aggie and Brawley, too.

Which spurred Doc to stand up and say his piece.

"If Brawley won't marry you, then may I have the honor, Mrs. Duldry?"

The widow woman Prudence floated to her feet as though she were drifting on a cloud. "You certainly may, Dr. Hinkle."

And for the first time since the ladies arrived, everyone involved in the matchmaking had that expression on their faces that they were befuddled by love. With one exception.

Malachi found his own Rosie in the fifth row of pews. She was looking at him, all right. She was giving him that cantankerous look that said she was displeased with him as always.

He hung his head. Though that tall, fine figure of hers was sure pleasing to the eye, he was actually in love with her. This was a lady who wasn't the least bit shy about speaking her mind, and he was especially enamored with the fancy accent she spoke her mind with. He could sit there for hours just listening to her yak at him. But regardless of what his heart wanted, and regardless of what the contract stipulated, he determined he wasn't going to force her to be his wife.

"If you don't want to marry me, Sweet Flower," he said with a breaking heart, "I ain't going to require you to do so." He heaved a sigh in anticipation of the worse. But nothing happened. His beloved, but sour-faced, Rosie just sat there with her arms crossed, looking sore with him as always.

Finally, Miss Aggie spoke up with the words Malachi dreaded.

"Rosie, ain't you going to ditch your bloke? You been wanting to ditch him all along."

Actually, that sounded even worse than he'd anticipated.

"Yes, Rosie," Prudence chimed in. "You're the only one of us who's got the money to buy her way out of the contract. Why haven't you done it yet?"

She does? Malachi scratched his beard. *This is mighty puzzling.*

But Rosie just sat there and studied him in a manner that made Malachi fidgety. He wasn't the prettiest puppy in the litter.

"Naw, I guess I'll keep the old bloke." Rosie waved a limp hand. "Besides, by the looks of the old coot, who else would want him?" She didn't exactly cast him the same adoring look the other women were casting their men, but Malachi perked nonetheless. "Does that mean you love me?" he asked.

Rosie came to her feet and planted her hands on those fine hips of hers. "It means I'll put up with you. Most of you, anyway, 'cause some things have got to go."

"Anything you say, Honey Blossom."

"First of all," Rosie said, "you're going to get rid of

that rat's nest you've got growing all over your face."

He was taken aback, and he fondly stroked his beard. It took decades to grow it that long, and he considered it his life's accomplishment. But he'd do anything for his beloved Rosie. "It's good as gone. I'll see Barber Joe first thing in the morning."

"And you're going to throw out those dirty old garbs. I'll buy you some new ones."

"Yes, dear." He had a feeling he ought to get used to saying that.

"And finally," she said, "that grimy old knapsack has got to go." She stomped to the front of the church to where he stood, and held out her hand. "Give me that filthy thing."

He hesitated. *That* demand wasn't so easy to comply with. Although the knapsack was a hump on his back, it'd been there so long, it had become a part of him. Without it, he'd feel like something had been amputated. But then again, without Rosie, he'd feel like his heart had been cut out and stomped on. So he reluctantly slipped off one strap, then he reluctantly slipped off the other, and he surrendered the knapsack over to Rosie. She received it with a scowl, and kept it at arm's length, as if she held a skunk by the tail.

"What have you been carrying in this dirty old thing anyhow, you old geezer?" With disgust, she opened the flap and looked. Then she took another look. Her eyes got wide and she suddenly clutched the knapsack to her bosom as if she were hugging the Queen's jewels. For a minute there, she seemed downright dumbfounded. Finally, she found her tongue, although her voice wasn't quite all there yet. "Where'd you get all this?" she hoarsely asked.

"California gold rush," Malachi said. He'd struck a

vein and cashed it all in. "Reckon I learned easy enough how to get it. Never did learn how to spend it."

"I can lend you a hand," Rosie said.

He was mighty obliged to have Rosie around to manage things.

~*~

Time stood still for Lillian. She gazed into Zachariah's eyes; he gazed into hers, and as far as she was concerned, all that existed was him and the sound of his voice, when he said, "I love you, Lilly."

Three words she thought she'd never again say left her lips. "I love you, Zachariah."

Everyone and everything had disappeared. It was as if she stood in the place he'd once described as *"the palm of God's hand,"* and she was looking up at a tall, gallant cowboy.

He wore a black frock coat, and a wide-brimmed hat rested low across his forehead.

She walked over to him, reached up, and snatched his hat. "There'll be no more hiding from me, Mr. Keane. I'm afraid I've found you." And with that said, she tossed the hat away.

His smile was as soothing as his voice. "I ain't afraid, ma'am." Then he bent down to kiss her.

But with a twinkle in her eye, she suddenly turned her back to him and crossed her arms. "But a girl ought to play hard to get—you reckon?"

"I surmise that indeed she does, Miss Rauling," he answered like a true English gentleman. Or close enough.

Lillian walked several paces away, and then

stopped. "Is this hard enough?"

"Maybe a few steps further."

"How about here?" she asked.

"That ought to do."

With that good running start, she threw herself into Zachariah's arms. He caught her, and tossed and twirled her high in the air, so that she threw back her head and laughed like a child. But a thoroughly different feeling overtook her as he gently lowered her to the ground. Though her feet touched the earth, her head was still in the clouds.

~*~

As was Zachariah's head as he looked down into a pair of eyes as blue and clear as the sky. The next thing he knew, his lips touched hers, and the scar he'd been so mindful of vanished.

~*~

Four newly-married couples cleared out of the church that day, along with the rest of the congregation.

The Reverend had deemed the romance going around was a little too romantic. He'd threatened to hold under holy hostage all those caught up in the amatory exchanges until they all agreed to get married.

It took about two seconds for them to hustle on up to the pulpit.

After the church cleared out, Zachariah lagged behind to spend a moment alone with Molly. He knelt beside her casket. "You were right all along," he told her. "I thought I'd kept that yearning hidden, but then again, I reckon you can't keep anything hid from a friend who knows you through and through." He bowed his head. "I'm sure going to miss your meddling, Molly."

He stood and looked toward the door, where Lilly waited for him. Her face was aglow with the promise of kisses that were so sweet he'd never get his fill of them. He smiled at her, and then looked over her head at the open sky above for one last word.

"Lord," he said, "take good care of my Molly here. She sure is a heap of trouble. But you'll find she's worth every minute of it."

Epilogue

Zachariah determined it would take a pound of faith and a ton of hard work to build a life suitable for a family. He also knew the kind of time it took for him to forage for mavericks from Texas to Montana wasn't suitable. He accepted the opportunity Marcus had offered him, got Hattie to stay with Lilly, and Clayton to check up on them during the time it took him to drive a herd from Ramsden to Dodge City, and ride back again.

Those months he was gone felt more like years, but it put enough money in Zachariah's pocket to fix the house up proper. And that wasn't all the benefits. The moment his foot touched home, Lilly threw herself out of the house and into his arms. As he twirled her around, she threw back her head and laughed like a girl. But that night, she was all woman. It seemed all the loving they'd done had chased Mr. Drummond out of her dreams for good, so that she slept peaceful and calm in his arms.

He made sure to split plenty of wood to keep her warm for the upcoming winter.

She was so proud she was learning how to cook, he didn't have the heart to tell her those little black things that looked like dried-up blueberries, weren't. She'd save them special for him to make sure he had the best of what she could offer. His eyes would water as he braved her peppercorn muffins, peppercorn waffles, and peppercorn pancakes, until he was compelled to excuse himself from the table, hightail out to the barn, and drown the fire in his mouth in a bucket of water.

He imagined the Good Lord Himself took pity upon his plight, when one day something prompted her to pick up the tin, cock her head at the word *peppercorn,* and sample her own fine cookery.

Zachariah shared his bucket with her, and they shivered on that cold December morning, soaked to the bone. His forced smile got her laughing, and her laughter got him laughing, so that they laughed like two silly schoolchildren.

But Lilly must have learned a thing or two from Molly about how to wrangle him into doing her bidding, because each Sunday when he was home, he'd find himself singing in that box of a church he'd helped build for her.

But when he was away driving cattle for Marcus, he'd find a place apart from the hands to sing his evening hymn and to thank the Lord that Molly got her church, and that Hattie found her way out of the saloon.

But mostly he thanked the Lord for Lilly, and he prayed to be able to provide for her.

God accommodated in that Zachariah always got the cattle to Dodge City in prime condition. But when prime condition only brought three dollars a head, that was a sign that opened Zachariah's eyes.

Times were changing.

Folks in the east wanted beef, and the cattle business had become so popular everybody was cashing in on it.

He rode along the street of that cowboy town, and took a good look around.

There were signs all over that advertised whiskey and women, and lured cowboys to use up the money they'd just made. Judging by the drunken cowboys that stumbled in the street, shot up the signs, and scared the locals—the cowboys had more than complied.

They made Zachariah ashamed of his trade, and caused him to remember why his father moved his family out here in the first place. People needed law and order.

And he wanted to be home with Lilly.

~*~

"Killing chickens." Clayton shook his head. "They can hang a fellow for that, you know."

Sheriff Zachariah Keane locked the jailhouse door. Behind it was an eleven-year-old boy wanted for shooting up three of Hattie's hens.

It had taken a posse that consisted of Zachariah, the boy's father, and Clayton a day and a half to apprehend the little mischief maker.

He could hide like a gopher. They were more concerned he'd get himself lost, than with the crime. The boy's father had whispered to Zachariah, "Learn him a good lesson for me." Then he waited outside.

"You can't hang me for shooting chickens," the boy challenged.

Zachariah walked up to the bars, all six foot three inches of him. He stared down at the boy. "How sure are you of that?"

The boy swallowed and backed away. He went as

far as the wall would allow, and then sat on the bed. Putting some distance between him and the Sheriff gave the little hooligan back his gumption. "I'm *very* sure of it."

"Can't hang you, huh?" Clayton reached into the desk, took out the Sheriff's log, and feigned reading. "Says here in the law book that if a man takes the life of another, he should be hanged."

"A chicken ain't a person," the boy answered saucily.

"It doesn't say a person," Clayton said. "It just says 'a life.'"

Zachariah gave the boy a long, quiet look. It was hard to keep a straight face. After a long moment of that quiet, came the statement of doom. Zachariah had a low voice he'd polished up special for this line. "So. Why'd you do it?"

That roused a wide-eyed look from the prisoner.

It wasn't as repentant as Zachariah wanted though, so he pressed harder. "Confession's good for the soul." He turned to Clayton. "I reckon you ought to go fetch the Reverend."

That got the boy's seat off the bed. "Why do we need the Reverend?"

"Don't you want to clean up your soul before…? You know," Clayton chimed in. He was good at this.

"All I did was shoot some chickens that belonged to some-"

"Watch your mouth!" Zachariah's booming voice scared the sass out of the boy.

His eyes grew wide.

Zachariah leaned against the bars. "Now. Tell me again. What did you do?"

"I shot some chickens that belonged to Miss Hattie

Brown."

"And you did it because?"

"I don't know. Guess I got bored. Or something."

Zachariah unlocked the cell door, and walked in. He towered over the boy. "You going to get yourself 'bored or something' again?"

The boy looked up, and his knees started shaking. "No, sir."

"Will I have any more trouble from you?"

"No, sir."

"I'll tell you what. Just to make sure you don't go getting 'bored or something' again, I want you here every day after school for the next month. You'll scrub my jail clean from floor to ceiling, and earn the money to pay Hattie for those chickens. Is that clear?"

The boy gulped. "Yes, sir."

"Now get on home."

The boy squeezed past Zachariah, and then dashed out of the jailhouse where his father was waiting to take him home.

Night had fallen and Zachariah was glad he could finally get on home himself.

The full moon was well overhead when Zachariah halted Thunderbolt on the crest of a hill. Something below had caught his eye, and he paused to look down on a pretty house with lamps shining from the windows, and a white picket fence running along the front. The site made him realize how time had crept up on him. The run-down house he'd started fixing up had, in fact, become a home fit for a family.

No sooner had he reached the gate, but a little girl in her night clothes came shooting out the front door and into his arms. Of course, he had to swing her in the air like she'd seen him do with her ma a hundred times before.

"I'm glad you're home, Daddy."

He put his big black hat on her little head. Beneath the rim, peered out a pair of eyes as blue as Lilly's. "It's good to be home, Little Molly."

He looked over at the doorway where Lilly stood, smiling at him. Her belly was round with another child on the way, and he was amazed at how she just kept getting prettier and prettier.

"Yup," he said. He couldn't take his gaze off her. "It sure is good to be home."

~*~

The carefree delight Lilly had once expressed toward her husband had matured to that of a mother's joy. Seeing her husband and daughter's love for one another had brought Lilly's life full circle. With a smile on her face, she leaned her head against the doorframe and let her gaze slide over their heads to the place she'd been watching from the window.

There she could still see, on the crest of the hill, her cowboy in the moonlight.

Thank you

We appreciate you reading this White Rose Publishing title. For other inspirational stories, please visit our on-line bookstore at www.pelicanbookgroup.com.

For questions or more information, contact us at customer@pelicanbookgroup.com.

White Rose Publishing
Where Faith is the Cornerstone of Love™
an imprint of Pelican Ventures Book Group
www.PelicanBookGroup.com

Connect with Us
www.facebook.com/Pelicanbookgroup
www.twitter.com/pelicanbookgrp

To receive news and specials, subscribe to our bulletin
http://pelink.us/bulletin

May God's glory shine through
this inspirational work of fiction.

AMDG

Free Book Offer

We're looking for booklovers like you to partner with us! Join our team of influencers today and receive at least one free eBook per month. Maybe more!

For more information
Visit http://pelicanbookgroup.com/booklovers
or e-mail
booklovers@pelicanbookgroup.com